Dark Plums

María Espinosa

Arte Público Press
Houston, Texas
1995

This volume is made possible through grants from the National Endowment for the Arts (a federal agency), the Lila Wallace-Reader's Digest Fund, and the Andrew W. Mellon Foundation.

Recovering the past, creating the future

Arte Público Press
University of Houston
Houston, Texas 77204-2090

Cover design by Mark Piñón
Original art by Leslie Nemour

Espinosa, María
    Dark plums / by María Espinosa.
       p.   cm.
    ISBN 1-55885-128-3
    I. Title.
    PS3555.S547D37   1995
    813'.54—dc20   94-36718
                                           CIP

The paper used in this publication meets the requirements of the American National Standard for Permanence of Paper for Printed Library Materials Z39.48-1984. ∞

For Walter Selig

Many people have given me support during the writing of this novel. I especially wish to thank Barbara Atchison, Josephine Michael, Helene Knox, Sally Headding, Lucha Corpi, and my daughter, Carmen, for their feedback and encouragement. Roberta Fernández has been a generous and insightful editor. My appreciation also goes to the Arte Público staff for their hard work.

Last but not least, my thanks to the Lafayette Cafe.

Heavy and dark are the plums.
From the sweet poison of their flesh
flows desire so intense
the heart could be engulfed
never to emerge.

Part 1

July, 1959

Chapter 1

A man in a pale green shirt was watching her. Adrianne could feel his gaze as she walked along Broadway in the steamy afternoon heat. In this humidity her bleached hair grew frizzy. She was tired from working at the office of Eureka Fabrics all day. Her high heels were beginning to hurt her swollen feet, while her dress, damp with perspiration, stuck too tightly to her large buttocks and breasts.

When the light changed, the man crossed the street, following her as she made her way uptown towards the Forty-Ninth Street subway stop. Three black teenage girls swung past him, laughing raucously, momentarily obscuring him from view. His attention made her spine tingle. This stretch of Broadway above Forty-Second Street never failed to fascinate her. The crowds seemed to throw out waves of electricity—poisoned reds and greens, golds and heavy purples. After walking just a short block, she would feel breathless and drained of energy.

Two boys with tight trousers and slick hair were standing at a hot-dog concession. They nudged each other, laughing, as Adrianne walked by. What is so peculiar about me, she wondered. Why were people always laughing behind her back? She knew they did in the office, just as they had in high school.

Gerald was the only one who hadn't jeered. Gerald, where are you? she wondered. What are you doing at this very moment? Do you ever think of me? She glanced now at every man on the street, as if by some miracle Gerald might appear among them. But he was back in Houston. "Gull girl," he used to call her in moments of tenderness, when he still loved her. "You have the breasts of a gull girl."

Noises of traffic and people, blaring music from a record shop, and a slightly nauseating stench all assailed her senses.

Further up 43rd Street a huge shovel swung through the air with a pendulous motion.

As she slowed to glance at her reflection in a window, the man in the pale green shirt overtook her. "Hello there," he said. Transfixed, Adrianne stood absolutely still while people continued to press on around them. Her image faded in the window glass. With his small eyes and narrow, reddish face, he reminded her of an animal that had been trapped underground.

Then he reached out and held one of her hands. Empty and lightheaded as she was feeling, there was comfort in his touch. As he moved a step closer, she held her breath. When he stroked her fingers, she fought an urge to press herself against him. His warmth was protection against the waves of human electricity all around her. However, she tried to wrench away. But he only gripped her more firmly.

"Come, follow me."

His voice was commanding, with a rough edge. He pressed against her, and in spite of herself, she wanted him to hold her and soothe the anguish inside her, even if it were only for an instant. Love me. Take me in your arms. Oh, this was crazy, she knew. Yet she felt as if the crowd all around her could suck her into itself and leave her hollow as a gourd, while this stranger's touch defined her body and gave her a sensation of being solid.

Discarding all caution, she went with him to a hotel room which had peeling cream-colored walls. The maroon carpet was stained; the ceiling was cracked; the old-fashioned sink in the corner was coated with rust; while the greasy gray embossed bedspread exhaled such a mixture of odors that, lying on it, she felt as if her life were touching all those who had lain here before. He put his arms around her and stroked her buttocks. His lips pressed hard against hers, and his tongue explored her mouth. At last he released her.

"Why don't you take off your clothes," he said.

Slowly she unzipped her dress and pulled it over her head. She removed her sweaty shoes, then peeled off her white brassiere and nylon panties. Sitting on the edge of the bed, she felt fat and unattractive. He took off his clothes, too. Pale and runty, he had a greenish cast to his skin, except for his ruddy face. A tattooed design of a woman encircled by a serpent covered one of his upper arms.

As he folded his clothes on the chair, he asked with seeming casualness, "Do you need money?"

Adrianne laughed. On an impulse she said, "Yes."

"How much?"

"Twenty-five dollars would help."

With the money she could buy the beautiful dark dress she'd seen in a Macy's window. Its bell-shaped skirt would make her look thinner, and its low neckline would reveal the cleavage of her bosom.

She felt giddy in the dim light which seeped in through the closed Venetian blinds.

"Do you know that asking for money is prostitution? I can have you arrested." His voice had grown menacing.

"If you're a cop, let me see your I.D."

"Don't get fresh. You'll regret it."

Maybe he was crazy.

She'd better do what he wanted, or he might hurt or even kill her. Why had she come here with him?.

As he stood naked in front of her, his cock, purplish and red and swollen like some prehistoric reptile, was pointed straight at her belly. Her fear and, perversely, her desire grew.

He gripped the back of her head and pushed her downwards. Kneeling on the carpet, she took him into her mouth. His odor was overpowering. His cock was so large that it was difficult for her to breathe as her tongue played against his pumping, slippery motions. She licked against the ridge. His testicles hung limp and full as she took them into her hand. His hands were pressing down hard against her head. Her knees were beginning to hurt. She thought of Gerald and the curious sweetish taste of his semen, the way he had of making her feel servile. She hoped this man didn't have any terrible disease. God protect me, she prayed. What was the point of living, anyway? Tears streamed down her cheeks as she pressed her hands harder against the stranger's buttocks.

"That's it, baby," the stranger moaned, swaying against her. Then she tried to pretend he was Gerald. She tried to disconnect this stranger's personality from the hard, swollen flesh inside her mouth. Finally, he started to come. His liquid gushed inside her mouth, sour like brine. If she didn't swallow it, he'd be angry, and God knows what he might do.

Moaning, he continued to press her against him.

Finally, he collapsed on the bed, pulling her beneath him. She tried to hold back her nausea. Sweat ran off him in rivulets, dripping from his body onto hers. When she wrapped her feet around his knobby legs, she realized with a shock that he was still wearing his socks. Afraid he might catch athlete's foot? In her strange state of mind, this seemed hilarious. The man revolted her. If she had a pocket knife, she'd slit his penis lengthwise.

He began caressing her vulva, then inserted a finger inside her, and her anger fed her desire as she grew wet beneath his touch. His mouth clamped on hers, his tongue probed between her teeth, and she inhaled his breath.

The man's face was rough with acne scars. His hair felt sticky. She felt that he could be cruel, like Lucille. She remembered Lucille's French perfume and those thin lips pressing against hers.

He pulled her hand down to his penis. "Help me, sweetheart."

She kneaded him between her fingers, and after what seemed an endless time, he hardened.

He was suckling her breasts. Momentarily, she felt that she floated out of her body and into his. She became his throbbing genitals. She looked at the world through his pale eyes as she guided him into her.

Adrianne could not understand it, but often she experienced what could only be called lapses of herself, as if she floated out of her body and into the other person's, and his will became hers. Now was one of those times, as she floated above both their bodies. She saw herself—a plump, flushed girl with bleached hair spread out in a tangled mass over the pillow, and she watched him—a rabbity man pumping away at her.

Spasms of desire within her grew in waves, and she felt like a huge cunt coming against his body. Coming, coming. God, let her come. Finally she found release. He, too, made an explosive sound and collapsed against her, crushing her breasts.

Limp inside her, his body was even more nauseating. He smelled like a fetid animal. Adrianne wanted to pull away, but he was holding her too tightly.

The blinds rattled under the impact of an air current through the slightly opened window.

"What's your name?" he asked.

"Stephanie," she lied, using a name she had mused over in her fantasies.

"You're a nice girl. I want to see you again. Where do you live, sweetheart?"

"With my mother in the Bronx." She felt a surge of pleasure at her inventiveness.

"You don't sound like you're from around here."

"I grew up in New Orleans," she said, elaborating on her story. "When my father died, we moved up North."

She thought of her mother Elena, brushing her hair with a silver brush. Elena was gazing off into the distance as she sat on the edge of the bed. *"Mamá,"* Adrianne cried. Her mother didn't seem to hear. *"Mamá."* The child's tiny hands parted her mother's fine, blonde hair. Elena gazed past the child, not seeing her, not hearing her, until finally she pushed her away with annoyance, murmuring, *"¡Cállate, Adriana!"*

She thought of how her mother's cheek, dry and soft, had pressed against hers that last afternoon at Houston Intercontinental Airport. "I love you, Mama," she had murmured. It seemed years, rather than just a few weeks ago. Standing next to her frail-boned mother, Adrianne had felt huge and awkward. That day her mother had worn pearls, a navy linen dress, stockings, and gloves, even though it was sweltering. *"Adiós, Adriana.* Let me know your address, when you have one," her mother had said coldly with her slight accent. Adrianne had felt indescribably hurt, but didn't know how to bridge the gulf between them.

The stranger continued with his questions. As Adrianne created the covering of a false identity around herself, she was lulled for a short time into feeling safe. Then she noticed a button over the bed to ring for the hotel clerk downstairs. Suppose this man freaked out? Suppose he wouldn't let her leave? What would happen if she pushed the button? She remembered that he had greeted the clerk as if they were old friends. No, Adrianne decided, it wouldn't help to ring.

"What's your name?" she asked.

"Red."

"Are you really a cop?"

Instead of answering, he took her finger into his mouth and sucked it.

"My wife's been in an institution for three years," he said. "I need a woman. I need someone like you, sweetheart. I love blondes with large tits."

She wondered what he could have done to drive his wife into a mental institution.

He began massaging one of her breasts. Pausing, he nuzzled her cheek and asked, "When can I see you again, Stephanie?"

"Soon," she said as she pondered how to make her escape. "I need to go to the bathroom," she told him. "Is it down the hall?"

"Yes. Get me a cigar and some matches from my shirt before you go."

She did so, and he lit his cigar and blew smoke rings up towards the ceiling. If she got fully dressed, she thought he might make trouble. So she just put on her dress and shoes, leaving her underwear on the floor. Then she picked up her purse.

He gazed up at the ceiling. The smoke wafted through the air.

"You don't have to put your shoes on."

"Yes, I do."

It was good that she'd decided to leave her underwear.

"Why are you taking your purse?" he asked suspiciously.

"I need to freshen my face."

Trembling, she shut the door behind her.

First she went to the bathroom and wiped off his fluid, which had already stained the back of her dress. Then she ran a comb through her hair and splashed her burning face with cold water.

Swiftly, she ran down the stairs and through the lobby. The clerk barely gave her a glance. As she ran out into the street, her breasts hurt and she began to feel a pain at her side. There was a bus at the corner. Just as its doors were closing, she boarded and collapsed on a seat.

Dazed after her escape, she made it home to her room on West 97th Street. The room was littered with kleenex, costume jewelry, and clothes. On the nightstand was a half-melted chocolate bar and two over-ripe peaches. Tiny fruit flies hovered above the fruit.

She would go into the bathroom, bathe, and wash off the stranger as she always did after these encounters. These had occurred more often than she cared to remember since her arrival in Manhattan only a month earlier. It frightened her to feel that she was losing control. On the wall above the bureau was a gilt-edged mirror. When she looked into it, her blue eyes gazed back at her with startling innocence, as though this afternoon had never happened.

In the tub, she splashed hot water over her entire body. She soaped herself, lathering inside and outside, as if she could soap out the contamination. The air had grown steamy when she heard a knock in the door. "Are you going to be long?" Max, who rented the room next to hers, asked in his guttural German voice.

"Yes. So leave me alone!" she shouted out angrily. Her former boundaries were restored. She didn't want to speak to Max or to anyone else.

Chapter 2

Max Gottlieb, a paunchy man with thick whiskers and white hair, sat on the edge of his bed trying to quiet the pounding of his heart by taking slow deep breaths. Through the thin walls he could hear water splashing and faint sounds as Adrianne bathed. The image of her naked in the bath disturbed him. Since she had rented the room a few weeks ago, her presence had increasingly grown on him.

Photographs of his wife and their two children stared reproachfully from the bureau. "Don't think about her, don't don't! After what you did to me!" his wife with her pale pointed face and large eyes said, even though all three of them had been dead for so many years. Their deaths had been caused indirectly by his involvement with another woman. By now consciousness of his guilt had dulled, but it still governed his entire life.

Although he could afford far better, he had lived in a series of cramped furnished rooms. His clothing was worn and shiny with age. He ate without tasting, looked without seeing. What right had he to physical enjoyment? As a young man he had been meticulous and sensitive to his surroundings. Now, the objects in his room were coated with grime, and it was heaped with half-rotted newspapers in Yiddish, Hebrew, and English.

More and more he neglected himself so that his greasy, stained appearance became an embarrassment at the shop where he had worked since 1944 as a watch repairman. They moved him away from the public into a back room where he worked alone under the glare of a high-intensity lamp.

The anguish of ill-fated timing. If he had known what his future was going to be, he would have chosen to be gassed in Dachau along with his wife and children. He repaired watches for a living, but he could never repair that gaping wound in his life.

If only he had gotten them out of Germany sooner. If only he had never met Monique. He was guilty not only of his ill-timed adultery, but guilty, too, because in the deepest recesses of his mind, he must have foreseen the future.

As he chewed on his upper lip, he realized with a slight shock that his mouth was empty. He must have forgotten to put in his dentures this morning. However, he'd skipped lunch at work today, and so he hadn't realized this until just now.

Breathing heavily, he raised himself from the bed and went over to the bureau. They were soaking in a glass of grey solution right next to the photographs. What a fool he was! What a sight he must have looked! He picked the dentures out of the liquid one at a time and adjusted them inside his mouth. The faces of Mathilde and the *kinder* gazed at him like the faces of saints in paintings by Grünewald: Jewish mother and holy children. Because he moved his fingers clumsily while he contemplated the photographs, he stuck the upper plate against a tender spot in his mouth and winced.

Through the walls he heard the bath water run out, and then he heard what sounded like sobs. Poor girl! Often he thought he heard the sounds of her muffled sobbing and moaning. She needed so badly a little tenderness. There was something about her like a bird with a broken wing, something damaged that looked out at him from her soft blue eyes. He imagined her half undressed, in a slip. She was ripe like a plum, although scarcely more than a child. Maybe she could be his. But how could she possibly be attracted, old and ugly as he was? He crunched the upper plate against the lower, and his jaw ached from the pressure. Only if she were deeply wounded would she find him attractive. Perhaps she had already suffered enough, young as she was, to understand the powers of guilt and pain and loneliness upon the human psyche.

Ordinarily, he would not have let himself dwell on Adrianne. But he was still weak from pneumonia, and he had in fact only returned from the hospital a few weeks ago. He had palpitations of the heart. The doctor told him to relax more and to start thinking about what he would do when he retired. "Find yourself a wife," Dr. Goldfarb said with a sly, conspiratorial touch on the arm. "Someone young and pretty and *zaftig* to take care of you."

The idea of dying alone frightened him, and an instinct for life reared up stronger after his nearly fatal illness. "Forgive me, Mathilde," he murmured. Her hands, composed of ash-fine powder, rose up to touch his heart. Her long, accusing fingers caused palpitations, and he felt all a-jumble inside his chest.

In 1946, just after the War, to his shame he had married a flaming beauty from Asbury Park, New Jersey. But the union only lasted a few weeks. How could any marriage have worked when he was doomed because he was a murderer?

He heard Adrianne walk down the hall to her bedroom, which was on the other side of his, and a little later he heard the clink of beads against her wooden dresser. He imagined her all fresh from her bath, ineffectually draped with a towel, while he knelt to caress her plump thighs. She would stand there, impassive, smiling slightly, while he caressed and kissed her all over. Her large soft breasts with tiny rose nipples would brush against his cheek ... Faugh! He was an old man. To think such dirty thoughts. Mathilde, forgive me. I need someone after all these years alone with never a woman to care for me.

Adrianne's high heels clicked against the wooden floor, and he gasped for breath. Before she went out he had to catch her, because she often didn't return until two or three in the morning. Sometimes in the middle of the night he awakened to the sound of her footsteps. He wondered who she went with. She seemed so lost and innocent, and she was hardly more than a child.

Again he sat down on his bed, waiting to hear the sound of her door open, to accost her before she could leave. He felt like a spider as he listened. He would capture her in his web, hold her there as she struggled in vain. And then at his leisure he would feed on her flesh, her affection, and on the gentleness he sensed within her.

When at last Max heard her door open, he jumped up, ran heavily out to the hallway, and planted himself in front of her. "Stop! I must speak with you!" he cried, heaving for breath.

She wore a low cut dress of green satin. Thick eye shadow, kohl rimmed around the lids, shimmering red lipstick, and strong perfume imprinted themselves upon him, even in the dim light, as did the glitter of her golden necklace and her

heavy oblong earrings. Poor child, he thought. She decks herself up like a harlequin, and I am sure men take advantage of
her, but all this cannot hide her innocence.

Standing so close, breathing in her sweetness, he grew
dizzy. Again his heart beat hard and fast.

"I've got to go," she said. "Leave me alone."

"Please, Adrianne, just talk to me a few minutes." He was
trembling.

"What do you want?"

"I want to be your friend."

"I've got to go."

"Where?"

"None of your business." She bit down on her lower lip
and flushed as if she regretted her harshness. He thought
that he had frightened her, because to speak in this way was
not natural to someone of her gentle nature. How pitiful she
was just beneath her painted, crackling surface.

She seemed to waver, and so he pleaded. "Let me take
you out to dinner and a show ... I always eat at the cafeteria
on the corner of 91st Street. Afterwards we can go to a Broadway show or anywhere you want."

She considered his offer as if she were trying to remember something. His voice was insistent. Just a few coins
remained in her purse, and there was only wilted lettuce and
milk in the kitchen refrigerator. Hunger gnawed at her.

Also, she had no definite place to go. While the walls of
her room oppressed her, the streets frightened her. She did
not want to repeat the afternoon's encounter with another
stranger. However, at any time her own mysterious needs
could erupt and overpower her. She was not in control. She
feared herself, her room, the streets. She feared everything.

In a vague way she had planned simply to wander the
streets as she did each night, talking to strangers, absorbing
something of them to nourish herself.

He stared at her now like an imploring dog. Although he
did not appeal to her with his old man's musty odor, his ill-fit-
ting clothes, and his protruding veins, he would not attack
her. She knew him only slightly, but when she was with him
she felt a sense of rootedness.

"Well, all right," she said hesitantly in her soft voice. "But
I have to get something in my room first. I guess I can put off
what I was going to do until later."

Almost as if by accident his hands stroked her buttocks when she turned to go back to her room, and she realized with a jolt that his hands on her felt good, just as the stranger's had.

Inside her room, a wave of loathing for herself and the world swept through her. His hands may feel good, but he is repulsive to me, she thought. Yet who am I—worthless, a slut—to resist Max's small demands? She stood a few minutes at the window looking down the narrow air shaft. She could open the window, jump out, and shatter her bones far below.

She could go now to Max who was waiting for her, or she could curl up on the unmade bed and never leave the room. She could say she felt too sick.

Fear oozed through her the way it always did. Beads of perspiration had broken out on her skin. She wanted to run away from everything, but to be alone at this moment was worse. The trash heap below, full of discarded things, beckoned her: sharp-edged rusty objects, a baby's overturned carriage with one wheel still attached, garbage crawling with rats. She was afraid to open the window, although the air inside her room was oppressively hot. A fly buzzing around the room grazed her forehead.

I am worthless, she thought. I love nothing. I don't love the sky or the concrete buildings with windows like hostile eyes. I don't love any human being. I don't love Lucille. I never loved Gerald. I only wanted him to love me.

Gerald was gone, forever out of her reach. Her pleading, her weeping, her fits of hysteria had destroyed any attraction she once held for him.

Everywhere now she looked for a man to break down her barriers so that she could love. Unlike Gerald, this man would accept her intense emotions. Yet since she was worthless, he would cast her down, dissolve her into molten liquid. Then she would be recreated whole, and he would love her. He would heal the pain inside her.

She sought out this man on every street corner, every subway car and bus, every cafeteria, coffee shop, and bar; but all she found were shadows of the man she wanted.

Still, she did not give up hope. With the certainty of an animal who lives by instinct, she knew that soon, very soon now, she was going to find him. She heard the doorknob turn and wheeled around to face Max.

"I am sorry to come into your room without knocking," he said, red-faced. "I was worrying if you are all right."

She was touched that he had worried about her. Perhaps he sensed that she had thought just now of killing herself. She could still say no, say she'd changed her mind. His panting apprehensiveness filled her with distaste. Nevertheless, a cunning created out of desperation urged her to go, whispered that in some way this would compress time and bring her nearer the end of her search.

He moved a step towards her.

"Max, let's get going."

Chapter 3

Inside the cafeteria, fluorescent lights gave people sharp, sallow faces. But the air conditioning was a relief after the heat outside.

Max felt dizzy and weak as they walked with their trays between crowded tables over to a vacant one by the wall. He hoped he wouldn't trip and spill everything. So jumbled were his nerves that he could scarcely see.

Adrianne had chosen beef stew along with a French roll and apple pie. He himself selected only a cottage cheese plate and tea, as Dr. Goldfarb had cautioned him about his diet. In truth, the excitement of being with this young girl had taken away his appetite. His heartbeat quickened. With a slight feeling of nausea, he looked down on the mound of cottage cheese bordered with raspberry gelatin and peach halves on a bed of lettuce. Adrianne began to eat with a ravenousness that startled him. When he got to know her better, he must speak to her about eating so much and so fast, as it was not healthy.

He wondered what to say to her. Two young men in rumpled shirts were gesturing to each other in sign language at the next table.

Trembling, he spilled a gob of jello on his necktie, then quickly wiped it off. Ah, he had forgotten how to be a social being. He had forgotten what it was like to eat with anyone else.

"I must watch my heartburn," he said, trying to pretend he had not spilled anything. The jello left a wet spot, and looking down, he noticed old stains from coffee or tea or grease on his trousers. If he wanted to attract this creature, who was young enough to be his granddaughter, he must buy some new clothes.

"Does it give you a great deal of pain?" she asked.

"Yes. Off and on. It's worse since I had the pneumonia."

"I'm sorry." Her voice softened with pity. What more can I offer him than my presence, even my body? she wondered. All he will ask of me is a smile and a little kindness.

She felt like a stuffed straw doll.

He would perceive only part of her. He would be easy to please, and perhaps she could make him happy.

He seemed depressed. However, she could feel the softness in her face and body attract him as she wondered how to begin drawing him out. During her nightly wanderings she had developed skill as a listener. Strangers' lives fascinated her. Their stories of failed intimacies, adventures, and losses made her own suffering seem more bearable.

"Max, what kind of work do you do?"

"I work in a watch-repair shop. And you?"

"I do clerical work," she said with a shrug, anxious to get the subject off herself. "Do you like your job?"

"In Germany I was not trained to repair watches. All this I learn over here. In Hamburg I was working as a lawyer."

"What made you change?" She swallowed another morsel of stew. God, solid food tasted good. This was the first real meal she'd had all day. Then she took a sip of coffee.

"Why do you ask?" Jerkily, he raised his glass of water to his lips, nearly spilling some.

"I want to hear about your life." She leaned forward. Her milky orbs swelled out over the green satin, beckoning his touch. Her hand gently touched his, and she said, "I can see you have suffered."

"Lately, I feel very bad. Whenever I climb the stairs to the apartment, my head hurts. I am so quickly out of breath, always tired. My doctor tells me I must retire soon."

"Oh, that must be hard for you. Why did you change your work?"

"I was an immigrant to this country. It was difficult to begin again. I did not know English well, so I took what work I could get." He sighed heavily.

Shadows of the past rose to haunt him.

The deaf mutes at the next table were staring at them. Were he and Adrianne so strange a couple? Was she so young and he so old?

"Do you regret you never became a lawyer here?" she asked. There was a quality about her that filled him with a desire to tell her things he had hidden for years, even from himself. Her voice had a low and pleasant quality, and her golden hair surrounded her full face like a halo. Her blue eyes were so gentle.

"Sometimes. But I have bigger regrets. The burden I carry in my heart is so much."

She leaned close while he groped for words to tell her about his past. Haltingly, he told her how he had married Mathilde in the 1930's. Then he told her how Mathilde and the *kinder*, Jacob and Miriam, died in the concentration camp at Dachau, where they were sent in 1941, just as they were about to leave for Switzerland. He escaped because he had left Germany a year earlier on one of the last ships out, hoping to get a job and raise money to bring over his family. However, in London he met Monique and had fallen in love with her. He had tried to convince himself that the situation in Germany was not as black as he had painted it in his mind and that his family could wait a little longer.

As he continued, he grew more tense and began to gasp for breath. Her passivity felt like delicate tentacles sucking at his nerve endings, releasing the torment he had held in for so long.

He told her how he awaited the birth of Monique's child with a feverish longing he had never known with the babies that came from Mathilde's womb.

Speaking more rapidly, he told how he delayed sending for his family until it was too late. Then he grew silent. How horrible to have spoken this way about his own dead babies. He clutched his cup as if he were trying to crush it into pieces, while drops of perspiration fell from his whiskers onto the table.

"Go on," said Adrianne.

Everything around him blurred. The deaf mutes had left, and the tables around them were empty.

"Finally, I sent for Mathilde and the *kinder*. She was so happy. She telegraphed me that she had train tickets to Basel. But before they could get out, they were taken to the concentration camp."

He felt black inside all over again with the memory. "I could no longer stand to be with Monique, because every time I looked into her face, I knew I was a murderer. I got a visa to come to the United States, and I left her."

"In New York, at first I found no work. Every day I looked. The dirt and the noise and the people in this city made me feel crazy. After three weeks, I got a job as a stock room clerk. I worked, ate, slept, like a machine. Whenever I think how my wife and babies died because I neglected them, it is too much to bear.

"Then in 1943 the letters from Monique stopped coming. After the war, I could never bring myself to search for her. I do not know if she and my son are alive, but I pray for them."

Tears long unshed streamed down his cheeks, mingling with sweat. As if he were holding onto the last remnant of sanity, he clutched the warm china cup more tightly. Long ago he would have killed himself, but he had grown to feel that the more bitter punishment was to live with the knowledge of what he had done.

"So you work in a watch-repair shop now," she said.

"Yes. I like to work with my hands." A wild hope surged up that Adrianne, like a princess in a fairy tale, would purge him of guilt.

He was silent for a moment. It was long past the dinner hour. How long had he talked?

"My poor wife and children." His voice was almost inaudible now, and he breathed heavily as once again their faces appeared in his memory. He looked overcome with pain. "If a heaven exists, they must be in it."

"I don't believe life ends when you die," said Adrianne.

Seizing her hand, he felt blood pulse through her warm fingers. Never before had he talked about Monique to anyone except Rabbi Zimmerman. Afterwards, the Rabbi had tears in his eyes, and he said a special *kaddish* for Mathilde and the *kinder* as well as for Monique and their son.

He wanted to press himself close to Adrianne, bury himself in her flesh and forget. If only the havoc inside aroused by his talking would go away.

Releasing her, he took out his handkerchief, wiped his face, and blew his nose. The few people remaining in the cafeteria blurred with the walls, the artificial lighting, and the oppressive smells of food.

Afterwards, he would lie awake, trying to find words to tell her things that now after all these years he wanted to tell someone.

"Every Friday night I go to Synagogue. Will you come with me some night?"

"Yes, I will," she said.

His pain momentarily made her own vanish. She wanted to weep for both of them, as well as for all those nameless strangers with whom she talked. Perhaps she could achieve some sort of salvation if she were kind to him. Now her own needs were overshadowed, as they had been with the stranger on Broadway this afternoon.

A faint odor of rose filled the space around her, apparently coming out of nowhere. It was not the cheap perfume she'd dabbed on earlier. The rose odor came out of the new vibrations into which she had risen.

Yet she felt that she had done something terrible in drawing out his pain.

She looked down at his gnarled fingers. His ridged nails, cut straight across, were edged with dirt. His hands were liver-spotted.

"Sometime I'd like to come with you, Max."

He glanced at his watch. "I have promised to take you to a Broadway show, but now I think it is too late," he said. "It is after nine o'clock."

"That's all right. We can go somewhere else. I'd like to go to a jazz club."

"Jazz?"

"There's a club on West 53rd Street. I've only passed by, but the music sounded good. Would you take me there?"

"With pleasure, *meine liebchen*."

"Let's go then."

When they left the cafeteria, Max hailed a taxi.

Chapter 4

Adrianne leaned back in the plush chair and let the music fill her. The saxaphone's wail swept through her tiredness and the piano notes satisfied her with their metallic hardness while a black male voice sang about love and loneliness. The music gave her a profound sense of release.

Memories of that day flashed through her mind. The long hours of clerical work at Eureka Fabrics. The stranger's cock in her mouth. The frightening interval in the hotel room before she had managed to escape. Max's hands on her buttocks. His sad tale and his need for her which seeped through the smoky air.

"Do you like this music?" Max asked.

"Yes," Adrianne nodded, her eyes closed. She could tell he didn't, but right now that didn't matter. While the music played, she was safe. The music was her refuge.

"This is very different from the classical music I know."

Although she knew he wanted her to look at him, she didn't open her eyes. Music gave her the strength to ignore the invisible pressure he was exerting on her.

When the musicians took a break, she opened her eyes and glanced at the bar. A tall, thin bartender with black hair and a flashing smile was mixing drinks. Without thinking, she stood up and said, "I'll be back in a minute. I've got to go to the bathroom."

As she wandered over to the bar, the bartender's eyes caught hers. He wore a soft blue madras shirt. His face gleamed with beads of sweat, and his hands moved swiftly as he filled glasses with liquor, ice, and soda.

"May I have a glass of water?"

Their eyes met a second time, and his fingers trembled so that the glass he was holding nearly fell.

"You're beautiful," he said. "You want water? Champagne? You name it, baby." He had high cheekbones and a distinguished face. "Tell me, are you over eighteen?"

"Yes," she said. "Actually, I'm nineteen."

He laughed. "Good thing the boss isn't here. He'd think you were jail bait."

She blushed and couldn't think of what to say. There was only one empty stool at the crowded bar, and she sat on it. People around her were wearing expensive clothing, several of the women in thin silk dresses and pearls. She felt shoddy in the green satin dress, which she'd bought at a discount store on lower Broadway.

"I'll have water," she said. "I have no money." Self-conscious, she fingered the satin rose at her bosom. How tacky it must look.

"Whatever you want is on the house," he said. "What's your name, beautiful?"

"Adrianne."

"Your last name?

"Torres."

"Adrianne Torres, you look tired. How about a rum and coke to pick you up?"

"Okay."

"You're gorgeous."

Again she flushed, but as his dark eyes bored into hers she forgot everyone around them. Somehow he was familiar. She wanted to tell him more about herself, but her mind went blank. Sensing her confusion, he reached across the counter and touched her hand. His fingers were warm, the skin calloused.

"Relax, baby."

"What's your name?"

"Alfredo Montalvo."

"Are you Puerto Rican?"

"No, I was born in Cuba."

"So, you're Cuban."

"Yes, I'm Spanish and Indian, with a touch of African in me."

He put ice cubes in a glass, squirted Coca-Cola, then added rum.

"I see."

Cigarette smoke was irritating her throat. The woman next to her, absorbed in conversation with her companion, didn't notice that her cigarette was practically in Adrianne's nostrils. The musicians, who were on their break, had gathered at a table in back. One had a very blonde woman on his lap. They were all black, except for the bass player.

"I was born in Chile," she said. "We moved to the United States when I was little because my father got a job with an oil company in Houston. But he died when I was twelve."

She thought of her mother, Elena, wandering at dusk through their house, opening the windows to let in the fresh night air. Elena would go through the motions a bit absently, deep inside her own world. Even before Julio's death, Elena's face had often been filled with sadness, and Adrianne had always felt as if she were somehow to blame for her mother's melancholy.

Alfredo put her rum and coke on the counter and gripped her fingers. His touch was warm. Then he went back to mixing drinks.

"You're lonely," he said.

"How did you know?"

"I can see it."

She wondered what it would be like to make love with this man.

The glass was icy in her hands.

"Two B&Bs," the waitress called out. She was a slender girl in a tight black sheath. When she whispered something in Alfredo's ear, the two of them both burst out laughing, and Adrianne's jealousy flared. At that moment she became aware of Max's eyes boring into her back.

"How's the rum and coke?" Alfredo asked.

The waitress disappeared in the crowd.

"It's good, but I should get back to the man I came with."

"That old man over there?"

"He's only a friend. I don't know him well. He lives in my rooming house."

"Baby, you're a free woman, and you could have your pick of just about any man here. You've been sending out sex signals to all of them. Do you know that?"

Again he touched her, this time caressing her face. And she could feel the magnetic current between them. "You don't have to be a slave to anyone. Most people are slaves, although they don't have to be. Look around you. They're all slaves except for the musicians. They're the only ones who really enjoy what they're doing."

"What do you mean?"

"Even if these people are wealthy, they're selling themselves. They sell their bodies and their minds and their time. Some of these men work eighty-hour weeks. As for the women, they're all selling themselves, every one of them, either at jobs or as housewives. They're *putas*, whores."

"I don't understand."

"Just think about it."

She fiddled with the satin rose on her dress. "Why do you work here? Are you selling yourself, too?"

"Yes," he said. "I'm selling my body and my time. I'm an artist. I need a job to pay the rent and buy canvas and paints. So, I'm no better than the others."

"I'm sorry," she said.

"See that painting over there across the room? The nude? That's mine."

Adrianne could see it only indistinctly in the darkness of the club. Above some tables was an unframed canvas, a mass of grey and pink tones that, when she looked attentively, depicted a huge reclining woman.

"I like it," she said.

"I sell my waking hours to this job, and the boss lets me put up one lousy painting. It ain't worth it, baby.

"By the way, don't look now, but your elderly friend is walking over here. Adrianne, come by tomorrow night around eleven-thirty. I've got to see you again."

He leaned closer and stroked her hand, gazing into her eyes. "Will you come tomorrow?" His intensity engulfed her.

"Yes."

"I can teach you who you really are," he murmured, just before she felt the heavy touch of Max's hand on her bare upper back.

"Hello, sir," Alfredo said. "How are you tonight?"

"Adrianne, I am tired. We must go."

"So, you're the young lady's friend. We've just been talking. How about a refill on the house."

"No," Max said abruptly. "It's very late. Come, Adrianne."

As she slid off the stool, Max seized her arm. She felt shaky. Once again she looked at Alfredo, but he was mixing more drinks and seemed not to notice her.

"I do not like that man," Max said as they walked outside.

They took a taxi back. When Max took her hand in his, she did not resist. I owe him that much, she thought.

After they reached the door of her room, Max stood still while she fumbled in her purse for her key. His heavy breathing made her tremble. At last she found the key and said, "Good night. Thank you for everything."

"Adrianne, very easily I could grow to love you," he whispered.

"Good night." She closed the door quickly, locking it shut. Alone at last, she walked over to the mirror where she took a good look at herself. The roots of her hair had grown out, she noticed, and the peroxide tint looked harsh under the ceiling light. Perhaps tomorrow she should apply a honey-colored rinse after work, before she met Alfredo. Thank God tomorrow was payday. She'd be able to cash her check and buy a package of rinse.

Max's desire touched and troubled her. As for Alfredo, thoughts of him obsessed her. Could he be the one she had been seeking?

Chapter 5

"Adrianne, what do you see in the old man you were with last night? Free meals? A few drinks?"

She flushed, feeling protective of Max, and she recalled how forlorn he had looked when she left him.

"He's a good man."

"He wants to get you into bed."

Adrianne's flush deepened.

The bartender went on swiftly drying glasses with a purple cloth. His face was sensitive, alive, and his movements graceful. People's voices mingled with the sound of a Cole Porter tune on the piano. The blues trio wasn't playing tonight. Smoke, alcohol, and perfume assailed her nostrils.

"Hey, I didn't mean to offend you." Alfredo gazed into her eyes. Once again she felt something familiar about him, although they had just met the night before. As though picking up her thoughts, he said, "You've got strong vibes, baby. I've known you in other lifetimes."

"Perhaps," she said.

Was this just a line he used? Strange he, too, should sense that he already knew her.

"Alfredo, I need those drinks."

"Coming right up, sweetheart," he said to the waitress who had whispered in his ear last night.

"I'll talk to you later, Adrianne. I've got to get back to work."

Adrianne looked down at her navy skirt and then surveyed herself in the mirror behind the bar. Tonight she wore a translucent white blouse with a plunging neckline, and she thought she looked all right, although she hadn't had time to tint her hair after all.

Alfredo filled a jigger with scotch, poured it into a glass over ice, then squirted in soda and placed it on the counter in front of a middle-aged man in a grey suit. A slave, she thought. Two slaves. Three slaves.

She tried to make out strains of piano music through the din. Soft and romantic, it almost hurt. Snatches of conversation caught her attention.

"...six and a half points a share..."

"...I hear he's leaving the firm."

"Al, two Buds."

"...got great tits..."

Several young men were thumping their glasses on the counter, and Alfredo said something to them that she couldn't hear. They began arguing with him in loud voices, but he ignored them as he continued his work. After a few moments they quieted down.

"Motherfuckers," he said, moving closer to Adrianne. "Those jerks can't see anything past their own selfish needs. If they opened their eyes and ears for a second, they'd go crazy. We're living in Sodom and Gomorrah, baby, even though it may not look like it."

Adrianne was startled by the violence of Alfredo's outburst. His fingers trembled as he poured white froth into large glasses.

"At this moment Eisenhower is close to pushing a button that will unleash the bomb. We're living so close to the edge. There are people in this city who don't have enough to eat. Men, women, and even children are shooting up heroin to escape their pain. Someday this whole system is going to crash. You'll see people dying like flies on these streets."

Adrianne suddenly thought of Max, of how he had suffered, and she was flooded with sadness for him as well as for the poor people of whom Alfredo had been talking. A shiver of fear ran through her as Alfredo continued in an angry voice. "People don't believe in God anymore. Their God is money. What about you? Do you believe in God?"

"I don't know. I don't go to any church."

"My mother went to Mass every Sunday. But she treated me like shit." He moved an ashtray in front of her. His nails were long, narrow, and square-cut. "What about your family. Are they religious?"

"My mother is." She twisted a tendril of hair around her fingers. "I don't know about my relatives in Chile. One of my aunts is a nun, but I've never met her. I've never met any of them. We left when I was so small, and we never went back."

"Really?"

"My mother doesn't want to go back."

"Does she understand that you feel cut off from your relatives?"

"No, she doesn't." Adrianne twisted harder at the tendril of hair, until it pulled at her scalp. Things looked blurry through the tears that had welled up in her eyes. "I don't think she cares. She's very efficient at her job—she's a librarian—but when she comes home, she's a different person."

Alfredo's hand was warm over hers. "I know what that's like, Adrianne. When my own mother dies, I'll dance on her grave," he hissed.

She stared at him. His eyes were flashing with anger. "I was born in Havana. When we came here, I was little, too. We lived with relatives for years out in Queens. My mother left my dad back in Cuba."

He began cutting a pineapple. He sliced off the skin, then cut the flesh into thin wedges. The sharp, shiny blade moved rapidly.

"Have you seen your father since you left ?" she asked.

"I visited him once. He was a good man. He wasn't crazy like the *norteamericanos* ...Adrianne, a little while ago I went to piss in the men's room. Someone had scrawled a message on the wall in pencil that read, 'I suck hot cock. Call me,' along with a phone number. One psycho is calling out to another across the city. Help me. Let me suck your cock. While I piss into the toilet bowl, I'm looking at this stuff on the wall. Can you imagine a man lonely or crazy enough to write down a message like that? What a crazy world. It's like we're living in a huge psycho ward."

The voices around her sounded louder. She heard a final chord from the piano, and then the piano player announced that he was finished for the night.

Alfredo lit a cigarette then offered her one, cupping the flame. "I'm off for the night as soon as I balance the cash register. Want to see my loft, Adrianne?"

"Sure," she heard herself say.

Chapter 6

They took the subway downtown. All the while she pressed against him, and the sexual current between them was so strong that Adrianne could hardly bear it.

They got out of the subway station at Spring Street, and he kept his arm around her while they made their way through dark streets, past unlit buildings in an industrial district, past a few huddled shapes that lay sleeping in doorways. When they reached his building, he unlocked the street door and they walked five flights up narrow stairs.

Alfredo's loft contained a large room with skylights and long industrial windows. Smells of paint, turpentine, and tobacco filled the air. Slowly she walked around, examining pictures and drawings that were stacked up against each other and that hung on the walls. A few reminded her of his painting at the Rose Bar, and these had harmonious shapes and hues. "Old work," he said with a shrug when she pointed out those pictures. There was also a series of male and female nudes with wolves' and tigers' faces. Some of these were sketched in charcoal; others were painted in brilliant oils and acrylics. There were paintings of trees that made her think of tortured human limbs.

He led her through the doorway of an unpainted plywood partition into the kitchen, where she sat down at a table next to a gas stove. The sink was jammed with dishes. In front of her was a butt-filled ashtray as well as a purple candle in a wine bottle coated with wax drippings. He lit a cigarette for her and one for himself, then poured them both glasses of Chianti.

For a moment he left the kitchen, then returned with a drawing pad and a pencil. "Hold that pose," he said. "I want to sketch you." He worked rapidly. Ash from his up-ended cigarette fell to the floor. From time to time he sipped at his wine. Her body began to ache. Finally, he showed her what he had done. Ochre lines revealed a figure slumped in dejection, with a sharp face and enormous eyes.

"That's me?"

"That's you, baby."

"But I'm so ugly."

"That's your opinion. Do you think my paintings are ugly?"

She gazed down at knife cuts on the stained wooden surface of the table.

"Well, the old paintings are beautiful. But the new ones ... yes ... to me some of them seem ugly. But they're very powerful," she stammered, unable to lie to him.

"That's the way I see the world. I try to get under the tinsel crap."

"What about the older paintings?"

"I paint what I see. I've changed, and so has my vision."

"I like tinsel," she said, looking down at a splotch of blue and purple on the table.

"You're still a child," he said.

"I've been through a lot."

"Are you really nineteen, Adrianne?" he asked, taking her hand and gazing hard at her.

"Yes, I really am."

"I thought you were younger," he said. "Your skin is so smooth." He let go of her fingers and brushed his hand against her cheek.

The bare light bulb overhead was beginning to hurt her eyes, and she shut them. In the distance she could hear the sound of night traffic. She thought of how one night Gerald had made love to her on a deserted beach outside of Galveston, and now she could almost feel his touch, feel the sand underneath, and feel the warm water in which they had swum under the dark, clouded sky. That night they had been so close. But then it had all shattered.

The click of a lighter brought her back to the present. Alfredo had turned off the light and lit the candle.

"That's better," she said. "The light was hard on my eyes."

She drank some of her wine.

In the flickering light, Alfredo's cheekbones stood out in his lean face. She thought he looked Indian. He pulled her onto his lap, and as he held her close, her longing for Gerald mingled with the waves of energy that coursed along her thighs and through her body. Then she drew away a little.

"You look frightened," Alfredo said. The warmth in his voice caused tears to flood her eyes.

"I've screwed so many men. I don't want to be hurt again. I want someone to love me," she blurted out.

Why had she said this? She was giving away her power, and she could see herself crumbling into particles in his eyes. His pupils seemed to contract. When he cupped her breast, she jerked away.

"Don't do that." His voice sounded colder.

She tried to speak, but she was shaking with sobs.

"Hey, baby." His voice softened again. "I won't hurt you. I won't ever hurt you," he said. His warm voice so melted her that she felt feverish with wanting him, and she pressed tightly against him, awkward as it was on the chair. "I've been with a lot of women. But this is different, and we both know it."

"How do we know?" she asked, feeling like a child in his arms.

"We *know* each other in a way that goes beyond any rational explanation. When I first saw you, an electric shock ran through me. Don't be frightened, Adrianne. Relax."

"I'm scared."

"What are you scared of?"

"I don't know."

"You've been hurt," he said. "It shows in the way you move and talk and even in the way you breathe. Men can sense that you're an easy lay. But I see something else in you. I see a beautiful woman I could love."

"Really?" She felt stupid. Her voice sounded so unsure. She took another swallow of wine and floated above herself, watching the girl, watching the man who gripped her as he leaned back against the wooden slats of the chair. He stroked her breasts. Aroused, she pressed closer against him, but tears were streaming down her cheeks as a wave of dread swept through her.

"What's the matter?"

"I feel so anxious all the time."

"About what, baby?"

"I don't know."

He was playing her game. He was drawing her out, and she was revealing too much. But she was tired of struggling to keep her secrets.

"I'm so tired of screwing different men. I want to love one man, and I want to be faithful to him the rest of my life."

Why was she saying this? The words had come out of her like swallows on wings of their own. She was hungry. Ritz crackers and cheese were all she'd eaten for dinner. At the Rose Bar she'd had a rum and coke, and now the wine was giving her a headache. "Is there anything to eat?" she asked.

"Not much. I'm just about out of food." He pushed her to her feet, then looked inside the refrigerator and took out a half empty can of beans. Quickly he heated the beans up in a frying pan and put them on a plate with a fork, along with a slice of white bread.

She ate the bread and swallowed a few bites of the beans.

"Is that all you want?"

"I'm sorry. I can't eat any more," she said, putting down the plate. Her stomach felt queasy, and she was far too excited to eat.

As they stood there in the kitchen, he took her in his arms, pressing his hands against her buttocks so that she could feel his hard cock against her belly. Reaching under her skirt, he ran his fingers along the inside of her thighs and underneath the silken fabric of her panties. He caressed her mound of flesh, stroked the pubic hair, pressed underneath to where she was wet, and slid his fingers inside. Aroused, she pressed even closer against him, contracting involuntarily against his fingers. When he led her by the hand through the narrow hall, she followed him in a daze to his room. He lit another candle. In its flickering light, she saw a mattress with rumpled sheets on the floor, and next to it was a bookcase crammed with books.

He knelt and slipped off her shoes, kissing her bare toes, while she rested her hand on his head for support. Then he unbuttoned her skirt, which fell to the floor. Rising to his feet, he pulled her blouse up over her head and unhooked her bra, holding her full breasts tenderly. She started to take off her panties. "Wait, let me," he said, as he slid them off, and pressed her all naked against him. She could feel how aroused he was. "You're so beautiful," he whispered. "You have a great body."

Then he took off his own clothing. He was well-formed and muscular, and his skin glistened with sweat. His cock looked very large. When he pulled her close, she felt herself melting as she never had before with any stranger. "I love you, baby," he whispered in her ear. He pulled her down on top of him on the mattress, rolled her on her back. By now she felt as if she were nothing but a huge wave of desire as he kissed her downwards from her breasts to her belly, then her pubic area and her vulva. He licked and sucked until she moaned with pleasure and gave a little gasp of release. Then he relaxed his hold and pulled himself up so that they were lying full length against each other. "I love you," he murmured again.

At first she hardly dared to breathe for fear of breaking the spell. Then she said in a low voice. "You hardly know me."

"I've never met anyone like you. I feel as if I've known you forever."

As they held each other, images of palm leaves floated through her mind, and she wondered if she were picking up his thoughts. She breathed in the smell of his sweat, mixed with musky cologne, wine, and tobacco. His black hair felt soft, almost silken.

Arching his upper body over her, he penetrated her slippery wetness. Sweat glued them together. As he thrust deeper, she began to feel like a swirling sea, all liquid inside, as she clamped the walls of her vagina tighter against him. He kept on thrusting. Deep inside her, he paused, and for a moment both of them lay still, while their breathing synchronized. It felt as if they were no longer two people. They were one. If only they could always be together like this, she thought. If only there were no lonely aftermath. When he began thrusting again, she felt as if he were filling her with his strength, and she ground her pelvis against him to get him even deeper inside her. "Fuck me until I die," she whispered. What a crazy thing to say! As they moved against each other, she felt as if she were sliding into a dark chasm, sliding, falling, until she could no longer hold herself back. Then she lay still. Again tears overflowed, and her face was wet when he stroked her cheek.

"What's the matter?"

"I don't know. I don't want you to leave me."

"I'm not going to leave you, precious."

She pressed her hands against his buttocks, dug her face into his shoulder. She felt like an octopus dragging him down beneath the sea as he continued ramming into her.

Then with a series of faster thrusts he climaxed.

Calmed by his orgasm, she sighed. The way he touched her, the warmth in his voice, the way he sensed who she was, all this was something she had never experienced before, not even with Gerald. Perhaps at last she had found the man who would be her guide as well as her lover. Perhaps he would marry her, and they would have a child.

His penis was shrinking now, and her thighs were sticky with his semen. She didn't move because she wanted to prolong the pleasure of feeling him inside her. She imagined his sperm traveling upwards to fertilize the egg in her uterus.

As if picking up her thoughts, he probed inside her vagina with his long fingers and felt her diaphragm. "Good," he said. "You're protected."

"Yes," she said sadly.

Dread encircled her like a serpent so that she could hardly breathe. She felt herself losing control of her center, her edges spilling out, as if she were some kind of soft putty he would be able to mold into any shape he wanted, and she sensed that she would be powerless to prevent this because she would need him far too much.

Chapter 7

At 9:15 the next morning Adrianne stumbled sleepily into the office at Eureka Fabrics. She put the paper bag with her doughnut and coffee on the desk and her straw handbag inside the bottom drawer.

Irene rolled her eyes to the ceiling. "Here's the party girl!"

"You're late," added Rose.

"I know," Adrianne said brightly, skittering over an abyss of fear. "The subway got stuck." She became aware of how wrinkled her skirt and blouse were from being thrown into a heap on Alfredo's floor.

Rose, five months pregnant, had pale skin and long curly hair. She took a sip of the Pepsi which always stood on her littered desk. "Why don't you ask your boyfriends to send you to work in a taxi?" she asked, exchanging a glance with Irene.

Adrianne laughed, but she felt panicky. Something was wrong. They treated her as if she were crazy.

The only phone in the office rang.

Irene picked it up. "For you, Adrianne," she said, handing her the receiver. Then she resumed flicking through some large worksheets. She was a bony woman with sharp features.

"Which boyfriend is it this time?" asked Rose.

"Who's keeping count?"

"Hi, precious," said Alfredo on the other end.

The sound of his voice swept away Adrianne's fatigue. Although it was awkward to talk, standing as she was against Irene's desk, she floated high above Irene and Rose.

"How are you, Adrianne?"

"Okay, Alfredo. Just a bit tired." She wobbled on her high heels.

"Last night was special."

"Mmmm," she murmured.

"Let's get together tomorrow night?"

"All right."

"Why don't you stop off at the bar around midnight. That's when I get off."

"Okay. I'll do that."

"I know you're working, so I won't keep you."

"That's okay."

"Love you, baby," he murmured, just before he hung up.

She replaced the heavy black receiver on its cradle. Did he mean it? *Love you, baby.*

Trembling, she began to type up orders that sales reps had written out in barely legible script. As she worked, she munched on her doughnut.

Again the phone rang.

"Bet it's another one of her boyfriends."

"Naww, it's my husband. Wants to check up on me and the baby," said Rose, smoothing the cotton of her maternity smock over her swollen belly. "He's kicking," she murmured.

"For you again, Adrianne."

Adrianne did not recognize the voice on the other end.

"Sure you remember me," the voice said slyly. "This is Don."

"Don ...Don?..."

"Nedick's ...a month ago on 37th Street."

In a flash she remembered an episode in the cellar of a delicatessen. He was a young man with dark hair, a punk's face, and a cynical grin. It had happened during her lunch hour. She recalled the fast rubbing of his groin against hers as he spilled semen inside her. They had stood against the cement wall, which smelled cool and fresh in spite of the heat. What had come over her? Why had she told him where she worked, let alone her true name?

"I would have called you sooner," the voice said. "I've been away."

"I'm busy, Don. I can't talk now."

"When can I see you?"

"I ...I have a boyfriend."

"That doesn't change anything."

She hung up. Hoped she wouldn't run into him again. Why was she involved in these encounters? At the time they seemed no more real than a lurid nightmare or an erotic fantasy. The stranger's bodies gave her a moment's comfort. But then all this was smashed by the reality of semen injected inside her, the odor of semen, the clammy feel of fluid, a collapsed penis, and afterwards, a harsh voice.

"Such a busy girl," said Irene. "So you have a new boyfriend?"

"Yes."

"Tell us about him."

Their eyes gleamed.

"Oh ...just a man."

"Just a man. Just a man," mimicked Rose and Irene.

"She uses us as personal secretaries," said Rose.

"Yeah. Saves on her phone bill. We oughta charge her."

Once more the phone rang. Apprehensively, Adrianne ran over to Irene's desk and picked it up. It was the same male voice. "Why can't you see me tonight, Adrianne?" he wheedled. "I'll show you a good time. Got a friend who wants to meet you. I want to see you so bad. I just *gotta* see you."

Conscious of the two other women, furious with them, embarrassed, she wanted to hang up, but she felt sorry for Don. Lonely aching punk. She was frightened, too, at the insistence in his voice.

"Well, maybe. Say, Don, maybe I can meet you at the same Nedick's stand," she said with cunning, aware that Irene and Rose were listening and wondering whom she met at Nedick's stand.

"Swell, Adrianne. Five-thirty?"

"Yes, that's okay." Get him off the scent. She'd take another route home. "All right," she repeated sweetly. Why she was so compelled by his urgency, she had no idea, except that she experienced herself now as a pure wave of energy, even as perspiration from her hand clung to the phone. "I'll see you."

She hung up again.

Irene handed her a kleenex. "You're perspiring."

"Just too popular," mocked Rose.

Adrianne laughed again, on the edge of her abyss. Now she was paying for all those encounters she'd had before she met Alfredo. She felt as if she had betrayed him. He must never know about this incident.

She had absorbed herself in typing the orders when her supervisor, Joyce O'Grady, came into the room. Joyce was a large, grey-haired woman in her fifties. Her skin was soft and pouched.

"Adrianne, I need to talk to you alone," she said.

Adrianne followed the supervisor into her small office. Shelves at one end were heaped with fabrics in many hues. Swatches of brightly colored fabric and a multitude of papers covered the desk as well as part of the floor.

"What do you want to talk to me about?" Adrianne inquired.

"You were late again today," Joyce began.

"I know. There was a subway tie-up."

"You're nearly always ten or fifteen minutes late. Last Thursday you were an hour and a half late."

"I'm sorry. I'll try to do better."

"I'm afraid you won't have a chance."

Adrianne swallowed, and her stomach tightened.

"I didn't want to fire you because you're a nice girl. I tried to protect you, honey, I really did. But when Mr. Schwab spotted your latest mistake, he hit the roof. He told me I had to let you go."

"What did I do?"

"*This!*" Joyce shoved two torn yellow orders at her. One, written in Joyce's large, circular hand, had red markings on it. The other, which had been typed and bore Adrianne's initials, was crossed with large blue-inked X's. "See here, August second."

Adrianne glanced at the original order and then at the ones she had printed, but at first both were blurs.

"The addresses match."

"Yes, I know. Look at the quantities."

With her pencil, Joyce lightly circled both numbers which had already been marked. "The original is for one hundred and fifty yards of Midnight Pima, and your order is for fifteen hundred yards. Mistakes do happen, but this is inexcusable."

Joyce handed her four more pairs of orders. "Just look at the addresses and the quantities. They've been incorrectly copied, and they're all signed with your initials."

Adrianne could not repress a smile. Somehow it delighted her to think of the commotion all the extra material had created when it was delivered.

A smile escaped Joyce's lips, too. "I'm sorry to see you go. I know you have a good heart, and the other girls in the office don't treat you right."

Tears rose in Adrianne's eyes. She liked this warm, motherly supervisor.

Joyce added, "Let me give you a little advice." She patted Adrianne's wrist. "There now, don't take it so hard. You'll get a week's severance pay. I tried to cover up for you. I wanted you to get at least twenty weeks in so you could file for unemployment. Don't tell anyone I said that," she muttered. "I want you to wise up," she continued, clucking like a hen and settling invisible feathers around herself. "All those men who call you ... a nice girl like you ... all they want is to get inside your pants. Believe me."

Adrianne stared at the golden cross which gleamed on Joyce's ample bosom.

"Find a decent man who respects you, and marry him. You need some steadiness in your life. Take my advice." Joyce squared herself in her chair like a soldier while she wrote out a memo for Adrianne to take to the Accounting Office.

Adrianne looked down at a swatch of dusty black velvet in front of her on the desk. What had caused her to make such stupid mistakes? She'd tried so hard. She could not do anything right. Something inside seemed to be trying to destroy her.

What would she do now for money? She couldn't face looking for another job just yet. She certainly couldn't use anyone here, not even Joyce, as a reference. What would Alfredo think of her?

Dazed, she walked back to the office she shared with Rose and Irene.

"I've been fired."

"We know," said Rose.

Heavy silence.

"Joyce told us this morning. She wasn't sure you were going to show up at all."

"Her boyfriends will take care of her."

The phone rang again. Irene answered. "For you, Adrianne."

"How are you, Adrianne?" asked Max.

"All right," she said. His voice gave her comfort. He seemed to send roots into the earth.

"Adrianne, I am sorry to call you at work, but so often now you don't come home," he said plaintively. "I wondered if

you will do me the honor of attending a concert with me this
Friday night."

"Oh, I don't know," she said. What if Alfredo wanted to
see her? Go with Max, pounded the voice inside as she considered that destiny depended on the slightest decision, a hair's
breadth.

"It is a concert of excellent musicians who will play
Beethoven and Mozart. Do you know this music?"

"Yes," said Adrianne. The prospect of listening to the
music filled her with joy.

"Then it is not only jazz you like?"

"No."

"I will get the tickets then," he said. "You give me hope,
meine liebchen."

"Another boyfriend," said Irene after she'd hung up. "A
new one, huh? Joyce told us to make sure you clean out your
desk before you go."

Trembling with anger as she felt their gaze on her, Adrianne took out her straw handbag from the bottom drawer of
her desk. She straightened out the other drawers and defiantly shoved a few pencils and paper clips inside her bag.
There was nothing else she wanted to take. She would leave
her faded magenta cardboard flower. Let them throw it out.

At the Accounting Office she received her check.

Goodbye, Rose and Irene.

Goodbye, Joyce, with your advice about not letting men
get into my pants.

Goodbye, office. Goodbye, everyone.

She walked out of the elevator and onto Sixth Avenue.
Although a light rain had begun to fall, she trudged along, not
caring that she was getting damp and chilled. How could
Alfredo love her if she couldn't even hold down a job?

Chapter 8

People were settling down in the concert hall and waiting for the music to begin. In the midst of them sat Adrianne and Max. Her face looked very white to him beneath the bright lights, and her cheeks were flushed. The way her low neckline revealed the curves of her breasts, sheathed in a black brassiere, tantalized him. She seemed sad, and her smile seemed forced.

"Is something wrong?" Max asked.

"I lost my job."

"Poor child."

He clasped her hand. "You are lovely," he said. His voice grew emotional. "Let me know if you need help. I have money."

"That's very kind of you, Max."

The musicians were warming up, and at last the concert began.

A Beethoven quartet was first, and Max unconsciously swayed in rhythm. The closeness of Adrianne's body stirred him. She didn't say anything about the music, but she was very still for a moment after the first piece finished.

He put his hand on her thigh. She did not move away. Max's heart felt too large for the space it took in his chest, and he had a sense of foreboding.

Next was a Mozart quartet in D major, serene but full of delicate melancholy.

Memories came back to Adrianne. She was making love with Alfredo all over again, and the intensity of it, the sweetness was overpowering. Then more troubling images arose from the past.

She was lying on an operating table, enveloped in the smell of ether.

"You'll be all right. Just close your eyes," said the surgeon, a friend of Gerald.

Afterwards they'd thrown the fetus into a garbage bin.

It would have been a girl, they told her.

During intermission, Max and Adrianne walked outside. It was hot and humid. Max wiped his brow with a handkerchief. "I am so sorry about your job," he said, trying to bridge the distance between them.

"I don't know what I'll do now," she said. "I just don't know."

"Don't worry, *meine liebchen,*" he responded, softly caressing her hand. "If you need help, I am here."

"Oh, you are good!" Perhaps she ought to give more of herself to him. Perhaps he was kinder and more decent than Alfredo.

Suddenly he felt dizzy. "Let's go back to our seats," he said. "I need to sit down."

During the Bloch sonata, sadness wound through him. He was acutely aware of Adrianne's flesh, while she seemed absorbed in the music. Long ago Mathilde had been a real wife to him, as had Monique. Old age caused him to seek a child-wife for his tired, flaccid body. How he had degenerated. Tears welled up in his eyes.

After the concert ended, they went outside again. People pressed against them. There were smells of sweat, smoke, and perfume, sounds of voices and traffic. They walked a little way up the block. Adrianne sighed. He was aware again, as he had been during the concert when he had stolen glances at her profile, of a radiant warmth about her that made him want to be close to her. Then he would have a reason to go on living. The heavy blackness would evaporate.

She looked nervous.

"You would like to go somewhere for a drink?" he asked.

"Oh Max, that's kind of you, but I'd better not. I have to meet someone."

He nodded, raging inside. "Is it the bartender we met the other night?"

"Maybe. Maybe not. That's my business." She hugged him. "I'm sorry. I should have told you earlier. Thank you for taking me to the concert. It was wonderful, Max," she said earnestly. "Goodbye. I'll see you," she added in a rush.

"Wait, Adrianne, before you go. Please take this money." He handed her five ten-dollar bills. As she hesitated, he added, "You will do me a kindness. I cannot take money to the grave. I know you do not have enough, so do me the honor to accept this small gift for a taxi and something nice for yourself."

With generosity he would overcome his rage. What right had he to possess her, after all? Perhaps by being generous to her, he could atone in some small degree for the past. Poor child, he thought. Perhaps she will not be mine, but I can still love her.

Swiftly she ran off.

He felt pain beneath his breastbone. The space in front of his eyes swam. He was dizzy, as he had been earlier in the evening, and as he walked in the direction she had vanished, fever shot through him. Feeling faint, he clutched at a lamp post for support while people swarmed past. What a fool he was to think she would ever love him!

Chapter 9

Adrianne found another job as a cook in a sleepy little bar in the West Eighties. There she worked from one in the afternoon until nine at night five days a week, grilling hamburgers and french fries, preparing salads and B-B-Q chicken and steaks.

In comparison to her last job, it was restful being in the small, greasy kitchen. The owner had told her that the restaurant was kept open for legal reasons, as only a few customers ordered food.

Two or three nights a week she spent with Alfredo. These were the high points of her life. As she worked in the kitchen or sat on a stool with nothing to do, waiting for orders, she would brood over what she might have said or done wrong the night before, and she would go over their lovemaking in her mind, trying to savor it all over again. When she and Alfredo were physically close, it was like being on fire, but afterwards she felt so isolated.

One night late after work she wandered into a bar on her way home. A bald man sitting next to her bought her two beers and talked in a drunken way about himself. Then he touched the bulge between his thighs, slyly, secretively, yet apparently so that she could see. She was revolted. "I've got to go," she said in a panic. Jumping up, she ran to the door. "Hey, wait a minute!" he shouted.

In the darkness she ran and ran until she was sure she had left him far behind. Her side ached with exertion. Then she slowed down, and her footsteps sounded against the pavement as if they belonged to someone else. She told herself that she should never have gone into that bar. Before she ran off, she had felt a surge of desire for that bald man. Alfredo, with his telepathic vision, would perceive that she was faithless in her thoughts and that she could crumble in an instant.

When she was not with Alfredo, not reassured by the strength of his presence, sometimes she felt as if her body would fly out into tiny pieces like dust and dissolve into the atmosphere. There was no center, nothing to hold her together. When she walked, she sometimes felt as if she were dissolving outwards into the strangers she passed on the streets. Only when she was holding someone close did she feel solid.

Her furnished room on 97th Street seemed suffocating, and as much as possible she avoided it, continuing to wander the streets after work. She hated her room, which was filled with the signs of her despair. Her clothing was heaped up in piles on the floor, on the bureau, and on the bed. The week before she had lost her door key and a twenty-dollar bill, which had been wadded up on her bureau for days. It was all she could do to get to her new job and concentrate on her simple tasks there.

If she moved in with Alfredo, she believed it would put an end to the chaos and uncertainty of her life. Then, too, Max would no longer plague her. Max's desire hung heavily in the air. This bothered her because she did not like to be cruel.

<center>~~~</center>

It was night, and the windows in the brightly lit loft were shiny and black like mirrors. To Adrianne, they had a slightly menacing quality. Street noises below mingled with Caribbean music on the radio. Alfredo sketched her while she lay on his old green couch. He was swaying to the music, but then stopped and looked at her intently.

"Why are you so down, baby?" he asked.

"Money," she murmured. "I never make enough to last the week."

"You could always try hustling," Alfredo waved his arms up towards the high ceiling with its ancient gas pipes. "You'd make a lot more than you do now. Hell, you could even support me. Then I could stay home and paint instead of busting my ass at that lousy bar and taking long shots at the track."

"I didn't know you bet." She tried to conceal the shock she felt at his references to hustling and the race track. He had never talked about these things before.

"Occasionally. There's always the dream—the pot of gold at the end of the rainbow."

She smiled uneasily. On the street below she heard men talking, laughing, and cursing. A fog horn sounded in the distance. *"Baila, baila, baila la rumba ..."* a man was singing over the radio, and just now she found this music jarring.

"Don't look so scared. I was just thinking out loud." Alfredo put down the charcoal and lit a cigarette.

She rolled over on the couch and drew her knees up against her bare chest, shivering. Smells of paint, stale cigarette smoke, and liquor filled her nostrils.

"I guess prostitutes do make a lot of money," she said, sitting up.

"Hey, don't break that pose. I'm not finished!" he shot at her. "Of course they do. They're not hung up with a lot of middle-class shit. Now hold still." He continued working for a few minutes, then paused, stepped back, and lit another cigarette.

"Do you go to the races a lot?" she asked.

"Once in a while. I'll take you to Belmont one day."

She yawned. Strangely, the tension she was experiencing made her sleepy. "Alfredo, I'm so tired."

"Hold on. I'm almost finished. Hey, baby, have you ever read Gurdjieff?"

"No. Who is he?"

"Gurdjieff was an Armenian mystic. A philosopher and a genius. He spent his life studying human consciousness. Gurdjieff writes somewhere that a person on the spiritual path ought to be able to make a living with his left foot. He meant that an artist shouldn't have to bust ass paying the rent at the sacrifice of his real work."

Alfredo added a few more strokes, then told Adrianne she could stand up.

She wrapped herself in a blanket which lay draped over the couch, then walked over to the easel. The floor felt cold beneath her feet. There she was, drawn in charcoal on butcher paper, bloated, with large breasts and buttocks and an anxious look in her eyes. Her nose looked longer and narrower than it was, and her cheekbones stood out.

"That's me?"

"That's one version of you. You've got a fantastic body and an expressive face." Alfredo drew her close and kissed her. His shoulder muscles bulged beneath her hands. As the blanket slid, she reached to gather it around her, but he yanked it off.

They went into the bedroom and made love. Burrowing against his shoulder, she savored his scent of sweat and cologne as she fell asleep.

Later he woke her. He had switched on a light. In his hands he held a worn volume of Gurdjieff's writings, which he had taken from the bookcase. Sleepily she rubbed her eyes. "Read this, Adrianne," he said, handing her the book. "It will open up your mind. Gurdjieff writes about how most people live their life in a kind of sleep, unless they make an effort to become aware. People don't question the rules. . . . How much do you make in a month, Adrianne? Two hundred dollars? You could make that in one night."

"But what a price to pay!" she said, upset that he had again brought up the subject of hooking.

He punched her lightly. "Some jerk fucks you. He doesn't have anything of *you*, he's only enjoyed your body."

"Alfredo, let me go back to sleep."

"Before you do, I've got something special for us." He pulled several books out from a bookshelf and produced a black lacquer box. Inside it was a small quantity of greenish grey tobacco and some thin paper. "Marijuana," he said. He rolled a joint, inhaled, held the smoke inside his lungs for what seemed a long time, and then exhaled. "Try it," he said. "Hold the smoke in as long as you can."

Again she was a bit shocked, as she had no idea that he smoked marijuana. When she inhaled, she coughed. He only laughed, thumping her on the shoulders, and encouraging her to take a few more drags.

"Marijuana gives me a relaxed kind of energy so I can work all night," he said. He put on his white jockey shorts, paint-stained jeans, and blue work shirt that lay heaped on the floor.

After a while she began to feel some of the effects of the marijuana. As she lay in bed unable to sleep, she saw vivid images in her mind. The Caribbean music was playing again. Rhythms and melodies sounded particularly distinct, as if time had slowed. She could hear him moving around in the studio as she drifted off to sleep.

Early the next morning he showed her the new canvas on his easel: a woman with two heads, four arms, and four legs, like an Eastern deity in brilliant hues of orange, red, purple, green, black, and yellow.

"Adrianne, this is for my show. Did I tell you the Harris Gallery is giving me a one-man show in October? It's a real break for me. With any luck, I'll sell enough work to quit my job," He drew her close. "I might even be able to support two people."

Her heart pounded as she thought that he must truly care about her. He was haggard; there were hollows under his eyes and lines in his face that she had never before noticed, and she realized for the first time what a strain he must be under. "You need to sleep," she said. She reached out and stroked the stubble on his gaunt face.

"Make me a cup of that Japanese tea by the stove, will you, *preciosa?*"

While he slept, she tidied up the loft and swept the floor. Later she washed the dishes in the sink, and she even cleaned what she could of the thick dust and bits of plaster from the ceiling which covered everything. Although she was exhausted, a sense of peace came over her as she worked. Pausing, she looked at Alfredo and watched his regular breathing. His face was peaceful. His lean body was curled up like a child's. *He trusts me,* she thought, and this gave her comfort.

Chapter 10

One morning the phone rang at the rooming house while she was still in bed. She heard Max pad down the hall in his slippers and answer. Then he pounded on the door. "It's for you."

"Who is it?"

"Someone named Lucille."

Adrianne stretched, rubbed her eyes, and put on her robe, tying the sash tightly around her. As she passed Max in the hall he brushed against her. Ignoring this, she picked up the phone.

"Adrianne, at last I've found you!" cried Lucille at the other end. "Why haven't you written to me? I finally got your address and phone number from your mother. I'm here in New York, at the Plaza Hotel for two weeks. Can you come and visit me today?"

Adrianne hesitated because Alfredo might call. "I may have to work tonight."

"Come for lunch then."

After she hung up, Max planted himself in front of her. Adrianne could hear the landlady and one of the other roomers, a Chinese student, talking in the kitchen. The landlady's elderly, matter-of-fact voice contrasted with the sing-song English of the student.

"Adrianne, for days now you avoid me. I must talk with you." He looked unhappy.

"Max, I just don't have time right now. I'm sorry." She felt cruel, speaking to him this way.

As she rode the crosstown bus and then a Fifth Avenue bus downtown, she wondered why Lucille had come to New York. The strangers around her in this midday heat seemed like shadows, except for their sweaty smells and raucous sounds. How different these voices were from the slower ones of south Texas, and from Lucille's. Across the aisle sat an old black woman in a cotton housedress, shiny with sweat. Adrianne thought the woman seemed to radiate a dull reddish aura of pain. She looked as if she mopped the floors of skyscrapers at night. At the 72nd Street stop, the woman opened her eyes an instant to look sullenly at her before an onrush of passengers blocked her from Adrianne's view.

Adrianne's memories of Lucille mingled with those of Gerald. She remembered the night she had first met Lucille. She and Gerald had gone to a party at Lucille and Barney's house. Lucille's husband, Barney, was a self-made millionaire, and Adrianne had been impressed with the elegance of the mansion and the guests. Unaccustomed to hard liquor, nevertheless she had three drinks to cover up the disturbance she felt because Gerald had never before ignored her like this, and he was openly flirting with other women at the party. A tall and handsome doctor, with his icy grey eyes and fair hair, Gerald seemed accustomed to being sought out by women. Adrianne had stood awkwardly in a dark corner, a trifle dizzy from the liquor. Suddenly an attractive woman in a white silk dress had swooped upon her.

"Who are you?" Lucille asked. "Honey, you look lost."

Lucille's voice was vibrant. She had taken Adrianne upstairs to her bedroom suite, with its satin upholstered furniture, and they had drunk still more and talked.

That night Adrianne found out that Lucille came from Alabama and that she had met Barney when she worked in Las Vegas as a show girl. Lucille had been vague about her past. In repose, a certain bitterness had showed in her face. But her manner was warm, even tender. Adrianne had found herself talking in a rush about Gerald and about the abortion. She had not felt able to confide in her few friends, nor in her mother.

"How old are you?" Lucille had asked.

"Eighteen," said Adrianne.

"Poor baby," whispered Lucille, clasping Adrianne in her arms. Aroused by Lucille's sympathy, Adrianne's emotions, which had been buried for months, came to the surface. Unaccustomed to tenderness, Adrianne sobbed uncontrollably. She pleaded with Lucille not to tell anyone about the abortion because she wanted to protect Gerald's reputation at the hospital where he worked.

Lucille had stroked her hair. "Relax, honey. It's not so bad. I had two abortions in Juárez. You're young and beautiful, even if you could lose a few pounds. There's nothing to be afraid of."

Adrianne shuddered. Was she beautiful in anyone's eyes? She felt overwhelmed that someone as sophisticated and elegant as Lucille should take an interest in her.

~~~

At last Adrianne was standing in the hotel corridor outside Lucille's room on the sixth floor. Nervous and inexplicably frightened, she smoothed her turquoise print nylon dress over her body, then knocked on the door. She had gained weight since living in Manhattan, and this was evident from the way the dress clung to her. Lucille would tell her to go on a diet. In her presence, Adrianne always felt a bit clumsy, yet she knew that Lucille cared for her with the warmth of the dream-mother of her childhood who used to come to Adrianne at night when she needed reassurance and love

In a flash, Adrianne remembered the afternoon their relationship had changed. At the time Adrianne had been working as a clerk in a small gift shop. She arrived at Lucille's late in the afternoon, exhausted from being on her feet all day, and she had lain back in a chair and closed her eyes for a moment. Lucille had started to stroke her hair. Then Adrianne felt the kiss that Lucille placed full on her mouth. When Adrianne drew back in shock, Lucille had whispered, "It's all right, honey. It's all right."

The door opened, and Lucille stood there, thinner than Adrianne remembered her, in a dark, dappled, clinging dress, its starkness relieved by a strand of pearls. Lucille's face was unnaturally pale, and her long glossy brown hair had been shorn off just below her ears.

"Oh, I'm glad to see you, baby!" Lucille's voice sounded strained. She pulled Adrianne inside, then shut the door. They embraced. Adrianne could feel the rise and fall of her friend's chest. Lucille kissed her on the lips, as she had so many times in the past. But Adrianne could sense that something was not right. Lucille's Chanel perfume mingled with a faint medicinal odor. She pressed against Adrianne, then abruptly pulled away, turning her back as she went towards the closet. "Honey, I haven't had anything to eat all day, and I'm starved. I thought we could have lunch in the Village."

Her voice still sounded artificial. After rummaging a bit, Lucille found a pair of delicate leather sandals. Adrianne noticed that her friend's fingers were trembling as she slipped them on over her stockinged feet.

They took a taxi downtown and got out at Washington Square. With their arms tightly around each other, they walked along the sidewalk, passing dirt mounds where slender trees, supported by wires, grew. The sky had turned grey. A gust of wind whipped the first dead autumn leaves from the square. The wind whipped through Adrianne's legs and blew her hair up around her face. Lucille pressed against her, nuzzling her ear, caressing one of her breasts.

"Dykes!" a man yelled. Adrianne's face reddened.

She and Lucille wandered into an Italian restaurant, where they sat down at a table by the window. Lucille ordered white wine. She adjusted her neckline which had slipped down over one shoulder, then leaned forward. "I needed to get away from Barney. I didn't call you any sooner because I had to be alone for a few days. "

"What happened?"

"Barney wants a divorce. If he files, I'll take him for all he's got. That bastard!" She paused and lit a cigarette with shaking fingers on which jewels glittered. "There's more, but I haven't drunk enough to tell you!...Tell me about *you*," Lucille commanded. She blew out the match.

Adrianne proceeded to bring her friend up to date. She described her jobs and where she lived. "I've met a man," she added. "He's an artist."

"You know nothing about men," Lucille said scornfully. "If he's anything like Gerald, he's bad news."

Although she felt hurt, Adrianne ignored this remark. "I'm hungry. Let's order," she said

Lucille's dark eyes had filled with tears, and a thin streak of mascara ran down one cheek. She dabbed her face with her napkin. "Yes, let's order. Where's the waiter? I'd like some more wine. Oh, damn, what's the use of trying to stay on top anymore?"

"What's the matter?"

"Do I mean anything to you?"

"Of course you do."

"Now that I'm in New York, would you like to live with me?"

"I don't know," Adrianne said hesitantly.

"Well, it was just a thought. Is your new boy friend treating you right? You've gained weight, and you look spaced out. Are you on drugs?"

"No, of course not." Was Lucille saying these things because she was jealous?

"I'm sorry about Barney," she said, trying to divert Lucille's attention away from herself.

"I'll sue him for everything he's got. He and his new wife can live in a goddamn shack. And I don't need your pity," said Lucille. Her eyes blazed darker. "Where is that waiter? Hey, there, boy, we need more wine."

The middle-aged waiter flinched and looked as if he were about to speak, but then thought better of it.

"Bring the menus, too, please," Adrianne added. Then she blinked. Was that man standing down there at the corner really Alfredo? He was waiting for the light to change, and he stood exactly the way Alfredo did, with one shoulder slightly curved.

"I'll be back in a minute!" she cried, running out of the restaurant.

He had walked halfway down the next block before she finally caught up with him and grabbed him by the arm. "Alfredo?"

It was indeed Alfredo, and he looked startled. "Adrianne, what are you doing here?"

"I'm having lunch with my friend from Houston, and I want you to meet her. We're just a block away."

Alfredo kept walking, but she kept pace.

"I've got an appointment," he said.

"Please! Just to say hello, Alfredo. She's my best friend."

"Okay, sweetheart. But just for a few minutes."

Triumphantly, she led him back and introduced them.

"Would you like to join us for lunch?" Lucille asked. Her eyes glowed with a mixture of attraction and distrust.

"That's all right. I'll just have a drink."

"You might as well order something to eat. It's my husband's money. We're getting divorced, and the faster I can spend that bastard's money the better."

"I'm sorry to hear that," he said.

"What the hell do you care?" Lucille said, gazing up at him.

"God, you're gorgeous," he said. He sat down between the two women. "Adrianne, didn't prepare me . . . I think I will have lunch, after all." Apparently, he was no longer in a rush to get to his appointment.

Lucille took out a cigarette from her gold-tipped case, and Alfredo lit it for her, cradling her hand in his. He gazed into her eyes.

"How could he divorce a woman as beautiful as you are?"

"Oh, come on!" said Lucille with annoyance.

Taken aback, Alfredo began to talk about contemporary art, and for a while he draped his arm around Adrianne.

Lucille and Alfredo discussed the work of contemporary artists, weighing the merits of painters such as Kline and Rothko. Lucille knew more about the subject of art than Adrianne had imagined.

Alfredo told Lucille about his up-coming show while Adrianne, ravenous, cut her steak into small pieces. The other two had ordered veal parmigiano, and the waiter had refilled the carafe with wine.

She was feeling left out. The attraction between those two created such a current that Adrianne could almost touch it. She began to feel as if she were living through a bad dream. There had been a hint of this on that first night when Alfredo had whispered and flirted with the waitress. God, please don't let him be like Gerald, she prayed.

The waiter brought the check, and Lucille paid. While waiting for her change, she took out another cigarette, and again Alfredo lit it, leaning very close to her. Adrianne thought there was a similarity in the cast of their features.

"Let me see your palm," said Alfredo, taking hold of Lucille's hand again. He examined her palm, stroking the lines lightly with his fingers.

"You had a difficult childhood," he said. "You've been abused. I see violence. You've done things you'd like to keep hidden."

She wrenched away, "Get your goddamn gigolo hands off me!"

Alfredo's expression so frightened Adrianne that, in a panic, she flung her arms around him crying, "Stop!"

He pushed her away and spoke to Lucille in a voice bristling with offended pride. "Lady, I can see why your husband wants out! You have no idea who I am."

"Adrianne, come on, let's leave," said Lucille.

Adrianne looked at Alfredo, silently begging forgiveness for what had just happened.

"Get out," he said, his voice as cold as ice.

"I love you," she whispered, but he was like stone.

"Come on," Lucille insisted. "Let's go."

Chapter 11

Inside the taxi, Lucille shivered despite the heat. "Your guy is a would-be gigolo."

"You were attracted," whispered Adrianne.

"No, I wasn't," said Lucille furiously.

The taxi driver braked suddenly as a car cut in front of them. The street was jammed with traffic. Adrianne became aware of the driver looking at the two of them in the rear view mirror. She wondered what he must think of the two women sitting so close to each other.

"I love him," murmured Adrianne.

"Ask yourself what he wants from you," said Lucille in a low voice. "He's an opportunist. I used to work the casinos in Vegas, and I met dozens of s.o.b.'s who came onto rich women the way Alfredo did to me. You have no money, and what have you got to offer? Is he with you for your brains? Your looks? Honey, be careful!"

"He loves me!" cried Adrianne. She was so offended that she was on the point of opening the taxi door and jumping out, but Lucille dug her nails into Adrianne's arm.

"I'm ill," Lucille whispered. "I don't think I have much longer to live."

"What kind of illness do you have?" asked Adrianne.

"I want you to stay with me," said Lucille, evading the question.

"Can you stay with me for a little while?"

Lucille's need wrenched at Adrianne. It was Monday, and she did have the day off from her job. Furthermore, after what had just happened, there was not much chance that Alfredo would call her tonight.

"Yes, I can," she said slowly.

Oblivious of the taxi driver, Lucille gave Adrianne a long, full, wet kiss. Then unexpectedly she announced, "I feel like shopping. Will you come with me?"

In a flat voice, Adrianne agreed to do whatever Lucille wanted.

They spent the afternoon at Bonwit's. Lucille treated herself to a silver mink jacket. For Adrianne she bought a black chiffon dress, slender Italian high heels, and quantities of lacy underwear. In spite of herself, Adrianne luxuriated in the new clothes. Perhaps they would make her more desirable in Alfredo's eyes. Long ago the dream-mother of her childhood fantasies had clothed her in bright dresses.

Back at the hotel, Lucille collapsed on the bed, sighing with fatigue. Room Service sent up a light dinner of consommé and salad greens. After they had eaten, Adrianne dozed off while Lucille was in the bathroom. When she opened her eyes, she saw Lucille standing over her in a peach silk negligee.

"Adrianne, I have something to tell you. But let's have a nightcap first. Scotch on the rocks okay? That's all I've got."

"I've already had too much to drink, and I'm sleepy."

"Honey, I need a drink."

Lucille would always be elegant, thought Adrianne as she watched Lucille walk across the room in her high-heeled slippers. She went over to a mahogany sideboard, picked up a glass, and filled it almost to the brim from a Cutty Sark bottle.

A fire siren shrilled. Lucille hobbled across the room to peer down through the blinds at 59th Street and the edge of Central Park. "It's incredible that they still have horses and carriages down there," she said. "We had a mule back home," she continued. "Did you know I was a farm girl? I left home when I was even younger than you—Alfredo did glom onto some things about me—I've seen too many men hurt women." Lucille gulped down what was left in her glass. Then she looked at Adrianne strangely. "Close your eyes and count to ten."

"Why?"

"Just do as I say."

Adrianne obeyed.

"Now, open them."

Lucille had pulled open the negligee, revealing her chest, where the skin was pink and flat. The nipples were gone.

"My God! Lucille, what happened to you?"

"Breast cancer. They butchered me."

Adrianne moved close to Lucille and held her. She felt roughened skin over ribs, where once Lucille's soft, full breasts had been.

"Maybe I'll find a plastic surgeon," Lucille murmured. "But what's the use?"

"Of course you'll find a surgeon," said Adrianne, wanting to reassure her even though she knew nothing at all about this situation

"What kills me is how Barney could choose this time to file for divorce."

"You're not going to die."

"What do you know about it? You're a goddamn fool."

"Don't talk to me like that!"

Lucille wrenched away. "You're repulsed by me, just as he is." She flung herself onto the bed and bit into the green brocade spread as if to keep from screaming. With her cropped hair and no makeup, she looked almost like a boy.

Through the thin silk, Adrianne stroked her narrow back. "I love you, Lucille. I want to you to live," she whispered as she took off her clothes and lay down next to her friend. They pulled back the covers and lay on top of the sheet, embracing each other.

"Adrianne, why do you give men, who are idiots, so much power over you?" Lucille chided. She licked Adrianne's earlobe. Then she softly kissed her eyelids, caressed her hair, her neck, and her shoulders before she lowered herself to take one of Adrianne's nipples into her mouth, sucking at it as hungrily as an infant.

If only I had milk to give you, thought Adrianne. If only I could give you back your breasts.

Lucille raised her face and buried it in the hollow beneath Adrianne's throat. Then Adrianne pulled her up and gently began to kiss her scars.

"Stop, goddamn you!"

"I'm sorry," Adrianne whispered.

"Don't do that!"

Adrianne burst into tears.

"Don't cry. Damn you, don't cry!" Lucille bit Adrianne's lower lip, then thrust her tongue into Adrianne's mouth. The strong perfume she was wearing could not mask her sickly odor. Lucille's thighs clamped around Adrianne. Feeling

Lucille's wetness, Adrianne reached down to stroke and comfort her.

Lucille whispered, "Honey, I want to go down on you." She shifted her body so that her head was between Adrianne's thighs. Closing her eyes, Adrianne began to let herself go, moaning a little and arching up so that Lucille's tongue could go deeper inside her. She pressed Lucille's thighs down against her face and shoulders, feeling the stubble where they had been shaved. As her own tongue penetrated Lucille's slippery, oyster-like crevice, she was almost overcome by the odor. But despite this, she gradually allowed herself to sink into pleasurable sensations

Afterwards, the two of them lay quietly with their arms around each other. Lucille soon fell asleep.

The noise of traffic sounded outside. Adrianne felt restless and hungry, and she had a headache. Stumbling around in the darkness, she looked for something to eat, but there was nothing except for a piece of toast left over from dinner. When she dialed the luminous numbers on the phone for room service, there was just silence at the other end. Finally, she felt inside her purse and found half a dozen gum drops that were stuck to the bottom lining. She ate them.

On the floor near the bed she found the Bonwit box with her new dress. She padded barefoot with it into the bathroom. There she turned on the light, took the dress out from its tissue wrappings, and tried it on. The chiffon draped over her so gracefully. It was with reluctance that she finally took it off.

Lucille's bottles of pills were everywhere in the bathroom, but Adrianne couldn't find any aspirin for her headache. She used Lucille's toothbrush and rinsed her face with cold water. To cool off, she decided to shower. As the water washed over her, she worried about whether Alfredo had phoned. If he had, would he suspect that she was spending the night with Lucille? Forgive me, Alfredo, she thought to herself. I'm sorry about Lucille. Please God, let Alfredo know I love him, she prayed. What if Alfredo never spoke to her again? If that happened, she vowed she would kill herself.

She returned to bed but couldn't sleep, disturbed as she was by all that had happened. Lucille tossed, twisted the sheet around herself in her sleep, and got up several times to go to the bathroom. Once Adrianne heard her vomit.

In the grey light of morning, Adrianne awoke from a dream in which Alfredo had offered her a plum. She was munching its flesh, even though she knew it was poisonous.

Lucille had already risen. She was in an armchair, dressed in a white half-slip and a padded brassiere. With her head bent over a hand mirror, she carefully plucked at her brows with a tweezer. The diamond and ruby rings on her fingers gleamed.

"Good morning."

"Good morning, honey. Excuse me, but I just have to catch a few old straggly hairs. I've got to keep myself pretty, you know," she said gravely.

Chapter 12

The next day Alfredo didn't phone. So when she got off her kitchen shift, Adrianne went to the Rose Bar. She found the place nearly empty, and there was no music. She called out, "Alfredo!"

He ignored her as he filled a glass with tap beer. When she cried out his name again, he looked at her with no sign of warmth. "Why are you here?" he asked bluntly.

"To see you. Oh Alfredo, I'm sorry about yesterday."

"I don't like you hanging out with that bitch."

"She's ill, and she's troubled."

"She's a ball-breaker. By the way, where were you last night? I called around ten, but you weren't in. Were you with her?"

"Yes."

"Tell me something, Adrianne, did you sleep with her?"

She hesitated. Gerald had never sensed what was going on between her and Lucille. Gerald left her isolated, just as her mother did. But Alfredo was reaching out to touch the tangled mass of chaotic emotions inside her, and this connecting made her feel whole.

Finally, she nodded.

"I thought so," he said.

"Do you still care about me?"

"Adrianne, you're sweet," he said, reaching out across the counter and stroking her cheek. "You turn me on just the way you are. But I don't want you hanging out with her."

"Alfredo, she'll be leaving in a few days. She just had surgery for breast cancer. She drinks way too much, and now that she's so sick, her husband wants a divorce. No one deserves to be abandoned like that."

"I need a Bud and a martini," said the waitress, who had just come up to the bar. She tapped her long fingernails nervously on the counter.

Dismissing Adrianne, he said, "I'm busy now, baby. Wait for me until I get off work."

Later, as they traveled back in the subway to his place, she was filled with anxiety. They were alone in the car. Beneath the overhead lights, Alfredo's face looked older and more tired than usual.

The subway rattled around bends, through the dark tunnel with its red and green lights. Lucille's mistrust of him had aroused in Adrianne an uncertainty that amounted to anguish. Thoughts of the baby girl she had aborted back in Houston haunted her. Lovelessness forces murder, she reflected. If only Gerald had loved her more, he would have wanted the baby.

She wouldn't let herself be hurt like that again. If Alfredo did not love her enough to share his life with her, then she would stop seeing him. That at least would end the limbo in which she was living now. Each day she wondered if he would phone. Who was he seeing? Had she alienated him in some way? Perhaps if they lived together, she would no longer feel as if she were about to fly into tiny pieces when they were apart.

"Honey, he'll use you however he can," Lucille's voice jeered. "He's a con artist. I wouldn't trust him at all."

"Alfredo, can I move in with you?" she heard herself say.

Her words sounded shrill. There was a long, painful silence. As the subway swayed around a bend, she knocked against his shoulder.

"Let me think about it."

At the Fourteenth Street station there was a delay because of some obstruction ahead. While they waited in the subway car, Adrianne gazed down with a kind of despair at her chipped pink nail polish.

That night she lay in his bed, unable to sleep until nearly dawn.

The next morning while they were drinking coffee and eating toast, he said casually, "We can give it a try."

"You mean about moving in?"

"Yes."

He spoke off-handedly, as if it were a matter of taking in a stray cat overnight, something he might do on an impulse, while to her the decision was a lifeline of certainty in the chaos around her.

"Really?"

"Why not?"

She could scarcely believe him. It seemed so simple. Over and over she rolled his terse response through her mind, trying to analyze it, trying to pierce through the words and the expression on his face to discover what he truly felt.

Chapter 13

The next day Adrianne called in sick at work and packed three large suitcases with everything she owned. She took a taxi to Alfredo's. He had given her the keys that morning, and as she unlocked the door to the building, excitement filled her. She sensed that this was a new beginning. They would be a couple, united and close.

This was the first time she had been here without him. The stairs creaked as she carried up the suitcases one at a time, leaving the others in the small entrance. Except for stacks of paintings and canvases on stretching frames, his studio was huge and bare. Flecks of dust floated in the air, lit up by the late afternoon sun. She could hear the sounds of machinery from the furniture shop on the second floor. As she looked out through the dusty windows at the narrow street, she saw two men carrying wooden tables out from the shop.

She was tired, and she would have loved to go out for some ice cream. Instead she took out a bottle of Dexedrine pills that a doctor had prescribed just a few days ago to help her lose weight. As she feared the possible effects of the pills, she had put off taking them, but now she swallowed one with a glass of water. She wanted to get thinner so that she would be beautiful for Alfredo. After taking the pill, she felt jittery and on edge. She longed even more for ice cream to fill her up and calm her, but she resisted going out.

In his bedroom she took off her sandals and lay down. It would be a long time before he came home. He had told her to wait here and not to meet him at the bar, as she usually did. She had an irrational fear that he would never come. Perhaps this was a trick, a trap, and she would wait for him forever until she ran out of food and until rats devoured the shreds of meat on the chicken bones that had fallen next to the garbage can.

Although she wanted to unpack, she didn't know where to put her clothes, as there was scarcely any space in the closet. She began to go through her suitcases, running her hands over the soft chiffon dress as well as the luxurious satin slip and the lacy panties and bras and garter belts that Lucille had bought her.

In her jewelry pouch was a gold locket on a chain that Gerald had given her long ago. Opening it up, she looked at his photo. How much suffering he had caused her! She half wanted to throw the locket in the garbage, but some clinging instinct forced her to put it back into the suitcase.

She fingered a cedar and silver rosary which had come down through her mother's family for generations, traveling to Santiago from a village in Germany. Just before Adrianne left home, Elena had given it to her as a keepsake. She thought of her mother's remote expression and her perfectly coiffed graying hair. Despite being religious, Elena was so cold and so lacking in compassion. Elena admitted only certain realities.

Adrianne remembered how her mother had ignored the probability that Adrianne and Gerald had been making love those nights Adrianne came home so late. Although Elena was courteous to Gerald in her cold way, she had been strangely lacking in curiosity, even as to how the two met. (It had been in the gift shop.) Elena had never seemed to notice that Adrianne gave a start whenever the phone rang, and that her daughter was on edge when Gerald failed to call.

From her luggage Adrianne took out an envelope containing several photographs. There was one of her mother Elena, who looked sad even as a young woman, and one of her father, Julio. Adrianne had inherited his large bone structure. However, his hair and eyes were as black as Alfredo's. In the photo, her father gazed at her with burning eyes. Nonetheless, she remembered him as distant, absorbed in his work as a geological engineer. She thought of the papers that had been continually heaped on his desk.

One night when Adrianne was twelve, the police called to tell them that a drunk driver had smashed his vehicle headlong into Julio's car, and her father had died en route to the hospital.

For months afterwards, Elena seemed almost unconscious of her surroundings and barely spoke to Adrianne. They were both submerged in grief. Then her mother began to erupt into fits of rage over small things—Adrianne's failure to wash the bottom of a frying pan, or Adrianne's breaking a dish. *"¡Eres una tonta!"* Elena would shout. As the months passed, Elena's rage became controlled. "I have something to discuss with you," she would say in a dignified voice before she began to scold Adrianne for yet another minor sin. If Adrianne shrieked in protest, Elena would upbraid her even more.

As Adrianne remembered all this, she was filled with a wave of anxiety. Suppose Elena were to call the rooming house and find out that her daughter had moved? She ought to let her mother know her new address.

With this in mind, she found a pad of paper along with a few envelopes in one of her suitcases. Then she sat down at the kitchen table, lit a cigarette, and wrote a note, saying only that she had moved in with a girl friend to save on rent, that they had no phone, and that she was doing well at her job. Adrianne feared divulging anything at all about Alfredo, as she credited Elena with a mysterious power to jinx things.

Suddenly, she realized that the cigarette ash had burned nearly to her finger, and she flicked it into the sink. She looked across the room at herself in the window glass. Her eyes looked huge, her features half-formed.

She still felt hungry. It took all her will power not to eat the banana lying on the counter among unwashed dishes. But she had to transform herself so that Alfredo wouldn't leave her the way Gerald had.

Returning to the bedroom, she heaped her clothing into piles on the floor. She had fallen into a fitful sleep when Alfredo's voice awakened her.

"Adrianne, are you here?" he called out.

"What?" For an instant she didn't know where she was, and she didn't recognize his voice.

"You left the door to the street unlocked."

"I did?"

"You've got to be more careful. Someone could get in. They could be hiding right now inside the building."

He stood in the doorway, glowering at her. In his arms he held white roses wrapped in green florist's paper. Above his open collar, sweat glistened on his face and neck. Even though he was angry, she found comfort in his presence.

"I'm sorry. I didn't realize I'd left it open."

He placed the flowers on the pillow beside her. "For you, *preciosa.*"

"Oh, Alfredo." She pressed them to her nose, savoring their fragrance.

His face softened. He leaned down, put his arms tightly around her, and rolled on top of her, squeezing her breasts. "Baby, it's good to come home to you," he said. The happiness she felt at this instant verged on pain. How could he possibly love her? She felt so inadequate, and the sense of some unknown sin she had committed haunted her.

Releasing her, he stood up. A fatigued look came over his face. She thought that she must be an added burden.

He glanced at the empty suitcases and piles of clothing on the floor as he lit a cigarette. "I wonder where we'll put all your stuff."

"Oh, I can get rid of some if it," she murmured. She had too many belongings. She wanted to efface herself totally and slip into his life without these encumbrances.

"Make me a cup of tea, will you?"

She started to get up.

"Wait! Are you my woman?"

"Yes," she whispered. "Oh, yes."

He kissed her with passion. Then releasing her, he whispered, "I love you." Her heart pounded. "As for you, *preciosa,* I think that you love me more than you know."

She credited him with more insight into her feelings than she herself had. He would be her savior. He would tear her open, revealing her to herself. Through him she would be purified.

"Go on, make me the tea."

"Yes," she said. She flung his maroon silk robe over her and ran to the kitchen. In her haste she left the flowers on the floor. She was only too glad to be able to fill some need of his, however small. As the needy one, she must cause the flame of her love to burn strongly enough for them both. She must sacrifice daily on the altar of devotion, anticipating all his needs. She must be as pliable as plasma, oozing around him, filling up the cracks and emptiness in his life, disappearing when he wanted freedom.

While she waited for the water to boil, she peered through the kitchen window above faded red cafe curtains. Craning her neck up, with her nose pressed against the glass, above the roofs of neighboring buildings she could see a few faint stars and a sliver of moon.

When she stepped back from the window, the glass ceased to reveal what was outside and became a mirror reflecting her image. Her own face looked haggard; she felt weak from hunger.

Chapter 14

That first week in the loft passed for Adrianne as if she were living in a dream, suspended outside of time. Everything was calm and uneventful. But she knew this calm couldn't last. The anguish inside her coupled with the tension and the violence she sensed in Alfredo made it impossible that these halcyon days should last.

After she got off work, she would go back to his place and prepare a midnight repast for him, which she kept hot in the oven—roast chicken and salad, or perhaps black beans and rice cooked the way he'd once showed her. While he ate, she would sip a glass of water. She was proud of sticking to her diet, although she felt hunger pangs when she watched him eat.

Every night when he came home from work, she would rush into his arms. He was affectionate, but she could tell that he was under pressure. His eyes were often full of torment and his face was drawn.

Every night that first week, they made love. In the morning when the alarm rang at eleven and it was time for her to get up and go to work, he would hold her for a while in his arms. Then he would roll over and go back to sleep.

She continued at her cooking job. When she got home at night, she was usually tired and had to push herself to do domestic chores.

While she waited for him to come home from work, she made stabs at cleaning the apartment, at laundering, mending, ironing. As she worked, she would muse over their futures, tormented constantly with hunger, nervous from the diet pills, often with a splitting headache. She wondered if she and Alfredo could possibly live on her take-home salary of $210 a month. No, that barely paid rent and utilities. They still needed money for Alfredo's canvases, his paints and frames, his clothing and food. If only she could get a better paying job, he could stay home and just paint. At other times, in periods of exultation, she had visions of babies, diapers on a rooftop line, Alfredo painting out his brilliant visions while she lay in bed and nursed their first baby. Alfredo would softly nuzzle the baby and embrace them both. He would sell his paintings and make lots of money.

That first week she lost five pounds. Now she was down to 158 pounds on Alfredo's scale, but she was tired and nervous.

Every night when twelve-thirty approached she would glance at the bedside clock. Then she would listen for the rhythm of his footsteps, heavy but rapid, on the stairs. If he were fifteen minutes late, she grew so afraid that her breath choked up and a chill ran through her. Death could come at any time, as it had with her father.

Two weeks after she moved in, Alfredo did not come home from work at the usual time. That night Adrianne was more tired than usual and lay down to rest. When she woke up and looked at the luminous numbers on the clock, she saw it was one o'clock in the morning. Where was he?

Putting on his maroon robe, she got up. She kept listening for the sound of his steps. In the harshly lit kitchen she took a chicken out of the oven. It was overdone and too dry. Nevertheless, she tore off a piece of meat with her fingers and devoured it. She was terribly hungry. If it hadn't been so late, despite her diet she would have walked down to the corner grocery and bought a whole German chocolate cake or a frozen boysenberry pie just to still the hunger which was like a wound blazing inside. She took a can of beer out of the refrigerator and drank some of it to calm herself down. She should take a Dexedrine, but it didn't mix with liquor and would keep her up all night.

The grocery was closed at this hour. She had no money to take a taxi to an all-night delicatessen. And she didn't feel safe alone on the streets at night in this part of the city. There was nothing to eat except the chicken in the oven, some rice on the stove, and lettuce in the refrigerator, along with a bottle of ketchup and a can of pinto beans. Grease covered her hands and face. She spooned some rice out of the saucepan. It also tasted too dry. The rice at the bottom of the pan had burned.

She stared at a watercolor that Alfredo had tacked over the stove. A man on a cross in a lush jungle was surrounded by huge birds, and above them all floated a woman's pale blue face and streaming lavender hair. Alfredo's visions were strange; she did not know whether she found the picture hideous or beautiful.

She felt trapped. The room was too bright. The wooden floor was cool beneath her bare feet.

When she turned on the radio, it gave off a lot of static. She tried to tune it to get a clear sound on the all-night jazz station, but the static continued, and so finally she gave up and turned it off.

The ghost of her father seemed to be watching her. An uncanny sensation. Her father wished her ill. He did not want her to be with another man. Although he had passed into the grave, he wanted to keep her as his alone.

If only Alfredo would at least phone. She resisted her impulse to phone the Rose Bar, to phone hospitals, police, the morgue. Everything was burning, tearing, devouring inside her, as if snakes were crawling inside the yellow walls of her brain, snapping and hissing, ready to poison her with their deadly bites. If she screamed out, no one would hear. The furniture factory below was abandoned at night.

Instead of screaming, she finished off the beer, ate some rice and chicken, and lit a half-smoked cigarette lying in the ashtray. She felt an even stronger sense that something outside herself was taking over her mind. It was forcing her to think these horrible thoughts, have these feelings. But this alien will was intertwined with her own; she could not separate them.

A malign presence pressed in on her. The kitchen was so bright; the beer tasted sour; the crucified man in the picture seemed an omen of evil. Perhaps she was the disembodied face. Against her will, perhaps she would cause Alfredo some deep harm.

She imagined him with a girl at this moment, their bodies entwined, whispering words of endearment.

Perhaps he had been run over, stabbed, or shot. Or perhaps, overcome with fatigue because he drove himself so hard, he had tripped and fallen into a gutter, cut open his skull on a ragged bottle edge. Perhaps he had been beaten up and robbed.

She went into the studio where the black window panes reflected her shadowy image. In the corner she found a sketchbook filled with drawings. There were lots of portraits of her. Nude. Clothed. Her face. Her hands. Ankles. Feet. She was touched, and a smile of pleasure swept over her face.

A strange humming noise filled the silence.

Could someone be hiding inside the loft?

Alfredo, please come. God, protect him.

After drinking another can of beer to numb herself, she finally dozed off on the bed, fully clothed.

The sound of footsteps awakened her. When she opened her eyes, she saw Alfredo moving in the dark. The clock showed 2:40 a.m.

"Alfredo, where were you? Tell me."

"Out," he said genially. His breath smelled of liquor.

All the anxiety and rage she had been suppressing erupted, and she grabbed him and dug her nails into his back. "Tell me Alfredo, where were you? Tell me!" she cried.

"Out."

"Where? Why are you so late?"

He wrenched himself away from her. "I lost my job."

"What happened?"

"They asked me to work overtime for the next month— twelve fucking hours a day! I told them to shove it."

"Oh, Alfredo."

He reached behind some books on the shelves for the lacquer box. Inside it was a joint which he lit, inhaled, and then passed to her.

She shook her head. "Marijuana costs money."

"Idiot! You know nothing about life," he snapped.

She burst into tears, and he put his arms around her. "Baby, I didn't mean to make you cry. Sometimes marijuana nourishes the soul."

"It's addicting."

"Don't worry, sweetheart. I can handle it."

He lit a candle and took off his clothes. They lay in bed together watching the shadows cast by the flame. Love and pity surged up in her as she looked at his tired face.

"I wish I could help you more," she said.

He laughed. "With your salary?" Then he sat up suddenly and looked at her. "There is something you can do. But I don't know if you have the guts."

"What?"

"A while back we talked about hustling. Remember? We were joking. But, Adrianne, it's no joke that if you were out on the street you could bring home in one night what you do now in a month. We'd be okay. Harris wants me to do six or seven new paintings in time for the exhibit. There's no way I can while I'm working another gig."

A shock ran through her. "You want me to hustle? I thought you loved me."

"Love's got nothing to do with it, baby. I'll love you all the more for helping me survive. I'm talking spiritual survival. How can I paint when I'm working forty hours a week in a bar?"

"You're doing it now."

"I'm not painting enough, and I'm wearing down. Sometimes I'll paint all night after I get home from work. Then I catch a few hours sleep. Baby, I can't go on like this."

He relit the joint, inhaled, and slowly blew out the smoke. "The God I worship is far beyond most people's limited understanding. This God wants me to create the visions He's inspired. Shit, if I'm working some half-assed job, then I'm copping out. Do you understand?"

"I can't do it!"

"They just touch your skin. What's skin anyway? Your skin's not you." Lightly he punched her arm.

"I don't want to screw anybody else," she cried. "I love you. I wanted you to be the last man I ever screwed."

He laughed. "You! Adrianne! Just a couple of weeks ago you were making it with Lucille."

"She's like a sister. That's different."

"Bullshit! It's all skin. Look, why romanticize fucking? You've fucked enough men in the past. Besides, when I met you, you were *giving* it away. All they touch is your skin. They can't touch the real you, because you belong to me."

His bare back was narrow, like Lucille's, only darker and more muscular. She smoothed his skin and leaned against him for a moment. "I don't want to," she said, even while a part of her was responding with an unhealthy desire. Hadn't she thought about working as a hooker before she met

Alfredo? Take strange men's money and run. Stop giving it away. Buy beautiful clothes and luxuries. Get back at men in this way for the hurt they had inflicted on her.

She inhaled on the joint, held it in while it burned her throat, then let it out slowly.

"Baby, it's hell to be living like this. If I don't paint, something in me dies. You can help me do what I was born to do."

"Let me think about all this," she murmured.

He took her face in his hands. "You're so young," he said. "You've got an innocence about you, like Marilyn Monroe. That's the secret of her charm. You've got it, too."

"Really?" she beamed with pleasure. Maybe it was the effect of the marijuana, but she could see rays of light around his head. She understood how badly he wanted her to do this.

"I suffered too much while I was growing up," he said. "But it opened me up and made me aware and made me an artist."

Was he a con artist like Lucille said? His eyes had a gentle look in the candlelight just now.

"What was your childhood like?"

He took a sip of cold tea from the cup on the floor. "Mama left my father in Havana and took my little brother Luis and me to New York when I was three. We moved in for a while with an uncle and aunt. I think Mama slept around with different men. She hated my father, and she took it out on me because I looked like him. She loved Luis. Then Mama remarried and things only got worse."

He took a deep breath, and a look of torment came over him, as if he were once again in the past.

"My stepfather was a janitor. He drank too much, and he had terrible, jealous fights with Mama. I don't think he had ever really learned to read, and it bugged the shit out of him to see me reading and drawing all the time. He used to beat me while Mama just looked on, although she never let him touch Luis. Finally, I got big enough to hit back, and I nearly killed that man. The next day I moved out."

"That's so sad," she said. Perhaps because her perceptions were intensified by the marijuana, his emotions flooded through her, filling her up so that she scarcely knew where she ended and Alfredo began.

"Did you ever see your father again?"

"When I was ten, I went down to Cuba for the summer. He was kind to me. *Un hombre verdadero.* I wanted to see him again, but I never had a chance.

"Then I started Cooper Union—never got a dime from my family. I was working my way through, and I saved up money for passage on a freighter to Havana because I wanted to see my father once more. He died just a week before I got there! Later, I learned that he'd tried to get me back after the summer I spent with him. He'd written Mama that he wanted me to come back and live with him, but she never showed me that letter."

"Oh, Alfredo."

"I learned about this from his relatives. They told me that he'd written me several letters, too. But I never got them. Mama destroyed them. All the time I'd been thinking that he didn't want me around, and maybe he didn't even like me."

"I want to help you!" Adrianne cried out in a burst of emotion. "I want to make it all up to you."

"Que Dios te bendiga, preciosa," He kissed her and held her in his arms. "I'm wearing down. I haven't had enough sleep in months."

She put her hand on his warm chest.

"Am I taking up too much time?"

"No, baby, no, but you do demand time."

She was silent for a moment.

"I'll do it for you," she said at last. "Because I love you."

"Do you know what you're getting into? It takes guts."

"I'll do it for you," she repeated. "Because I love you more than anyone in the world."

"You're beautiful."

"I'm scared. I don't want to go to jail."

"I'll protect you, baby. Whether something is legal has no connection with whether or not it's right. Madmen make up the rules. But God is watching over us. He knows what's in your heart."

They lay against each other in silence. She had never felt so much harmony between them. Their energies flowed into each other; they were indeed one larger being. Shadows cast by the candle flickered.

"Our bodies don't last," he said. "We're born, and then we die. What happens when you fuck a stranger? Nothing really."

"I think so," she said, still in the realm of vastness into which the marijuana had propelled her.

"There's no emotional bond. They just get to feel your body, that's all. They never touch the real you."

She gripped his hand. Gradually the realm of light had vanished. Now she was in a desert, and the only human being who could touch her lonely core was Alfredo.

"It scares me though," she said. "It's so dangerous."

"Not if you use common sense," he said. "You're intuitive. When you're scared, you even get psychic, right?"

"How do you know?"

"I *know* you in my bones. Baby, you and I belong together. You won't be hustling long. We'll save up money so we can split. Then soon, with any luck, my paintings will start to sell. We'll leave New York. It's a different world on the Caribbean Islands or in South America. We'll travel. We'll get married."

Her heart thudded with excitement.

"I know about South America," she said. "I told you, my parents are from Chile."

"We'll go there, *chica*. We'll go to Cuba, where Castro is creating a whole new society."

He was kneeling over her now, and very gently and sensitively and slowly he made love to her until finally she let herself go in a flooding orgasm.

"This is spiritual," she whispered.

"You can shut it down and make it just physical," he said. "That's what Gurdjieff would do."

He got up and worked in the studio while she slept.

Not until the first morning light shone in through the air shaft did he finally lie down again. His body curved around her. As he breathed against her shoulder, she stirred and turned to him.

"Alfredo, will you still love me?"

"Of course, baby. I'll love you all the more," he mumbled into her hair. "Now let me get some sleep."

Part 2

September, 1959

Chapter 15

Adrianne clung to Alfredo's arm as they made their way uptown along Broadway. It was muggy and overcast. They had both slept little the previous night. As she walked, her spike heels wobbled. She realized that she'd forgotten to take her diet pills. Since waking up, she had consumed only tea and half a piece of toast. With almost no food inside her, she felt dizzy, nervous, and tired from the marijuana she'd smoked last night as well as conspicuous in the tight blue jersey dress and flashy brass earrings that she'd bought this morning at Klein's on the Square.

It was four in the afternoon when they went into a bar that was dark and smoky, thick with odors of beer and roasting meat. Alfredo ordered two draft beers.

"Want something to eat, baby?"

"No, thanks." She wanted to show him she was strong-willed about sticking to her diet, even though the smell of food made her ache with hunger.

There was stubble on Alfredo's face. Marked with fatigue, he looked older.

"Are you sure you can go through with this?" he asked.

"Yes."

He nuzzled her fingers and lit another cigarette, although in the last hour he'd already smoked five or six.

After he had eaten, they continued walking uptown until he stopped and said, "Here's your turf, baby. I'll hang around for a while." He motioned to the bar behind them.

Why had he chosen this neighborhood, this particular block? A cluster of tough-looking men at the corner filled her with fear.

The next block felt safer, although she didn't know exactly why. Perhaps it was the Spanish grocery store on the corner. She went into a hotel a few doors down from the grocery. There she rented a room from a young, pimply-faced

hotel clerk who sat behind the desk of a small lobby which
had a stuffy, sweetish smell. The room was nineteen dollars a
week. Luckily she had enough money with her to pay for it.
Alfredo had gone over all this with her earlier before he
cashed his severance check at the corner grocery.

"I may have a few visitors," she said, giving the clerk a
big smile. "Is that all right?"

"That's your business," he said, apparently bored with the
transaction, and he returned to reading his *Police Gazette.*

Going outside again, she stood a few doors away against
the window of a lingerie store, and as she swung her handbag
slightly, shifting her weight occasionally from foot to foot,
waves of people flowed past. She had a headache from the
beer, and her stomach ached with hunger, although at the
same time she felt curiously weightless and adrift in space.
Standing at the other corner were two young women wearing
tight dresses and spike heels like her. One was tall and blond;
the other was plump with long, wavy black hair. Their hostile
stares frightened her. She hoped they wouldn't hassle her
about invading their territory. All the people looked somehow
deformed, incomplete, ugly, their skins sallow beneath the
polluted gray sky. The air was so heavy that it felt as if a
storm were about to break.

A man in a brown suit with horn-rimmed glasses approached. He looked her up and down, as if mentally undress-
ing her. "Wanna have some fun, sweetheart?" he asked.
Maybe he was a buyer in the garment district. He didn't give
off vibes of being a cop or a weirdo, so she decided to chance it.

"You got twenty dollars?"

"Yeah, sure."

"Come with me," she said.

She hoped to God he wasn't a cop. She would treat him as
if he were part of a dream, and indeed she felt as if she were
now living inside a dream. All this wasn't real. Only Alfredo
and she together were real.

The hotel clerk glanced at them as they walked through
the lobby. She'd better slip him a bill later on, as Alfredo had
told her to.

They walked up three flights of stairs into her newly
rented room, narrow like a box car with its fresh, unrumpled
bed. Sink in a corner. The room smelled of Lysol. Beige
drapes and worn, greenish carpet. Chenille bedspread, creaky

springs, mattress sagging with the weights of all the bodies that had lain on it. Old mahogany dresser.

"You can put the money on the dresser," she said airily, as if she were acting in a play. Alfredo had told her how to handle the money part—to ask for it first. He had told her what to say and do. God, she was dumb—that he had to tell her!

The stranger undressed casually as if he were used to going with prostitutes. At least he seemed safe. And he actually put some bills on the dresser. Didn't dispute the price or threaten her, nor did he object when, still in her underwear, she washed him off with a damp washcloth.

She took off the rest of her clothes.

"Mmmm, you're nice," the man, said almost dreamily as he ran his hands along her thighs.

They got underneath the sheet. Fondling his cock, she slipped a thin rubber condom over it, as Alfredo had advised her.

"Do you have to do this, doll?"

"Yes."

Then he was on top of her, weighty, hairy, solid-smelling. It was quick and uncomplicated. She was surprised to feel within herself a slight stirring of desire, even an orgasm.

Five minutes and it was over.

Finished.

He left.

She sat on the bed and stared at the flowered wallpaper for a long time, still naked, shivering a little. Since she had lost weight, she felt chilly a great deal of the time. Finally, she went over and picked up the bills on the dresser—a ten and two fives. Carefully she placed them inside her wallet. Then she returned to the murkily lit Flamingo Bar where Alfredo said he'd be, and she found him at a corner table.

"How'd it go?" he asked.

"Okay." She reached inside her purse and handed him the money.

"Great, baby. You're doing great," he said as he slid his hand along her nylon-sheathed leg. "Are you going to be all right on your own for a while?"

She nodded. She felt as if he were leaving her alone on the North Pole surrounded by a vast expanse of ice that merged with the sky, and her blood was freezing in her veins.

"See you later. I've *got* to get some work done for the show. Be careful, sweetheart, and take a taxi home."

He could he be so casual about all this?

How could he concentrate on painting while she was out here alone on this chilly street corner in front of a discount luggage store? She had moved south a block, as it felt safer.

It grew colder, and she shivered in her jersey dress. Finally, she decided to return to the Flamingo and have a drink. There she gave herself the luxury of ordering spaghetti and meatballs to still her hunger pangs. Then feeling bolder, she accepted a proposition from a hulking man in a dark blue suit and loud tie who was sitting next to her at the bar. The fat, red-faced Irish bartender looked at her curiously. Would she have to pay him off, too?

After the big man there were five more men. There was a Puerto Rican whom she met near the Spanish grocery. He was delicately built, almost like a girl, in contrast to the previous client whose heaviness had nearly crushed her. Then there were two businessmen and several men of varying ages with slicked back greasy hair and tight pants. She was beginning to lose count.

The hookers she had seen earlier disappeared for a while. Later on in the evening she would see one, then the other.

A youth with a pasty face and twisted body in a wheelchair lingered for a long time on the sidewalk in front of the hotel and watched her. When he did not return her smile, she began to feel uneasy, and when she heard a police siren, she cringed.

A policeman strode down the street with his nightstick dangling at his side. Quickly, she walked to the grocery store, bought a package of cigarettes, and walked around the corner. Was he following her? After another block, she turned her head to look. No one was in sight. She walked on, waited, picked up another man who was plump and grey-haired. She took him back to the hotel. A few heaving thrusts, and it was done.

It seemed amazing that all the men paid the twenty dollars she requested, except for the Puerto Rican who told her he had only fifteen. She was exhilarated with her prowess. At least some part of her was valued. How many girls could make so much money in just a few hours? How many would

have the guts to escape from a life of drudgery in this way?
Alfredo was right. The world belonged to the daring.

After the last man had left, she sat alone in a kind of stu-
por. Then she washed herself all over, dried herself with the
small hand towel, and, naked as she was, started to cry
uncontrollably.

How absurd it was to have refused poor old Max her
body.

She wished Alfredo were here with her. She wanted to go
home to him, but she ought to bring home more money than
she had taken in so far.

Feeling too tired to move, she curled up and fell asleep.

She didn't know how long she had been sleeping when a
knock on the door awakened her.

Nervously, she wrapped the chenille bedspread around
her and in the darkness went to the door.

"Who is it?"

"Toby. The desk clerk."

"What do you want?"

"We need to talk."

"I'm tired."

"It's important."

She opened the door a crack. In the light of the hallway,
his face had a yellow cast. His black hair was slicked down
with pomade.

"What is it?"

"Let me in a minute." Stepping inside, he switched on the
light next to the door, then glanced at the unmade bed and at
her.

"You've had a lot of visitors today."

He was looking her over strangely. She realized one of
her nipples was visible because the bedspread had slipped.
Hurriedly, she pulled it up around her.

"You told me that was okay."

"One of our permanent guests might complain."

What kind of permanent guests does a hotel like this
have, she wondered?

He stepped towards her, and when he touched her upper
arm she wanted to shriek. Backing away, she grabbed her
purse, which was lying on a chair. Quickly, she took out a ten-
dollar bill and gave it to him. Now he'll go away, she thought.

But he just stood there. When he touched her arm again, she had goose pimples.

"You've got a great body."

"Please go. I don't feel well."

"You want me to get you anything?"

"No, no, leave me alone."

She opened the door, and to her relief he walked out, although he was smirking.

Much later, after she had forced herself to go with several more men and had eaten a roast beef on rye at an all-night Horn & Hardart's, she went home in a taxi.

It was dark inside the loft, and Alfredo was asleep. When she put her hand on his chest—she could feel his rhythmic breathing. He stirred as she turned on the bedside lamp.

"Alfredo, Alfredo," she murmured, stroking his hair.

"Huh? What is it?"

"Alfredo, it's me. I brought you lots of money."

She flung the bills from her wallet onto the blanket.

He sat up and rubbed his eyes. "Huh? What happened?"

Then he counted out the bills. Two hundred and twenty-five dollars. "Not bad, baby," he said. "Did things go okay?"

"Yes."

He folded them up and put them underneath the lacquer box hidden behind the books.

She exulted that she had conned the world. Then suddenly fearful, she asked, "Alfredo, do you still love me?"

"Yeah, sure I do."

"But I've been with all those men."

"Cut the crap. You belong to me."

Clinging to him, feeling his touch, his voice, her life again took on coherence. When she got into bed, he caressed her with extraordinary tenderness. It was worth all she had gone through tonight. If he kept on loving her, she would hustle for him for a hundred years, she thought sleepily.

Chapter 16

Adrianne and Alfredo took a cab to a Japanese restaurant where they sipped saki and ate tidbits wrapped in seaweed, using chopsticks, while Japanese music played in the background. Adrianne felt buoyant. In the last week she had made over a thousand dollars.

Alfredo was attired in a new charcoal flannel suit, while she was wearing the chiffon dress and Italian pumps that Lucille had given her. Over the dress, she wore the black rabbit-fur coat that Alfredo had just helped her choose at Bendel's.

They clinked glasses and drank as more food was brought to their table—beef teriyaki, salad flavored with sweet vinegar, and rice. Oh this is the life, she thought hummingly. Soon he will marry me and how happy we will be in a Caribbean hacienda. Then the familiar black chasm opened in her imaginings, and she felt panic. "Do you love me?" she asked, although she knew he hated her to ask. Anguish shaped her question.

"Yes, sweetheart."

Over there in a corner, she thought she saw a trick that she'd been with a few days ago, and she didn't give a damn. She whispered this to Alfredo. Fifteen minutes with that man over there had paid for the meal. Hilarious. Ironic. Everything swirled around and around. Even though her fur coat was warm, she shivered.

"I know you're a hundred per cent for me," he said in a gust of exhilaration. "One of these days we'll settle down and have those babies you want. Here's to us!" He raised his glass to hers.

An anxious kind of joy flooded her. He must love her, she thought. He must trust her. Otherwise he wouldn't show her where he kept marijuana and cash hidden, wouldn't talk as he did about his work and his dreams, wouldn't reveal as much of himself as he did.

"I wish you didn't have to hustle," he said. "As soon as people start buying my work, I'll be able to support you."

"Alfredo, I love you so much"

He averted his eyes, and again she felt panic.

They consumed an entire bottle of saki and were both a little drunk when they left.

Chapter 17

White walls covered with Alfredo's paintings were obscured by crowds of fashionably dressed men and women whose voices filled the air. They wandered through the Fifty-Seventh Street gallery, sipping wine and nibbling on morsels of cheese and crackers as well as hot hors d'oeuvres, which a waiter passed around on silver trays.

Voices—harsh like birds of prey, New Yorkese, Bostonian, effete, shrill—assailed Adrianne. When she peered around a woman who was wearing an enormous felt hat with a long feather, she glimpsed Alfredo's huge semi-abstract jungle painting. A few days ago she'd helped him carry all the paintings up here from the rented van. She fingered her left knee where she'd bruised it, tearing her jeans on a rough frame edge.

Snatches of conversation reached her ears.

"…more concrete than Motherwell…"

"…paranoid awareness…"

"…picked a fight at the White Horse…"

As she watched them talk, his canvases treated as no more than a backdrop to their thoughts and voices and egos, she could understand why Alfredo despised these people and how he despaired of getting through to them.

Among all these people, she alone knew Alfredo. Only she knew this man whose work they were judging. She alone slept with him and knew the feel of his flesh, knew how he tossed in his sleep when oppressed by nightmares.

She knew the secrets of so many men, their whispered confessions, as though she were a priest or psychiatrist. Confessions of failures in intimacy, confessions about erotic dreams, guilts, and regrets.

Why then did people despise prostitutes, who gave far more of themselves than priests or psychiatrists ever did?

Why was prostitution against the law? Alfredo would say it was because New York was like a gigantic psycho ward.

Now he came up to her, accompanied by a balding man who wore a bright red tie. "Adrianne, I'd like you to meet the man who owns this gallery. Harris, this is my girl." Alfredo's tweed jacket felt rough against her bare arm.

"Hello, Harris," she said.

"She has an extraordinary face," said Harris, appraising Adrianne as if she were a piece of sculpture. His voice had an effeminate tinge. "We've got quite a crowd. A reviewer from *The Times* stopped by a little while ago. That man in the turtleneck over there next to "Woman with Wolf's Head"— that's Gus Liebowitz, a big collector. Come over and meet him. Adrianne, you're charming," he said by way of farewell.

"Hi. Are you with Alfredo?" asked a soft voice. Adrianne turned around and gazed into the face of a beautiful mulatto girl, perhaps eighteen or nineteen, who was slender but full-bosomed. She wore a beige angora dress and pearls. "I've heard about you from Alfredo," she said. Gently, she embraced Adrianne.

"Who are you?"

"My name's Sonya. I'm a friend of his." Sonya laughed at Adrianne's questioning look. "Don't worry, there's nothing between us. We're old friends, and a few weeks ago we ran into each other again."

Adrianne had a fleeting vision of nestling against Sonya's soft breasts and belly, of lying for hours with the healing tenderness promised by Sonya's touch, so different from the male harshness of the streets.

"Adrianne, this is Dominic." Sonya introduced a slender man with dark hair in an Italian silk suit whose harsh face was pitted with acne scars. "Dominic is going to buy one of Alfredo's paintings." Sonya cuddled against him.

"So, you're Alfredo's girl," said Dominic. His voice was abrasive, and Adrianne immediately distrusted him. She wondered what connected Sonya and Dominic, because they seemed so different from each other. Dominic took hold of Adrianne's arm with a familiar gesture. "I understand you're in a rough line of work," he said. "Maybe I can set you up in a better situation."

"What do you mean?" She felt as if he had hit her in the pit of her stomach. How did he know what she was doing?

"We'll talk later," he said.

Then he and Sonya wandered off.

After a moment, she realized that the crowd was thinning. Someone had turned on a Vivaldi record. She found a chair to sit on, and her visual awareness of things dimmed as she descended into the Baroque music, which was almost unbearably sad but beautiful. Alfredo must have told them she was hustling. Who else had he told? She felt betrayed. Then she let the music take hold of her senses, trying to grasp each note as if this could give her clarity and heal the anguish inside her.

Chapter 18

"Not one review," said Alfredo. He lay sprawled across their mattress with its new satin sheets and purple quilt. Beneath him lay the crumpled Sunday papers.

"That opening wasn't worth shit." He flicked cigarette ash onto the floor.

"What do you mean?"

"Don't act so fucking stupid!" The violence in his voice sent a tremor through Adrianne. She lay a hand on her belly, feeling the silky texture of the beautiful pale-pink negligee she had recently bought. At Elizabeth Arden's, she'd had a facial, her hair styled, and her hands and feet manicured. However, she wanted to look beautiful for Alfredo alone, without there being other men.

Alfredo got up. She heard him piss in the bathroom, then go into the kitchen. He came back with a bottle of beer. Lately he'd begun drinking early in the day.

He scrutinized her and, appearing to pick up her thoughts, said, "You've made yourself look pretty sharp with your new clothes and the help of Elizabeth Arden." He paused for a moment. "Remember Dominic? You met him at the opening."

"Alfredo, why did you tell him about me?"

He pulled her head back and looked down into her eyes. "Dominic runs a house. His girls make a lot more than you do. You'd be safer there than you are on the streets."

"I don't want to work in a house."

"You're crazy." He yanked her hair so hard that she cried out with pain, but he kept right on pulling her back until she was afraid her neck would snap. At last he released her. She screamed, then burst into tears. This was not the Alfredo she knew.

"Now, baby," he said, his voice softening as if he realized he was going too far. "I love you, and I don't want you getting messed up on the streets. It's dangerous out there."

"Do you really care for me?"

"Of course I do, sweetheart."

"How did you meet Dominic?" she asked.

"Through Sonya."

"How do you know her?"

He arched his brows and gave a half-smile, drank some beer, then offered her the bottle. But she shook her head. "I meet lots of people," he said. "She wandered into the bar a while back, just like you did, and we began talking."

"Did you ever make love to her?"

"No. We're just friends. She's a nice person."

"Does she work for Dominic?"

He swallowed more beer. "Yes, she does, and she can teach you a lot because you're still rough at the edges."

She pondered this. The idea of becoming more polished appealed to her. On the other hand, his talk about the call girls just now jabbed her in the heart. She had been hoping that any day now, as soon as enough of his paintings sold, he would tell her to stop hustling.

Again she felt her belly. It was nearly flat because she had lost so much weight. If she were pregnant with Alfredo's child, her belly would swell again. Their unborn child, laughing, dark-skinned, with brilliant eyes, floated away in an invisible wind. Poor child. Will you ever get born? As for that other infant conceived back in Texas, just now she could hear it crying. A girl, they said. Carcass rotting in a trash heap somewhere.

Turning over on her side, she moved against his ribs. "Alfredo?"

"What?"

"I want to stop hustling."

"Soon you will, baby." He kissed her on the forehead, lit another cigarette, and took another sip from the bottle that lay on the floor beside him.

"The critics play fucking skull games," he said, going back to his former line of thought. "They don't really *see* a painting. They see a name, or they see a style that's 'in.'"

"Your work is powerful."

"Shit. I can spend my time better at the track."

"Alfredo! This doesn't sound like you."

He leaned over her, his face twisted with pain. "Stop bullshitting me. Nobody *knows* Alfredo Montalvo."

Tears welled up in her eyes and a lump came into her throat. What was causing him to change into a stranger? Anger surrounded him in flaming, invisible clouds which frightened her, so that she wanted to get away from him this very minute. "I'm going to shower and go out for a walk," she said. She rose and walked across the room. Just as she was going through the door, he threw one of her slippers at her.

"Cunt! *Puta loca!*"

Sobbing and jittery, she ran water over herself with a shower hose while she stood in the rusty tub Alfredo had picked up in a Brooklyn junkyard. For two months now she had denied herself food and kept herself going on the diet pills. Pain was something she had learned to live with: aching hunger, pain from her high heels jabbing into her as she waited long hours on street corners. Now the pain from Alfredo's contempt and fury was too much for her to bear. "He's hurting a lot. He's upset over the show. I need to be patient. He loves me. He loves me. He must love me. I know he loves me," she kept reassuring herself.

As Adrianne was drying herself off with a huge new rose-colored towel, Alfredo stalked naked into the bathroom. He snatched the towel from her grip and held her close.

"Baby, you know I care about you. If I act crazy sometimes, it's because this city is driving me out of my mind. That art gallery was full of phonies. Maybe Dominic and Sonya—a Mafia man and a hooker—were the only honest people there."

He sat down on the toilet seat, pulled her onto his lap, and suckled at her breasts. *"Melones.* Your breasts are beautiful melons. I ought to paint them all by themselves," he said after he came up for air. Tenderly, he caressed her full breasts. How handsome he was, with his smooth, olive skin, his sensitive face. She rubbed her hand against his forehead.

"Are you my woman?"

"Yes," she whispered.

One of his hands moved down her body, and he began to rub her with a circular motion that aroused her. Then he stopped, looking anguished. "Not one fucking review!" he cried. "Those assholes." His nails dug into her skin. "Not one sale. Not one review."

She clenched his fingers, pulling them away. "Give it time. The show just opened. Dominic said he's going to buy a painting."

"*Mierda!*" he spit out. "That's just Dominic's way of thanking me. He'll make a lot of bread peddling your ass."

"You sold me, Alfredo? Like a slave?"

"You *are* my slave."

"What do you mean?"

He let go of her, leaned back against the toilet tank, and reflected. "Baby, you've never faced that slave core of yourself. Until you do, you'll never be free."

"I don't understand."

"Something inside you has always wanted to be a slave, because you *are* one. We have to live out who we are before we can change. Most people never face who they are. So they stay children all their lives, fucking up the world."

"I still don't understand."

"Someday you will. But first you need to be a slave completely. Then you'll become a magnificent woman. You'll grow beyond slavery, and you'll leave me. Someday you'll realize I was your teacher."

"I don't want to leave you! I want to marry you and have your children."

"You may just do that, sugar. That may be part of the whole trip."

"I don't like Dominic."

"Why?"

"I don't trust him."

"You don't need to trust him. I'll deal with him." He looked into her eyes. "Baby, tell me, 'I'm your slave.'"

"I'm your slave," she murmured uneasily.

"If you leave me now, Adrianne, you lose your last chance of making it. You were on the verge of cracking when I met you."

He stroked her pelvic bones. "You've gotten almost skinny," he said. "Got a cashbox between those thighs."

They both laughed uproariously, filled with a strange burst of energy.

"Let's see how you do a blow job with a trick."

She stared at him.

"*Puta!*" he cried. "You're nothing without me!" He struck her across the face. "Go on. What are you waiting for?" He pushed her down to the floor and thrust his erect cock into her mouth. "Blow me, baby."

The linoleum floor was cold. Her face stung from the blow, and her neck was sore as she leaned her head backwards, then cupped his testicles in her hand. Tears streamed down her face as she began to suck him while she stroked his balls and thighs, licking and sucking. Her knees ached, and she wished he would come. He was taking such a long time. She tried every technique she knew, every titillation between anus and scrotum, until finally she heard him breathe faster, and then the semen came in thick spurts that she swallowed. While she licked him off, he pressed her head against his thighs.

Chapter 19

She was carrying a tube of contraceptive jelly, along with black lace panties and an extra pair of nylons. Her large handbag also contained three bras to return to Saks, because Alfredo said they looked like nursing bras. At the bottom of her bag lay a thin book on the history of European music, which she had found the other day in Brentano's. The book stirred old memories. As a child she had loved to play the piano.

As she waited for a taxi, it began to drizzle, cold and icy, half-rain and half-sleet. Despite her fur coat, she shivered. Her slender heels dug into her feet; her toes were cramped, and the small of her back ached from the way the shoes pitched her forward so that her spine over-arched.

Three p.m.

A taxi stopped.

"Ninety-seventh and Park, please."

"Good morning, miss," said the doorman. She knew that Dominic and Cecily gave him generous gifts.

Adrianne went up in the elevator with a middle-aged woman swathed in mink who got off at the eleventh floor. At times she wondered if the other inhabitants of this building knew or cared what went on. She, as well as the prostitutes she worked with, appeared to be simply three or four fashionably dressed young women who shared an apartment on the fifteenth floor. When men in heavy overcoats visited them, this aroused no great stir as they were indistinguishable from other strangers who lived in the building.

Cecily nodded to Adrianne as she walked inside the luxurious apartment with its dark, polished furniture and thick carpets. Cecily had reddish mahogany hair, and today she wore a grey knit adorned with an elegant gold necklace. While she talked on the phone, she was paying bills which were stacked up on the desk in front of her.

Was there any essential difference, Adrianne wondered, between typing for Eureka Fabrics and acting as a human receptacle for sperm and confessions? Either way, as Alfredo would point out, she was a slave, but here the pay was better.

~~~

A sweaty stranger pressed on top of her and pounded against her numb vagina walls. For a while, she used to fantasize about food when she lay with strangers, as she had been constantly hungry. But with the Dexedrine pills the hunger gradually lessened. Now her mind went blank, or else she soared far away from her body and thought of the ocean or a song she had heard on the radio. When the stranger climaxed, she gave a fake moan of pleasure, then drew her face away and buried her nostrils in the sheets, drifting off half-conscious into a world of pine forests.

Cocks in her cunt, her ass, her mouth. The varied tastes of semen, like seaweed or cheese or slightly sweet. A blow job was more personal than straight screwing. Far more offensive to take a stranger's cock into her mouth and swallow his semen than to take his fluid inside her vagina. After each encounter, she washed her mouth out with Listerine.

Semen ran down her legs. Strangers' fluids filled her. Where did she end, and where did they begin?

~~~

The smell of Sonya's nail polish filled the living room. A spike heel dangled from one of her feet, and she surveyed the fresh scarlet tint.

"Want a game of rummy, Adrianne, when my nails are dry?"

Irritated at the interruption, Adrianne looked up from the chapter on the harpsichord in the eighteenth century. "No, thanks. I'm reading."

Cecily said, "You shouldn't do your nails out here in the living room."

"I forgot," muttered Sonya. The expression on her broad-planed face was impenetrable. Why did she work here? Adrianne wondered. Although Sonya went places with Dominic and screwed him, she didn't seem to be in love with him. Did she do this just for the money?

Vanessa, a strikingly beautiful woman in her late twenties with chalk-white skin and glossy dark hair, wandered out into the living room. Her last client had just left.

"I've got some kind of infection," she said.

"Vanessa, dear, I've got you scheduled all through this evening's shift. Wear your diaphragm, and make sure they use condoms. You'll have to wait until tomorrow morning to get a checkup. Girls, don't any of you forget your weekly medical checkups."

While Cecily was talking on the phone, the buzzer rang. The elderly Puerto Rican maid, María, who was afflicted with arthritis, limped to the door. Then a man came in and chose Sonya.

While she waited, Adrianne read about Clementi. When her father was alive and they still had the piano, she had practiced Clementi exercises for hours. Now one of the melodies she used to play floated through her mind.

The next trick summoned her. He was a thin man with receding hair.

Fifty dollars a shot.

An expensive house.

~~~

"Hey, don't tell Alfredo, okay?" Dominic was feeling her all over. Then he took off her clothes, and he made love to her slowly, with surprising gentleness. She noted that he left his socks on, though, as many tricks did. Close up, with his acne-scarred face, his lips on her body, Dominic took on a different aspect.

Afterwards, he took out a small plastic bag of heroin from his vest pocket.

"This stuff relaxes you, doll, and you're very tense. Try some."

"No, thanks."

"Don't be scared of it."

"I'm afraid of getting hooked."

"You can't with one shot. It's here any time you want. Just ask me."

~~~

"So tired," Adrianne would moan at night in Alfredo's arms.

"Baby, you're doing fine."

She wanted to tell him about Dominic, but she didn't dare as she did not know what Alfredo's reaction would be. She nestled more tightly against him, but he soon stirred, got up, and went into the kitchen, probably to get some beer. She heard him pace back and forth, and then she heard him moving canvases.

~~~

While Sonya, Vanessa, and a new girl named Eileen ate a pork-chop dinner which the maid had cooked, Adrianne sipped her broth and munched on celery. Then she lit a cigarette. She had lost thirty pounds. Her hip bones protruded, her waist was slender, and her large breasts hung pendulous. She felt as if her heart were seeping through her breasts, as if soon her heart's blood would drain out completely and she would vaporize into mist.

Eileen's left eye involuntarily twitched. Both her eyes were reddened, as if she had been crying or were on drugs. Dressed in a tight purple sheath, she was small, with skinny legs and dull blonde hair.

After dinner, the girls relaxed for a while. Business generally picked up around seven.

Eight hundred a night. Sixteen tricks. Fifty-fifty split with the house.

"Safer then the streets," said Alfredo.

"But so boring," Adrianne said.

Despite its luxuriousness, the Park Avenue apartment oppressed her.

Days flowed into nights flowed into days. At closing time Alfredo would come by to pick her up in the new black Cadillac that he had recently bought. It had red leather upholstery, a fine radio and other luxurious options, and was costing them eighty dollars a month in parking tickets.

Her wrist watch said ten-thirty p.m. Sonya's eyes were glassy before she leaned back against the couch and closed them. Then she stumbled into the bathroom where she stayed for a long time, and Adrianne wondered if she were on heroin.

Vanessa went off with a trick.

Waiting.

Her turn.

A flabby man in his sixties. She stimulated him for what seemed an endless time. Knock on door. "Time's almost up," Adrianne whispered.

Finally, his penis stiffened and he grew so excited that he ejaculated before he totally entered her. His copious fluid spilled out all over the sheets.

Wash herself off. Say goodbye. Next trick. "Hello, darling." A diminutive Oriental man.

Then a potbellied, middle-aged man with something strange about his manner, a hint of repressed violence. With him, she skittered on the edge of panic. Be very careful, an inner voice told her. "Think of me when you're screwing. Remember, I love you. You're doing this for *us*." Alfredo's voice sounded in her mind, wrapping around her like a cocoon.

At one a.m., Adrianne vomited into the toilet bowl.

Alfredo was late. Just as she was about to step into a taxi, he pulled up, reeking of liquor. He told her he'd gone to the racetrack and then out for drinks with old friends.

Chapter 20

Late rainy afternoon. Forty-five minutes before the end of her Wednesday shift. They were closing up early tonight for some reason, and so the evening shift of girls was not coming in.

"I don't ever screw my wife," the trick said in his effeminate voice. With thinning fair hair and a paunch, he appeared to be about forty. His British tweeds and underwear lay in a heap on the carpet.

"Why not?" asked Adrianne.

"She's beautiful ... used to be a showgirl ... but she simply doesn't arouse me."

While Adrianne pondered this, he inhaled a pinch of snuff from the small box he'd placed on the night table. Then he coughed. There was a brown residue of snuff around his aristocratic nostrils.

"Tell me, why do you work here?"

"Oh, I don't know." She was tired of being asked.

"Fondle me."

Despite her efforts, his penis remained flaccid, and most of his attention went into sniffing the tobacco while he lay on his back and she vainly attempted to arouse him by stroking and pumping.

"Tell me some stories to excite me."

She looked at her wrist watch in the dim light. "You've only got a few more minutes."

"What a shame. You're so charming. Your name again?"

"Stephanie," she said, using what Cecily termed her "professional" name.

"There's a special quality about you, Stephanie. Perhaps I can get you a part in the film I'm doing. I'm producing an experimental film with a Hungarian director."

He was probably putting her on. Nonetheless, he intrigued her. Perhaps she should give him a little extra time.

But it was already five-thirty, and she had a sudden premonition that if she failed to meet Alfredo tonight at six, something terrible would happen in their relationship.

Falling rain began to hit against the windows behind the heavy brocade drapes.

"Look, I have to go. Your time's almost up."

"Mmmm, just keep on stroking ...oh ...oh, I'm finally getting hard ...just a little more, you sweet thing."

Someone knocked on the door to signal that it was time for him to leave.

The man was alternately stiffening and going limp. Often Alfredo was late. He might not even get there until seven, and she didn't relish the idea of waiting for him on the street for an hour in the cold rain. The new Cadillac, at least, was warm inside. Let him wait for a change.

"What pleasure do you get out of this life, Stephanie, tell me." His eyes gleamed with avidity. "Does it give you a thrill?"

Adrianne sensed he wanted her to say yes, that she had twenty orgasms a day, that she adored fucking, sucking, being mauled, intimidated, even spat on, that she loved living in fear of disease, of violence, and of arrest. He wanted her to say that she didn't mind being bored while she waited interminable periods of time in the living room between tricks. He wanted her to say she liked standing on the cold street while she waited for Alfredo at night, liked taking penicillin shots for clap, and that she liked having the gynecologist stick a cold steel instrument or an impersonal gloved finger inside her every week.

But maybe this stranger really was producing a film. Maybe she could become a film star, and then her whole life would change entirely.

"Yes, it excites me," she said. Then she began to tell him about her tricks and began to get carried away by her own words. She heard a soft-spoken, wide-eyed girl who wasn't herself at all murmur, "It excites me to take a man's cock in my mouth. Would you like that?"

"Later," he said. "Tell me, you beautiful creature, have you ever made love to a woman?"

"Well, a few times." Again the soft-spoken girl took over, and she felt herself sheathed inside some other personality who was trying to please this man by telling him what he

wanted to hear. She told him something about Lucille, changing her name, looks, and background because she felt she
must protect Lucille from this stranger's obscene personality.

As she talked, his organ swelled larger. "Tell me, do
Negroes have bigger cocks?"

"Oh, some do, some don't."

"What was the longest it ever took a man to come?"

"I don't know. Maybe a couple of hours."

She remembered a trick back in November while she was
still working the streets whom she had to stimulate for a very
long time. She sensed murderous rage growing out of his frustration, and he seemed at a point where he might injure or
kill her. In a state of intense fear, she had done everything in
her power to satisfy him while she prayed for protection.

"Why are you so silent?" he asked, inhaling a pinch more
snuff.

Then she made up a story she thought would please him,
in which she elaborated on every detail of an imaginary,
day-long erotic encounter. She heard herself as if it were
someone else talking—this soft-voiced girl going on and on.
He became more and more excited. In her hand, his penis was
hard and huge, his breathing quickened.

She felt imprisoned in her lies, deprived of her identity,
stifled like a mummy wrapped in gauze layers, a phony china
doll. Yet, because this man had managed to plumb a few
drops of truth out of her, she was strangely disturbed.

He reached a pitch of excitement; his pupils dilated as if
on a drug, wide-open eyes listening to a fairy tale about other
men's powers. Finally he mounted her and came. Then he
rolled away and fell into a light sleep with a blissful expression on his bloated face.

Throughout the rest of the apartment, it was unusually
silent except for the clang of a pail against porcelain. María
must be cleaning up. It had grown dark outside. Light no
longer filtered in through the draperies, and outside the rain
fell harder.

She switched on a lamp.

Alfredo, are you still outside waiting? Don't go, she
begged him in her mind. She needed Alfredo with special
intensity right now because she felt phony and isolated, more
used than if this trick had fucked her all day and all night.
Something had been taken away. Her soul had been robbed.

"Wake up. I have to go now," she said.

"Huh?"

He sat up and rubbed his eyes.

Hurriedly, she dressed while he put on his clothes with maddening slowness.

There was no one in the living room, but the door to one of the bathrooms was ajar, and she smelled disinfectant and saw María with her long white braids scrubbing the floor on her knees. "Good night," she called out to the old woman.

"Buenas noches, señorita."

Cecily's desk contained cubbyholes where at the end of each day Cecily would put envelopes for the girls with the money they had earned. Her envelope was missing. Had one of the other girls stolen it? Had the maid taken it? Had Cecily forgotten to leave it for her? She would have to wait until tomorrow to find out.

"What about the movie?" she asked the stranger as they waited together for the elevator. "You said maybe there will be a part for me."

"Movie? What movie?" he asked, startled. But when they got inside the elevator he immediately recovered himself. "I'll invite you to my next party. The director is sure to be there," he said. The amused edge crept back into his voice. "I'll speak to him about you, beautiful creature."

"How can I get in touch with you?"

"I'll call you."

"You can leave a message for me here."

"I'll do that, sweet thing. You're a nice girl. Don't believe all the stories you hear," he added, chucking her under the chin.

They had reached the ground floor.

He pranced away through the rain to hail a taxi.

She knew he would never call, and she had been conned because she was a fool.

"Alfredo was here," said the doorman. " He just drove off a few minutes ago."

In the rain, she waited a long time for a taxi, and when she got back to the loft it was cold and dark and empty.

Chapter 21

"Cecily, where's my money?"

"I put three hundred and seventy-five dollars into an envelope for you last night."

"I didn't see it."

"It was there."

Adrianne wanted to scream and throw the silver ashtray on Cecily's desk into her face.

"She'll rip you off any chance she gets," Sonya had warned.

The next few hours for Adrianne passed in turmoil. Alfredo hadn't come home the night before, and she wondered where he was. Was he with another girl? Had he gotten into an accident? She wondered if Cecily really had put the money out and if someone had stolen it. Her stomach hurt; her period was several days overdue; and her head ached.

Even if this place were safe, she was getting fed up. Eileen and Vanessa had gotten close to each other and were acting a bit nasty to her. She missed Sonya, who had called in sick.

There was a general tension in the air, and Cecily was agitated. She smoked cigarette after cigarette and talked a long time with Dominic over the phone.

Adrianne's last trick, a tall, stooped man with grey hair, a professor, had just left. She looked at herself in the ornate Spanish mirror. On the bed behind her were rumpled sheets that she needed to straighten out. Used tissues were everywhere. Was this red knit dress the right shade? With her dark blue eyes and her flushed cheeks, perhaps a deeper red with more purple in it would look better. Her bleached ringlets stood out like a halo around her face. She looked into her eyes as if for the answer to some mysterious question. Then she heard rough male voices.

They were talking to Cecily. "Get your hands off me! Let me speak to my lawyer!" Cecily was shouting. She heard Vanessa's and Eileen's shrill voices and sounds of scuffling.

"Got 'em handcuffed, Sargent."

"*Yo no he hecho nada!*" the old woman María wailed.

Adrianne glanced towards the windows. Outside was a fire escape. Her beautiful new silver fox coat, which she had bought only last week at a wholesale furrier's, was flung over an armchair. Panic plunged her mind into a state of crystal clarity. Hastily she put on her shoes, flung on the coat, grabbed her purse and pulled open the window which led onto the fire escape. Carefully, she shut the drapes and closed the window behind her. Wind whipped against her, nearly knocking her down. Her heels were going through the steel grillwork. She took them off, moving much more swiftly than she did in normal life, and stuffed the shoes into her purse. Then she made her way down the wet, slippery steps, clinging to the rail, going down landing after landing. Snowflakes were swirling about. She could see into lighted rooms on some floors where drapes or blinds were not pulled shut. She hoped no one would report her. When at last she reached the bottom landing, she was a full floor above the ground. Below her were neatly covered garbage cans in a cement courtyard. She flung her beautiful new fur, lining down, onto the cement to soften her fall, lowered herself to a window ledge, then took a deep breath and jumped.

Landing on her buttocks, she was shaken and bruised. She got to her feet, put on her high heels, and ran out the alley to the street. There she saw a police van with flashing lights. Moving more slowly, she tried to look casual so that she would merge with the crowd. She squeezed onto a bus just as it closed its doors.

Chapter 22

Wind was blowing through her hair and through the lining in her coat. "Baby, you're beautiful." The memory of Alfredo's voice caressed her and warmed her bones, enveloping her like a blanket. Whether his words were true or false, she wanted to believe them. "I love you, precious. Long ago in Greece, temple priestesses used to give their bodies to strangers. They knew it was a way to gain wisdom."

"Hey doll, want to warm up?" asked a squat, fleshy man with strong whiskey breath. He wore a windbreaker and a tweed cap.

Adrianne smiled at him. "I need twenty-five dollars."

"No problem, doll." He flashed a roll of bills.

And so once again she walked up the grey, carpeted stairs she had climbed so many times before in the last few months. He followed close behind and occasionally brushed against her as they ascended. Each discoloration on the wall was familiar to her, as was the smell of Lysol superimposed over grime embedded in the structure of the building.

A few other hookers also rented rooms. Older men and women lived here, too. Adrianne thought that the older people seemed to be permanently in exile. The place was familiar to her now, even comforting, if only because she had created daily rituals. Habit built up such a strange sense of safety. This Eighth Avenue hotel seemed more real to her than the Park Avenue establishment ever had, and it seemed safer because it was less insulated from the world.

The man behind her heaved. His leg brushed her buttocks. Noises of street traffic came faintly through the walls. On the third floor an old woman opened her door and stood in the archway in her pink chenille robe, parchment cheeks flushed with rouge, brassy curls half-concealing her face. The woman gave her a look of disapproval and went inside her room again, perhaps to listen to the sound of Adrianne's activities, her ear pressed against the wall, or to listen to the sounds of the hooker and her trick on the floor above.

The man's hands were on Adrianne's buttocks, and he felt beneath her skirt while she turned the key in the lock. "Impatient pig," she thought to herself. Then his hands were between her thighs, caressing and squeezing her bare skin above the stockings.

"Wait!" she cried.

It was getting close to midnight. A feeling of lovelessness choked her. If only Alfredo were with her. Lately he'd been so preoccupied with other things, and he was painting less.

God help her. After each client, she felt more bereft, stripped of another shred of identity. Her life had become like a dream, a delusion. Perhaps one day she herself would disappear. Then only a phantom would glide up the third floor and into her double bed. Bits of her would remain glued to a thousand men.

She switched on the light. Twenty minutes ago she had hastily made up the bed after her last trick. He had been a large man who kept murmuring, *"Querida, querida, mi amor,"* his eyes tightly shut, as if he were trying to envision some sweetheart abandoned long ago.

She carried a knife in her purse as well as a loud whistle, and she let herself be guided by instinct. Alfredo said this kind of life was sharpening her psychic powers. So far she had escaped harm, and she had escaped arrest when the cops came by on foot or in their vans. Still, her nerves were always on edge, like antennae, as she gave instructions to herself. "Not that corner. Stay away from that hooker—stay in your room for thirty more seconds—when the light changes, turn left quickly—don't say yes to that man—walk in the other direction." Stimulated by terror, she had grown acutely sensitive to people's vibrations and to the slightest suspicious movement around her.

Now she took a good look at the stranger beside her. She wondered whether she had made a mistake in bringing him to her room. On the street, his appearance had been somewhat obscured by darkness. He had a flushed, round, rough-skinned face. Slump-shouldered, with protruding blue eyes, his unusually small mouth aroused in her a faint sensation of fear. She did not trust people with such small mouths.

Just last week, a girl had been bound and stabbed to death in a hotel down the street. Adrianne glanced nervously towards the fire-escape window, which she always kept ajar in case she should need to escape as she had needed to do from the apartment on Park Avenue.

The trick embraced her, pressing against her groin, then planted a wet whiskey-smelling kiss on her mouth while he kneaded her buttocks.

"Wait. Put the money on the dresser first," she said. Pulling away from him, she watched as he reached into his pocket, then took out three bills from the roll he had displayed on the street. He walked angrily over to the dresser where he slapped them down.

While he undressed, she wet a washcloth with cold water and wrung it out at the sink. He sat down on the edge of the bed in his underwear and began drinking from a Seagram's pint bottle. She knelt before him. Before he had time to protest, she opened his wrinkled boxer shorts and began to wash him off, examining him carefully. In spite of her precautions she'd caught the clap twice. Alfredo no longer made love to her except with a condom, and never went down on her anymore.

"Hey, why are you doin' that?" The trick's face was contorted, and his voice was strained. "I ain't got no disease. Filthy bitch. You got all the diseases of the city right inside you."

Holding back her rage, she murmured, "I do this with everyone. It's for your safety, too."

"Safety, hey, hey," he chortled. "If I wanted to be safe, I wouldn't be with you."

She pretended she was hearing a sound track from a movie. He was only an actor. She was an actress going through her role. As she washed him lingeringly, he started to stiffen, and his toes wriggled on the carpet. "Mmm," he said. "That feels good." Biting her lips, she suppressed a sob.

"Hey, take your clothes off, doll," he said. "You been washin' me long enough. I wanna see what you look like." Back from the undergrowth of her own mind to his pinkish skin and wrinkled testicles.

While she undressed, he took off his underwear. His body was nearly hairless. Then he grabbed her and felt her all over, pulling her down on the bed and suckling her tits as he gave her awkward little kisses. He was hard now, and she guided him inside her. For an instant she tried to imagine he was Alfredo, but he smelled different. He was damp with cold sweat. She felt that his sperm inside her could create a monstrosity. Suppose her diaphragm had even an infinitesimal hole? She always smeared lots of spermicidal cream on it, but just to be sure, she should inject more with the plunger after this creep left. She should have made him wear a condom, too. She thought of women who were raped, impregnated with unwanted fetuses, and tears came to her eyes. To have the child of the man you loved growing inside you seemed the greatest blessing a woman could have. Even if he hated or deserted you, if you had his child growing inside your womb, it would be all right.

Her long-lost baby girl seemed to cry out. Bones discarded, the baby's infant soul floated above discarded cars and refrigerators.

The stranger kept thrusting against her while she held back sobs. She wished she could get pregnant by Alfredo and then leave him and have their baby alone somewhere. But she was not strong or clever enough to do this. Tears scalded her cheeks. She wanted to slice this man's horrible penis off with a knife. Chop it with a cleaver. He breathed harder as he started to come, then heaved and lay still. Sticky fluid trickled out from her onto the sheet.

"You're so heavy," she said. "Let me get up."

At the sink, she washed off the semen from between her thighs. Then she sipped a glass of water. As she swallowed, she realized in a sudden dreadful flash that Alfredo's loving her was only a delusion. She was a fool. Yet she was addicted to Alfredo. She needed his presence, his voice, his body pressed against hers, even a few minutes a day. She needed this, even though he was throwing away all the money she brought him on booze and expensive clothes, on the car and the track. Maybe on other girls. What an idiot she was to believe even for an instant in her dreams.

The trick was still lying on his back. He stared at her as she stood by the sink, overcome with her revelation.

"Bring me a glass of water. Come back here. I gotta talk with you." His face was contorted with pain, and there was anguish in his eyes. "I gotta talk to someone."

She walked back to the bed and sat beside him. Out of
pity, she stroked his shoulders. As she did so, she noticed that
his skin was marred by moles and blemishes. His pale body
exuded a state of being unloved, just as Alfredo's exhuded a
state of being desired by many women, despite his mother's
rejection. She could feel it in the texture of Alfredo's skin and
in the aura around him. Now on the contrary, touching this
stranger, she was repelled.

Tears glistened on the man's face. He was shaking, and
she felt frightened.

"Gimme that bottle."

She handed him the Seagram's bottle, and he gulped
down the whiskey before offering her some. The strong liquor
burned her throat. She set it down on the nightstand, and he
clasped her, his alcoholic breath surrounding them.

"Don't leave me!" he cried, quivering. "I gotta stay with
you. Gotta be close to someone."

"What happened to you?" she asked. Despite the overly
dry warmth of the room, she shivered. Alfredo would be furious at her for staying so long with one trick.

His clammy hands pressed against the small of her back.
"I just wanna hold you again. I wanna hold you close. I need
to talk to someone."

"I've *got* to leave," she said.

"Don't leave me." He clasped her so tightly she could
scarcely breathe. "Don't leave me. My wife threw me out.
Understand? She threw me outa my own house. Got a
restraining order from a fucking judge so I can't see my own
kids. I'd like to blast that jerk's brains out."

As he reached once more for the bottle, he loosened his
grip and she rolled over to the other side of the bed. Then she
stroked his forehead, which felt feverish.

"I'm sorry."

He held the bottle with a trembling hand and looked
down at her with his pale, angry eyes. "I don't even know your
name."

"Stephanie," she said, using her usual alias.

"My name is Eddie. Stephanie, that's a beautiful name.
And you're a beautiful doll. Tell me, Stephanie, can I be your
man?"

"You don't even know me."

"I can tell you got a warm heart." His voice was pleading. He grabbed the fingers of her left hand. "Can I be your man?"

She stroked his chest and his rough, pitted face.

"I have a boyfriend."

"Yeah? He know you do this for a livin? Hey, say somethin'. Why are you so quiet? I can tell he knows. I can see it in your face. Probably takes all your money. He don't love you or he wouldn't be lettin' you do this," the man drummed in her ears. "Come home with me, Stephanie," he begged, finishing off the bottle, his hands unsteady, eyes rheumy. "Come home with me. I'll treat you good." Then suddenly, as if startled out of sleep and talking to himself, he added, "But you're a whore. What am I doin', askin' you to come home with me? I gotta be out of my mind. I could stick a knife up your filthy cunt."

Then he gripped her so hard that she winced with pain. "Forgive me," he said. "Don't be afraid. I ain't gonna hurt you. I'm askin' you to come home with me. I can tell you got a good heart. You're a good girl. You won't be no whore with me."

"Stop!" She cried.

"Your boyfriend don't love you. He don't give a shit about you. You're nothin' to him. Just trash."

The phone rang.

"Hi, precious."

"Alfredo!"

"Are you okay?"

"Huh?" Her voice trembled.

"Sounds like you're in trouble. I'll be right up, baby."

How grateful she was for Alfredo's presence. He had a sixth sense. He must love her, she thought desperately.

"My man's on his way up here," she said.

But Eddie was already getting dressed with jerky, pathetic movements. He stumbled into his trousers, and his hands shook as he tied his shoelaces and tucked in his shirt.

As he stood there before her fully dressed, prepared to leave, he pressed his face into his hands. Adrianne wondered if he realized that at this instant she both pitied and loved him simply because he was aware of his loneliness. Their bodies were two shadow-selves. Underneath the isolation of their bodies and minds, they were all one. Everything in this stinking universe was one. Beneath the surface, Alfredo was as lonely as Eddie. Men exposed to her their hidden secrets and anguishes. Yet they despised her for offering her body, even though they desired it. At this instant she felt like the mother of all human beings. The world was crazy, just as Alfredo said, and she was helping save men with a few drops of her heart's blood.

Chapter 23

Every time the phone rang in the loft, Adrianne was apprehensive, thinking it was the police who were finally catching up with her for working at Dominic's. That establishment remained closed.

Above her, the radiator pipes hissed. Outside, the sky was grey, and it looked as if it might snow. Still in her robe, and shivering with cold, Adrianne sat down on the couch and wrapped herself in an old Army blanket. The loft was barer of paintings than it had been before because so many were in the gallery, either on exhibit or in storage. One of the few that remained was a recent one of ape-like humans groping each other beneath skyscrapers. Another pictured a raw heart circled by a heap of nude, writhing bodies.

Alfredo inhaled on his cigarette and stepped back to survey the canvas he was working on. It consisted of somber masses of color: dark red, brown, shades of grey. He paced back and forth, evidently disturbed.

"Shit!" he said. "I want to leave this fucking city. People here are such phonies. Harris used to tell me how much he believed in my work, but he hasn't promoted it."

"Really?" she said uneasily. Last Friday, after he had smoked some marijuana, she'd heard him shouting angrily at the art dealer over the phone, and she had wondered with anxiety whether Harris would continue to show Alfredo's work.

"Where could we go?" she asked, lighting a cigarette of her own and putting the match into a jar lid that served as ashtray.

"Somewhere far away, baby. South America. Europe. Maybe Cuba."

He ground out his cigarette butt beneath his heel, lit another one, and took a sip of rum from the bottle. He'd been drinking more lately, and by early afternoon he was never quite sober. Lately, he'd scorned ashtrays and took pleasure in grinding out the butts beneath his feet. He had also begun staying out all night, which wore her nerves to the edge. He had not come home until eight o'clock this morning.

"Where were you last night?" she asked.

"None of your business."

"You treat me like shit."

He laughed. "Baby, you've got to give me some slack."

Tears sprang to her eyes.

Ivory legs were forming on the canvas. He brushed on more shadings of ivory. In spite of her anger, she admired his long, slender fingers and the graceful way he moved. He was handsome, even in his worn, paint-splattered jeans and ragged sweater. With deft strokes, he added a torso and arms. Then there appeared an elongated face framed by red hair.

Outside it had begun to snow. Tiny flakes swirled, barely discernible in the white sky. She wished he would put down the brush and hold her. She wanted him to tell her he loved her, to reassure her about his absence last night.

"I hate it when you spend the night out. Where were you?"

"I went to the moon."

"Tell me really, where were you?"

Just then the phone rang in the kitchen. Alfredo went to answer it.

"Sure, baby," Alfredo said. He laughed, then lowered his voice. She couldn't make out the words, but she could hear his seductive tone.

Her heart pounding, she stood up and took a few steps. There was a brown hairpin on the floor. She stooped to pick it up. It wasn't hers. Had the woman on the phone been here last night? Had she inspired the new painting?

Alfredo came back into the room.

"Who were you talking to?"

"None of your business."

"Does this belong to her?" She showed him the hairpin.

"Ah, Miss Sherlock Holmes."

"Stop it!"

"*Déjame tranquilo!* When you're fucking the whole world out there, am I supposed to live like a monk?"

She lunged and bit his shoulder. He grabbed her hair and slapped her Then she collapsed on the floor, sobbing as she rocked back and forth, hugging her knees to her chest. He put down his brush and began cleaning up. "I can't work when you act like this."

"I'm sorry."

She could not keep back her sobs. They tore out of her as if they were something alien.

He left the room for a few moments, and when he returned he had on a suit and his new cashmere overcoat. He looked somber as he reached down and pulled her to her feet. "Come on, baby. Sit down here with me. Take a deep breath." He pulled her over to the couch and sat her on his lap, then lit a cigarette for both of them and finished off the rum.

"I worry about your drinking," she said.

"I'll worry about that. Don't fuck me up with your hysterics."

"I'm sorry."

"Who's your master?" he suddenly asked in an altered tone that frightened her.

"You are."

"You're learning," he said. His voice softened, and his arms tightened around her. "You mean a lot to me, *preciosa*. That's why I'm hard on you sometimes."

"Do you love *her?*"

"Now, I don't want you getting jealous. You're my woman, but I've got to have some slack. Sweetheart, I want you to meet her. Then you'll feel easier."

"I hate hustling."

"Soon we'll split this scene." He pushed her gently off his lap, went over to a window, and looked out onto the street. When he turned around, his face was filled with sadness. "As soon as we get the cash together, we'll split."

"Where is the cash all going? I give you everything I make."

"Look at all the things we've bought, sweetheart. You've got a silver fox coat, the wardrobe of a princess. We've got a Cadillac. A hi-fi."

"But where's the rest of the money? Is any of it in the bank?"

"I've gotta be careful or the IRS will track us down. I'm taking care of things."

"How much have you lost at Belmont?"

"Trust me, baby," he said. "If you don't trust me, then you can walk out the door right now!" She knew he was lying, but she needed him too much to question him further. He had walked up very close to her, and his intensity overpowered her so that she could barely think.

He lit another cigarette. "I'm making plans for us. We'll go to Havana and stay with my father's family. We'll get married and have those babies you want."

Lies! All Lies! She began crying again, in spite of her attempts to hold back the tears.

A small voice inside her whispered that she, Adrianne, had sinned and that only if she stayed on with Alfredo would she work out her salvation. It was as though she were inside a dark tunnel and only he could lead her out. The price was believing in him.

"I don't want to hurt you, baby," Alfredo was saying as he stroked her hair.

She dried her eyes.

"That's better, sweetheart."

He slapped her lightly on the buttocks. "Now get dressed. Tonight I want you to meet Michelle, but first you've got work to do. It's already four-thirty, and it's time for you to hit the street."

Chapter 24

The lights shone brightly in this all-night Horn 'n Hardart's, lighting up things that should remain hidden. It brought secret thoughts and vices out into the open as it illumined lines, shadows, and subtle emotions in people's faces. Above the stainless steel and formica, the fluorescence, and the din of voices, little could remain hidden.

Alfredo and Michelle sat across the table from Adrianne, his arm around the pale girl whose long red hair was loosely gathered in a chignon. Michelle wore a camel coat that was open to reveal a low-necked black velvet dress. She had thin brows and green eyes.

Adrianne wanted to scream at Alfredo to get his hands off Michelle. She was outraged. Her thoughts swirled; her blood pounded; and she was eating a hamburger, fries, salad, and cheesecake. To hell with struggling to stay thin.

The root of all anguish is that each person needs so much to be loved, she thought. This realization made her think of Max. Long ago, she had dined with him at a Horn 'n Hardart's like this. Lucille, Max, Alfredo, and even this girl Michelle, were all seeking a kind of love that could reach into the center of their beings. Even her tricks were trying to buy love.

She rubbed her fingers, which were still cold from being outside, and put them around her coffee cup to warm them.

"...when I got to the audition, they gave me a script that was so faint I could hardly make out the words, and then they told me I wasn't putting enough emotion into the lines," Michelle was saying.

Alfredo nodded.

"And when I left, the director's assistant told me that all along they'd wanted someone fifteen years older."

"Tough," said Alfredo.

"Where did you two meet?" Adrianne asked.

"The Cedar Street Bar," Alfredo said. "Michelle was acting in an off-Broadway play. Afterwards, she would come in
for a drink."

"What play?" asked Adrianne.

"Experimental," said Michelle. She glanced away.

"I work on the street. That's a different kind of acting,"
said Adrianne, clutching her cup.

"I do a little hustling, too, when I run out of money. Usually I work the Plaza Hotel area."

"I tried that once, but I almost got arrested," said Adrianne, remembering how two plainclothesmen escorted her out
of an elegant hotel lobby near the Plaza one afternoon, shortly
after Dominic's place was busted. After that, she'd decided to
go back to her old Eighth Avenue territory.

"Someday I'll go with you. I'll show you how I work it,"
said Michelle.

So Alfredo was going to be Michelle's pimp, too. Adrianne
knew it from the proprietary way his hand caressed Michelle's shoulder .

A chill ran through her.

She took another sip of the hot coffee and then another
bite of the hamburger. But she could scarcely swallow it. She
wished they were in a place where she could get something
alcoholic.

Michelle's eyes seemed glazed.

"Alfredo, this coffee gets me on edge. I need something to
slow down," said Adrianne.

"Let's go home where I can relax with you fine women,"
he said expansively, spreading his arms around the back of
his chair and Michelle's.

Michelle went to the restroom, and while she was gone,
Alfredo turned to Adrianne. "Now, baby, there's no reason to
get upset. She's nothing to me. Michelle is going to be our
ticket out of here."

"You're using us both."

"Baby, you're my woman," he whispered. He kissed her.

Just then Michelle came back. "Come on, let's go, sugar,"
said Alfredo.

Adrianne's body felt heavy, glued to her chair. She made
an enormous effort to stand up.

They drove back to the loft through thick snowflakes
which covered the city in softness. Thelonius Monk was play-

ing on the car radio. All three were wedged in the front seat, Michelle between Adrianne and Alfredo. Although the heater was turned up, Adrianne shivered with cold.

After they got back to the loft, Alfredo lit up a joint and they smoked while they sipped cognac. Michelle lay back on the sofa against Alfredo, while Adrianne sat on a faded orange cushion on the floor. It pained her to see them physically close like that. She inhaled deeply on the reefer whenever Alfredo passed it to her, and slowly her perceptions began to change. She floated high above her body. After they smoked the second reefer—a Panama Red—she could look down and see they were each in an isolated desert.

Slowly Alfredo began to undress Michelle right there in the studio. Adrianne could see that Michelle had pear shaped breasts, a long torso, and slender thighs. "She's beautiful," Alfredo said to Adrianne, turning Michelle around like a mannequin. "Great bones," he added.

He began kissing one of Michelle's nipples, reaching for her white panties to slip them off.

Adrianne watched them grapple on the floor. Alfredo reached out and grabbed Adrianne's ankle. He pulled her down and kissed her lightly on the lips. "Baby, I want you, too." He pulled off Adrianne's clothes, and then his own.

"Greedy!" The marijuana was lessening her pain.

They all made their way into the bedroom. As Adrianne floated higher on the marijuana, she began to feel a new kind of power inside herself. It soothed the hurt. It made her feel as smooth as glass. After she had wrapped herself in her silk robe, she looked down as though from a mountain top at the two of them on the mattress.

"How's my baby?" Alfredo said in a cajoling tone, taking time out from his exertions. "Looks like you got a buzz on."

Adrianne merely smiled, determined not to give him the satisfaction of seeing her upset. She gazed at Michelle's pale legs wrapped around his dark thighs. Michelle's haunches were as firm as a child's.

Adrianne floated as she watched Alfredo hover over Michelle then come down on top of her and glue his mouth to hers. Fascinated, she could not take her eyes away as Alfredo moved his face down, now kissing her navel, her curly reddish pubic hair, and burrowing between her thighs.

He raised himself. "Baby, why don't you join us. Michelle digs chicks, don't you?"

"Mhmm," murmured Michelle. She giggled. Then Alfredo began laughing, too. They were all high.

Alfredo wedged her between them and slipped off the robe. Michelle began to caress her breasts and thighs. Although she felt no desire for Michelle, she responded, following the odd etiquette of their situation. Michelle's tongue wedged between Adrianne's lips. Adrianne began to relax and to note the differences between the qualities of their touch. Michelle was on top of her now, while Alfredo groped her genitals.

At first Adrianne felt numb, but gradually their touches were awakening a desire she thought she had lost, screwing so many men.

"*Preciosa.*" Alfredo's fingers caressed the nape of her neck, and his voice reached across an expanse of desert to seep into her bones. But he had rolled onto Michelle again and was humping her. Adrianne realized that tonight he wasn't bothering with a condom. His breathing grew faster, and then finally, mercifully, he came. Both Michelle and Alfredo sighed with satisfaction. Soon after that, the two of them dozed off.

Adrianne stared at the luminous clock. Half asleep, Alfredo reached out to cup one of her breasts. Perhaps Michelle was only transient while she, Adrianne, and Alfredo were forging a deeper connection by means of the other girl. Alfredo must love me, she thought with desperation. The marijuana was wearing off, and tears were welling up in her eyes, moistening the pillow.

Was it only an illusion that he loved her? To tear herself from this illusion would be to skin herself raw, to be wounded by exposure to the very air. Without the comforting cloak of illusion, events like this evening's caused unbearable pain. How comforting it was to let the illusion that he loved her— loved her far more than he was aware—creep over her with the warmth of cashmere.

After a while Adrianne could bear it no longer and put on her bathrobe. She walked through the studio, which reeked of paint and linseed oil and cigarette smoke. Why did she notice these odors so strongly just now? In the kitchen she poured herself more cognac to calm her nerves.

When she turned on the radio, Frank Sinatra was singing.

His voice and the romantic words he sang made her sob again. She let the tears roll down her cheeks while she sat there at the kitchen table and sipped the burning liquor. Then she looked up, and while music played on, she gazed out the window at the tops of buildings and at the sliver of night sky until finally darkness began to melt into the grey light of dawn.

Chapter 25

A girl screamed overhead. Adrianne heard the girl's pimp swear at her. Then she heard more screams, and something crashed in the room above. "Don't, please don't! Don't hurt me!" The girl screamed again.

"I wish she'd shut her goddamned trap," said the trick on top of Adrianne. He was very fat. In fact, he was nearly suffocating her as he thrust inside her.

The next day Adrianne passed the girl in the lobby downstairs. Pencil thin, with pale skin and long bleached hair, she wore a black sweater and skirt. She was limping on her spike heels and her right arm was in a sling. Coming close to Adrianne, she whispered, "He sprained my elbow. He beat me so hard with a hanger I can't sit."

"I heard you scream. I wanted to help," said Adrianne.

"Thanks, but this is between him and me," said the girl, clutching her injured arm beneath the sling.

Why didn't the girl leave him? Why didn't she herself leave Alfredo? They were both slaves, Adrianne thought, even as a voice inside her murmured, "Stay with him. Through Alfredo, you will be saved."

When she thought of leaving him, all she could see was a vision of herself freezing to death in an Arctic wasteland.

That afternoon a cold wind blew in, and the temperature fell to ten degrees. Her face and hands felt icy, and Adrianne could not face the thought of working that night. She wished Lucille were here with her—Lucille as she used to be before she got so sick.

Acting on a bold impulse, she decided to take a taxi to a lesbian bar in the Village. There she sat at a long wooden table. A stench of beer mingled with the smell of sawdust. She had never been in such a place before, and she looked around with curiosity. Mostly butch women filled the place. They wore trousers, thick jackets, and leather workboots. Only a few had on makeup and feminine clothing. Several couples danced to songs by Patti Page. Their faces seemed harsh.

Bursts of laughter came from a group of women sitting near her. When the jukebox fell silent, the bartender, a cheery woman who must have weighed over two-hundred pounds, sang the chorus from "You are my Sunshine."

Feeling relaxed after two glasses of burgundy, Adrianne shook a candle in front of her. She watched as the wax dripped down into a porcelain holder.

"Hey, what's the matter? You high? You afraid to speak?" a girl across the table jeered. Adrianne saw that the girl had African features but light skin. She looked even younger than Adrianne. "You're dressed like a hooker," said the girl.

"That's what I am."

"I thought so," said the girl. She had a small delicate face and brown hair. She wore a black T-shirt under a huge worn leather jacket. "I used to turn out," said the girl. "Only I had one experience that shook me up so bad I won't do it no more. I only hustle women now. They're safer. That is, I don't exactly hustle, but they help me out if you know what I mean." She looked at Adrianne as if for reassurance. "By the way, my name's Tina." She inhaled on a small corncob pipe.

"I understand what you're saying. Only I still dig men as well as women."

She became aware that other women at the table were listening, eyeing Adrianne with hostility. They must view her as a traitor.

The candle cast flickering shadows over Tina's face. "Come home with me," she said. Her frail child's hands reached out for Adrianne's.

Adrianne pitied her, but shrank from the coldness of her fingers.

"Don't be afraid of me," said Tina. She let go and looked at Adrianne with a slight glimmer of fear in her own eyes, as if she sensed exactly how Adrianne felt.

"Okay," said Adrianne. Why not, she thought, pushing down the knot of fear inside her gut. Let Alfredo wait up all night for *her* for a change, if he came home at all.

"I turned out for a man once," Tina said softly. "I told you. I was only fourteen." She took a sip of her beer. "But now I won't have anything to do with men. They're evil. All of them. Wise up. You can stay with me for a while if you like. Come on, let's get out of here." Tina's voice sounded a little frantic. When Adrianne looked at the glaze in Tina's eyes, she realized the girl was on something besides beer.

"Bet you have a pimp," said a round-faced woman with glasses who sat on Adrianne's left.

Adrianne flushed and swallowed.

"Bet you give him just about every cent you make."

"What does it matter," said Adrianne.

"You're a sucker for him, I can tell."

"Don't let her get to you," said Tina.

Adrianne ordered another glass of wine and was silent as she listened to the women talking and laughing around her. Gradually, they forgot about her. Then in an alcoholic daze she once again felt Tina's soft hands, a little warmer now. "Come home with me," whispered Tina. "Maybe you can help me out a little, if you can spare any change."

Alfredo would be furious if she not only didn't come home, but walked in tomorrow morning without any money. Let him be furious, she thought. She was growing tired of giving. She was a sucker. Let him wait. Again, she pushed down the panic that was growing inside her.

"Come on," pleaded Tina. Her eyes were dark velvet. There was something soft and honest about her to which Adrianne responded

As they walked out of the bar, Adrianne glanced at their reflections in the mirror behind the counter. There she was, a big, strong girl, yet thinner than she used to be, even though lately she'd gained back some weight. Her bleached hair had grown down to her shoulders. She wore her silver-fox coat and her burgundy leather boots. Although she looked physically strong, inside she felt very fragile and at this moment almost without will. There was Tina leading her by the hand in her huge man's jacket, olive trousers, almost hipless. Tina's delicate mouth tightened into a thin line of tension.

Outside, it was colder than before. As they shivered along MacDougal Street, vague questions about the nature of love ran through Adrianne's brain.

They took a taxi to Brooklyn. In the taxi, Tina kissed her. The girl's tongue tasted of peppermint from a lozenge she had been sucking, but underneath the peppermint was a smell of tobacco and flesh.

When they got out, it was dark and streetlights were on. Three elderly black men were warming their hands in front of a fire in a trash can. Their belongings were heaped on an abandoned sofa with partially torn-out stuffing which stood a bit back from the sidewalk.

"Got a quarter, got a dollar?" cried one of the old men. Adrianne fingered the clasp on her purse.

"Come on," hissed Tina. "Speed it up or the rest of them will be on you like a pack of animals. A whole lot of them live right in front of my building."

Tina's building was half-abandoned. Some of the windows were boarded up, but Adrianne noticed a mailbox which had mail sticking out of it at the entry. They climbed several flights of stairs to the apartment where Tina lived. Adrianne tripped over something before Tina lit a match. Through dark, narrow hallways they walked amidst an overwhelming stench of urine and garbage. Adrianne could scarcely breathe. She would have turned around to run back, but she knew she would not be safe on the streets outside. And so she huddled inside her coat with its scent of Chanel Number Five.

In the apartment, the wooden floor was littered with old newspapers. There were smells of rotting food, no electricity, and only a candle for light. A stained mattress was piled with clothing.

They took off their clothes and huddled on the smelly, clothes-heaped mattress beneath Adrianne's fur coat. Tina's skinny body wound around hers. She had small breasts, and her bones protruded.

Making love to Tina was like making love to a frightened, tender, and yet lustful child. Tina's cold feet and boyish body pressed against her as Adrianne heard rats scampering through the walls. Tina's peppermint-smelling tongue wove aggressively into Adrianne's mouth. Her small childish hands excited Adrianne along her inner thighs, then moved to Adrianne's genitals. In spite of her youth, she had a woman's sensitivity as to what would stimulate or soothe. Gradually, Adrianne forgot the surroundings and the stench of everything. She immersed herself in the lovemaking.

As the two of them held each other, some of the men Adrianne had lain with or sucked off or satisfied in various perverse ways during the last few months flashed through her mind. Each had wounded her. Even Alfredo wounded her in the way he made love to her, which lately was brusque and unfulfilling. If only she could press against Tina long enough and hard enough, perhaps she would somehow be healed. She bit Tina's tongue so hard that Tina gasped with pain. "Hey!" she cried. Then Adrianne soothed her with gentle strokes, and eventually each of them found release.

Later, in her sleep Tina cried out, and Adrianne clutched her closer.

Adrianne dreamed that Alfredo and Michelle were fucking right next to her. She tried to throw herself between them, and Tina mingled with the two. Their limbs interwove like tree branches. One of the branches stuck down her throat and was choking her. She sat up, struggling for breath.

When Adrianne woke up the next morning, wind was blowing through a jagged, broken window above her.

Tina was not there.

Adrianne huddled deeper inside her covering of clothes, but she couldn't get warm. "Tina," she yelled. No answer.

On the wall was a poster of a naked girl on a beach. The girl was blonde, sprite-like, with pointed breasts, a sea nymph who leapt and danced with arms raised high in front of the ocean waves.

She heard a toilet flush. Tina came back into the room with a man's black overcoat over her shoulders carrying a tin can, a syringe, and a roll of gauze. Again Adrianne called out, but Tina did not seem to be aware of her presence as she walked over to the window and poured something from the tin can into the syringe. Then she sat down crosslegged on the floor and injected the needle into her arm. A beatific expression came over her face. At that moment she looked beautiful.

Adrianne stumbled around naked, shivering as she looked for her clothing. Tina had slumped back against the wall and breathed heavily through her mouth. Her eyes were shut. The needle and syringe lay next to her on the floor.

After Adrianne had dressed, she knelt down and kissed Tina's forehead. The girl's skin felt feverish, but her breathing seemed to have returned to normal. Hurriedly, Adrianne left the building, sighing with relief when she felt the cold fresh air outside.

As she was walking along the street, a man on crutches called out to her for spare change. He wore a large cardboard sign around his neck with letters in black crayon that read

"ACCEPT JESUS AS YOUR SAVIOR OR DIE FOR YOUR SINS." Adrianne put a few coins into his tin cup while he wheezed something at her that she didn't understand.

The smells of rotting garbage and incinerator fires prevailed, although the air was so cold. A layer of powdery snow had fallen which softened everything.

She could take a taxi to the airport and fly. Where? Home to her mother? No. Then she would be even more alone. Elena was so cold and so self-absorbed.

What if she were to take her earnings tonight and get a room in the city far away from Alfredo, where he couldn't find her? Perhaps she could get a straight job as a cook or a clerk typist. If she lived alone, would she again experience the walls of her room threatening to suffocate her? Would she again suffer unbearably in the way she had before she met Alfredo?

Suddenly she thought she could hear Max's soft voice whisper, *"Meine liebchen. Poor child."*

Max would despise her if he knew what she did for a living. She thought of other people who had crossed her path.

Slave mentality, jeered Alfredo in her mind.

Give me my fix, said Tina.

You're a damned fool not to leave him, Lucille would say.

Adrianne had called Lucille in Houston a few days earlier only to learn from the maid that Lucille was back in the hospital.

Lucille, I want to be with you, and now you are dying, Adrianne thought as she continued walking through the cold.

Chapter 26

More often now, Alfredo didn't come home until dawn. Half-awakened by his entrance, Adrianne would hear him undress and take off his shoes with a thud. She would hear bathroom noises. The mattress would creak, and he would touch her thigh or her breast, as if simply to make sure she was there. Then he would roll over and go to sleep. She wanted to cry out with pain because she wanted him to caress her and whisper words of love.

When she got home this morning the sheets had been torn off the bed and stuffed into a pillow case, ready to be taken to the laundry. Adrianne could smell coffee and bacon. Alfredo's breakfast dishes were piled in the sink, and he was standing in the middle of the studio, dressed to go out.

"Did a rich trick keep you up all night, baby?"

"No. I slept with a girl. I was so tired, and I felt so sick of men. I went to a lesbian bar. Alfredo, don't be mad."

As he stood there in his suede jacket, wearing a muffler and grey flannel trousers, he looked distinguished and a trifle older. Morning sun streamed down through the skylight, illuminating the lines in his face. On the wall there was a new painting, half-finished of black, purple, and ivory abstract swirling forms.

"I ought to beat some sense into you." As he moved towards her, his look frightened her.

Adrianne laughed nervously.

Suddenly Alfredo's fist shot into her face. In seconds, she was on the floor and he was kicking her.

"Stop!" she screamed. He kicked her ribs. She curled up in a ball. All her muscles tensed as she waited for the next blow. Then she heard his footsteps recede. Sobbing, she held her hands against her face.

After a while, she limped to the bathroom and looked in the mirror. Her face was bruised, with a purplish swelling under her right eye. Her ribs ached where he had kicked her. Had he broken any?

When she heard his footsteps again, she trembled.

"Don't be afraid!" He came up from behind and slipped his arms around her waist. "Come on, baby, let's take a look at you." His face was somber. "Let's get some ice."

He led her into the kitchen where he wrapped a lump of ice in a dish towel and had her hold it beneath her eye. Then he led her to bed where he undressed her tenderly. After a while, overwhelmed with shock and pain and confusion, she fell asleep beneath the soothing power of his hands.

When she woke up it was late afternoon, and she realized that the apartment was empty. Wrapping the quilt around her, she got up and went into the bathroom to pee.

In the kitchen, she fixed herself tea and toast. Her stomach felt queasy. She returned to bed and turned the radio to some classical music, which soothed her. Then she dozed off again until Alfredo awakened her by gently shaking her shoulders.

"What is it?"

"Don't cry, Adrianne. I love you."

"How can you treat me this way?"

"I do it because I love you," he said. "You need a firm hand."

"No, no, no," she sobbed, afraid to speak freely. How unfair he was. She would leave him, yes, she would when she got well, but for now she would say nothing about it.

"I've got something for you." He took a small white box out of his jacket pocket. "Open it."

The box had a Tiffany label. Inside were two perfect pearls wreathed with tiny diamonds. "For the woman I love," he said.

She fingered the earrings. "They're beautiful."

"Let's see how they look." He helped her put them through her ears, then he put his maroon robe around her and led her to the bathroom so she could see herself. The bruise beneath her eye had darkened, but the earrings gleamed. He stood behind her in the mirror, half-a-head taller. There was something scornful in his expression.

"You stay out all night. Why can't I?"

"That's how it is," he said, fixing her with his eyes. "We'll put some makeup on over those bruises so you can work tonight."

"I can't go out like this. My ribs hurt. Maybe you broke them."

He felt her body. "Nothing's broken," he said. " Tonight you work."

"I hate hustling."

"It's only for a short time, so be patient. You and I are going on to better things, but we need to save up some money first."

He lit a cigarette, offered her one, then blew out the smoke and took a deep breath. "I don't want you getting upset about what I'm going to say. *Preciosa,* you know I love you. You're my woman, *verdad?*"

"Yes."

"We're in a tight spot just now. Michelle is moving in. She can help us out with expenses."

"What?"

"Now don't get excited." He put his arm around her. "She's just moving in temporarily. She has to move out of her apartment by the end of the month."

"I'll move out!" She stubbed out her cigarette, clutched the robe tighter around her waist, and walked over to a window where she looked down at the moving cars and people. She could throw herself out onto the street below. She could leave him tonight. She could go back to stay with Tina.

She would pack her suitcase and get out of here. But then what? She had visions of standing alone on Times Square with frozen icicle tears on her cheeks, feeling as if she were flying apart. He was like a slippery eel, like the god Proteus in an ancient legend she'd read about in high school. You had to hang onto him to keep him from changing shapes. She had to hang onto him or she would drown. If she only hung on long enough, something good would come of it.

"What happens to all the money I bring in? Where's it all going?"

"We've got the Cadillac. The hi-fi. Your fox coat," he uttered his usual excuses. "Your black rabbit. Those earrings set me back three-hundred dollars."

"How much have you lost at Belmont?"

His eyes clouded with anger and he tilted her chin up. "If you don't trust me, you can pack right now and leave!"

"I don't want Michelle to move in. It hurts me that you want her here!"

"We need the money."

"Bullshit!" she cried out in a burst of bravery. "It's bullshit that we need the money. You want to screw her."

"Watch your mouth, bitch!"

Furious, she swallowed her anger and went into the kitchen. He followed her.

"I love you," he said softly. "I want you to be all that you can be. Just remember that whatever happens, I love you." He began caressing her beneath the robe. "You're a slave," he murmured as he stroked her. She put her hand out to steady herself against the stove. He caressed her breasts, her belly, her buttocks. "You've got a beautiful ass. You'll keep right on being a slave, baby, until you understand what it's all about."

"Then what?"

"Then you'll be dynamite. I love you, and I'm going to make you into a dynamite woman."

"So you make me suffer because you love me?"

"Yes."

"That's crazy."

He didn't seem to hear her. Letting her go, he reached for a half-empty bottle of rum on the kitchen counter and drank from it. Then he walked out of the kitchen.

She would leave him. Yes, she would leave, she decided.

She stood motionless, staring as if in a trance at the stove, then at the bottles and jars crowded on the counter.

A few minutes later she walked back into the bedroom. He was smoking a joint and he passed it to her. "This will take away your pain," he said. "It will make it easier to work tonight." He put some Miles Davis on the hi-fi. Then they lay down and smoked. The marijuana relaxed her. He opened the maroon silk robe and tenderly kissed her breasts, her earlobes, her neck, and finally her mouth. "Soon we'll leave the country. We'll get married in Havana."

If only she could believe him.

She inhaled, held the smoke, let it out. Let out all the doubts. Let her mind go black. Higher. Get higher. But he was wrong about the grass. It wasn't easier to work after you'd smoked. It was a lot harder when you came down again.

He made love to her slowly, with the music playing in the background, and afterwards she lay quietly and felt as if the molecules in her body were subtly changing. A new kind of power was surging through her, even though her ribs still ached. In her altered state, things seemed easy. Easy as pie. By and by she would lay all those men until she reached the sky and touched them with her gigantic fingers. She and Alfredo were floating on top of the world.

At the edge of her consciousness Miles Davis' trumpet sounded. The music sounded so beautiful when she was high. The intervals were longer between the notes. Time was expanding. She could forgive Alfredo because she, too, was expanding.

However, when she looked closely at his face, she saw that it was tinged with a brutality that had not been there when they first met. "He is growing weak through his brutality to me, and I am growing strong. When the time comes, I will leave. Then I will be the strong one," Adrianne said to herself. The balance between them was shifting. Maybe the beating this morning, horrible though it was, awakened something in her that had been paralyzed.

After a while Alfredo got out of bed. He went into the kitchen and brought Adrianne a plate with cold steak, salsa, potato chips, and a mug of coffee. "It's late," he said. "Come on. I'll drive you uptown."

~~~

An hour later she was back at the Flamingo Bar on Eighth Avenue, sipping Courvoisier for her throat, which felt a little sore. A middle-aged man with a goatee who was sitting three bar stools away said, "Have one on me."

"Thanks."

The man moved closer.

She smiled at the bartender and slipped him a bill for his part of the take.

Chapter 27

Michelle moved in. In order to squeeze out some closet space for her belongings, Alfredo packed some of his own clothes into a duffel bag. Adrianne experienced the other girl's presence as a slow-motion nightmare. Sometimes it was all she could do to keep herself from attacking them both with her fists and screaming.

A few days later, Michelle started working the upper East-side hotels and bars. "Why don't you come with me, Adrianne?" she suggested.

Adrianne refused.

At times she would picture Michelle with a knife sticking out of her chest and blood all over, or she'd imagine Michelle's fingernails being torn out with pincers.

Some nights long after Michelle was asleep, Adrianne would clutch Alfredo, and if he were in the right mood he might make love to her tenderly and quietly. As they rocked against each other, she would feel that a deep bond like a subterranean river connected the two of them.

She and Michelle usually both woke up around midday. Often, Alfredo would have gone out. Then she and Michelle might play with each other's bodies, caressing and kissing. At such moments Adrianne felt the sense of power that she imagined a man would feel with a woman. However, at times Adrianne felt that she and Michelle were secretly measuring each other, like opposing warriors. She observed Michelle's smallest gestures as she tried to master the secrets of Michelle's charm.

She tormented herself with the fear that Alfredo cared more for Michelle. Were they planning to abandon her, in spite of Alfredo's whispered promises? Some nights the other two did not come home until nearly dawn, and then they would come in laughing, high on marijuana or some other drug, and Adrianne would question the set-up all the more.

Generally, Michelle was friendly but reserved. Her self-containment unnerved Adrianne. But there were moments when the other girl's green eyes were full of pain.

"Do you love Alfredo?" Adrianne asked one morning while they were drinking coffee.

"I'm not in love with him."

"Why did you move in here?"

"I had nowhere else to stay. Besides, I'm a Gemini, and Gemini's are curious."

"About what?" Adrianne wound a tendril of hair around her finger. Michelle looked particularly frail as she sat there in her translucent nightgown. At that moment Adrianne felt she could stick a knife through one of those taut breasts, straight into Michelle's heart.

"I wondered what it would be like to live with a man and a woman."

"How do you feel when he fucks me?"

"It's beautiful. I float with it."

"Why don't you get your own man?"

"What makes you think he's yours?"

Seeing the disturbed look on Adrianne's face, Michelle said, "I'm sorry. He is your man, after all. Don't be afraid, because I won't be around for long." Michelle grew more serious. "I was married once, but it didn't work out. I don't want to be involved like that again. I want to float ...split when the going gets heavy or when I get bored, whichever comes first. You see, I don't *want* Alfredo. I don't want you to walk out and leave me here alone with him." She cluched her cup more tightly between her hands as she looked directly into Adrianne's eyes.

During the next few days, illusion curled its soft petals through Adrianne as seductively as a drug. She persuaded herself that Alfredo loved her. Alfredo loved her so much that the two of them would only be more strongly mated as a result of their shared experience with Michelle.

"You need a girl around," Alfredo said. "You need the softness of another girl." He would sketch Michelle and Adrianne in bed together in amorous poses.

"Doesn't it upset you to see us like that?" she asked.

"No, baby," Alfredo said. "It turns me on."

For her part, the only way she could endure it when Michelle and Alfredo made love was to detach herself, as if she were in a dream or nightmare.

The tension inside her built.

One morning when Alfredo was out and there was no toilet paper in the bathroom, Adrianne shrieked at Michelle for never buying any. Afterwards, she was ashamed of herself. She had sounded like her mother, Elena, in the early days after Julio's death.

She tried to anesthetize herself so that she felt nothing. She tried to numb herself to the tricks and to the sordidness of her working life. However, she became irritable despite her efforts at self-control. All her antennae were opening up. She'd stepped up the diet pills to prevent herself from eating too much. Now she ran on nervous energy, and a curious lightness filled her.

She found herself psyching out the tricks in rich detail, trying to pick up their fantasies, thoughts, and fears while she went through her physical contortions. This helped her to feel more in control. She felt as if she were drawing on a deep source of vitality. However, it also exhausted her, and she needed twelve to fourteen hours sleep a night.

Why, she asked herself, when she could penetrate the minds of strangers (even as they penetrated her body), couldn't she understand Alfredo? Why did she need him so much?

Chapter 28

She dreamed of an arctic cloud, and this merged with early infantile memories. As a baby, no one had ever touched her enough. She half-remembered howling for hours on end in her crib, crying out to be touched and fondled.

"Mamá ..." she heard herself sobbing while Elena, in pale satin, lay back against bed pillows and gazed right through the child, as if she were transparent. Her mother was apparently entranced by the red roses on the mantelpiece.

"Cállate, Adriana," scolded the servant as she pulled the child away. *"Tu mamá está enferma."*

They were still living in Santiago then, in the big house that belonged to her father's family. But her father had already left for the United States.

One night Adrianne and Alfredo went out alone to a jazz club. A trio was playing blues, and the music filled her with its substance. "We've got to stop this way of life," she said. "I can't stand it anymore. Since Michelle moved in, you've almost stopped painting."

He sipped his rum and soda. "I've got to treat you better," he mused, rubbing his calloused finger along her inner arm. "You know I suffer when you do, baby, even though I've been kicking you in the ass. We've been leading crazy lives. Something has to change."

"Yes," she said.

There was a glimmer of light, she thought, at the end of the tunnel.

The hard piano notes and the muted sax rubbed along her bones.

The next day she came down with severe menstrual cramps. Michelle hit the streets. but Alfredo let Adrianne rest. He stayed home with her, cooked her chicken broth, filled her hot-water bottle, and then went out for a short time, only to return with several long-playing Beethoven records. He massaged her stomach, and later on in the evening when she was feeling a little better, he made love to her. To her surprise, she had an orgasm and let herself flow with it as if waves were breaking over her, breaking her into pieces, carrying her with their flow.

Afterwards, she felt very sleepy and relaxed, healed in some mysterious way. She dozed off. When she woke up, he was in the studio painting. He worked late into the night while she lay awake in bed listening to Beethoven symphonies, trying to penetrate beneath the sound into something she could not fathom, something that held the keys to an essential mystery.

She got out her old wooden rosary, prayed with it, then put it under her pillow.

She dreamed of a small child of indeterminate sex, bundled in leggings, snow jacket and mitten, its face and head hidden by a green woolen visored cap. The child was running clumsily past her along Eighth Avenue. A huge black Doberman leapt forward, and in a flash there was a crunch of bones. The child shrieked. Blood seeped through the child's torn layers of clothing as it lay sprawled on the snow. Just before dawn she awakened and clutched at Alfredo for warmth. Instead, she felt Michelle's soft breasts and Alfredo's fingers on the girl. Adrianne bit into her pillow to keep from shrieking out loud. She could smell the fresh menstrual blood which stuck to her thighs.

If she didn't get out, she would go crazy.

To escape them both, Adrianne holed up in her hotel room. When Alfredo called, she told him that her period was still painful and that she needed to be left alone. She slept a great deal—a dull, heavy sleep—and went out to the movies.

On the third day when she peered through the drapes, the sky was swollen with heavy clouds. The turquoise-colored walls of her room closed in oppressively. She rushed out into the street bundled in her good fur coat, her leather boots, and her gloves. Her hair streamed over her face, obscuring her vision. A fierce wind nearly swept her off her feet.

The Flamingo Bar was empty except for an old man, and so she went outside again. The streets were nearly deserted. She enjoyed the force of the wind. It seemed to release all her pent-up feelings. She might take a subway down to the Brooklyn Bridge. Then she could jump off the bridge and end this nightmare, which seemed to roll on and on like celluloid film. But if she were to die now, perhaps the film would only roll on into the next life.

Why did one man have the power to arouse so much anguish in her, she wondered.

On the corner of Eighth Avenue and Sixty-Third Street, she glimpsed a woman who looked like Eileen from Dominic's. Even in her heavy coat, the woman looked painfully thin, with matchstick arms and legs and a haggard white face half-hidden by enormous glasses. Eileen had been almost plump. Nonetheless, Adrianne called out across the street "Eileen!" The woman turned her head.

"It's me, Adrianne."

The woman did not recognize her. She seemed drugged. A man in a topcoat, head down against the wind, nearly stumbled against her. Adrianne watched the woman clutch his arm while the man shook her off and hurried on.

Bracing herself against the wind, Adrianne kept on walking. She thought of Max, the old German, and she was consumed with a sudden longing to be with him. Ah, she was a fool not to have chosen him because he had truly cared for her. To be loved seemed a treasure beyond price. But she was not worthy of Max, she thought. The wind was bitter as it blew against her face, chapping her skin.

As she rushed along the street, with no idea at all where she was going, she told herself in desperation that Alfredo *must* love her, and Michelle was only a cruel test.

"It is only an illusion that he loves you," whispered a voice inside. But the illusion felt warm and soft, like gossamer. "Pity," a voice that sounded like Max's whispered. "Have pity. Be kind to yourself." Her fingers and toes were numb with cold, and her boots hurt her feet. Although she was aware of the cold, at the same time she did not seem to be part of her body and a strange peace began to fill her. She wandered uptown into an unfamiliar neighborhood along Tenth Avenue.

"Pity," whispered the voice through the freezing wind.

It took all her strength to keep on believing in Alfredo's love because she had to battle constantly against her perceptions. "Love on earth is an illusion," whispered the voice. "Love causes anguish, and only our illusions shield us from its pain." The voice's presence enveloped her, like a cloud in its embrace.

Chapter 29

"Palmist, psychic, and spiritual healer," said the hand-let tered sign outside the first-floor apartment with its dull green scuffed door on West 84th Street. Adrianne rang the bell. A heavyset, swarthy woman, whom Adrianne thought looked like a gypsy, opened the door.

"Yes."

"Can you read my palm? Or do a psychic reading or a healing?"

The gypsy woman looked at her dubiously and said, "Come in."

They walked through a narrow entrance into the living room which smelled musty and was crowded with furniture. There they sat down at a round table covered with a fringed red cloth

The gypsy wrapped her black shawl more tightly around her large breasts. She wore a dress of flowered silk. A silver amulet hung from a heavy chain around her neck.

Adrianne looked at the woman's full face and noticed a large mole on one cheek. The gypsy's wavy black hair, streaked with grey, hung below her shoulders. "How much is a reading?"

"It depends. What do you want?"

"Well, a palm reading," said Adrianne with hesitation.

"That costs three dollars."

Adrianne fumbled in her purse and found three single bills.

"Gimme a dime—a quarter—something silver. That brings luck," said the woman in a husky voice.

Again Adrianne rummaged and found a quarter.

"I am Rosita. Relax. Don't be frightened, honey. Tell me your name."

"Adrianne Torres," she blurted out. Then too late, she wondered why she had told the woman her last name. Lately she was so scattered, hardly aware of what she was doing. She'd been going around in a daze, acting on compulsions and blurting out stupidities. She was barely able to cope any longer. Couldn't cope with the tricks. Couldn't cope with Michelle or Alfredo.

"Adrianne Torres is a nice name. Don't be scared, Adrianne. Relax."

Adrianne looked down at the worn Persian rug. A light patch near her feet had been bleached of color.

The woman smelled of garlic.

Don't come so close to me, Rosita, she thought. You're appraising the value of my fox coat, which I should not have worn, and the pearl earrings with tiny diamonds that Alfredo gave me.

"Your mind is wandering," said Rosita, bringing her back to the present. "Relax. You gotta trust me." It was as if the gypsy could read her thoughts. Jarring. Her head ached.

Rosita asked her to hold out both hands flat on the table, palms up. She examined the lines closely with a magnifying glass which cast white circles on Adrianne's skin. Then she took Adrianne's right hand between her soft warm ones, turned it over to look at Adrianne's oval polished nails, and then back again.

"There is darkness around you," said Rosita. "Darkness around you for a long time. You got children?"

"No."

"You had one that died?" Rosita looked closely at her.

"Yes."

"Hmmm, I thought so. I see your whole life like colors in a pattern. This is a dangerous time for you. You could have a bad accident or even die. You gotta be real careful, honey." She looked away, concentrated in thought. "I'm telling you what I see."

Sighing, Rosita took her hand again while she gazed into a crystal globe on the table. Rosita's fingers were pudgy. She wore a thick gold wedding ring. Her nails were square with chipped blood-red nail polish. Adrianne could feel pulsations through the gypsy's fingers.

"You love a guy, but he don't treat you right."

From the look of pain on Adrianne's face, Rosita must have known she'd hit the mark.

Mark.

She had always been an easy mark. A thousand lovelorn people must have passed through Rosita's door.

Spit in her face.

Run. Hide her face in Rosita's lap. Adrianne was trembling. She should have eaten a solid meal instead of taking only a cup of coffee and doughnut at noon.

"Help me, Rosita, I'm going crazy," she felt like blurting out. Adrianne loosened her grip from Rosita's and groped in her purse for a cigarette. "Mind if I smoke?"

"Go ahead."

Psychic shit, Adrianne was sure Alfredo would say. Who cares? Can't cope. Can't cope.

"You look frightened, honey. Trust me. Rosita ain't gonna hurt you."

Adrianne inhaled and tried to stop trembling. She was crazy to have come here. She should have gone to a shrink.

> *"Alfredo, let me stop taking diet pills."*
> *"You'll gain weight."*
> *"So what."*
> *"Listen, baby, I'm your brains. You don't know how to wipe your ass without me."*

She wished she could be born again as a fragile, undersized girl, wasp-waisted, with huge dark beguiling eyes and silken hair. Then people would realize when she was hurt and they would want to protect her. No one did now. Even though she'd lost more than thirty pounds since last summer, she was still large and people seemed to think her sheer size protected her. She wondered if Rosita's stolid appearance also hid a refined sensitivity.

Her head ached.

"Can you help me clear away the darkness?" Adrianne asked.

"You gotta trust me."

"I do."

Rosita looked at Adrianne intently and said, "You don't know how to trust."

"I want to trust you."

"That's what Rosita needs to hear."

Only unhappy people went to fortune tellers. Maybe she should run away right now. All around her were dangers.

Some evening her sensing radar might be off and she might pick up a murderer who would stuff her mutilated body into a garbage can.

Then who would give a damn? Alfredo would rage and say it had been her fault because she should have immediately sensed the trick's character. He would rage and get crazier. Would Alfredo love her more if she died? Should she pack herself into an airtight container and have herself shipped to him?

Weird thoughts.

Help me, Rosita.

In a nearby room, a baby started crying.

"You belong with me, baby. When you're with a trick, just think of me and know that you're doing this for both of us."

Every girl needs a man. Without one, she is nothing. She is alone without ballast, a cipher, a freak. Adrianne's thoughts swirled her away from the room and then back again into the ruddy brightness of the crystal.

"Can you help me?"

Rosita spoke slowly. "You need a healing service," she said. "But it cost plenty money. I gotta pay my helpers. I don't know if you got the money. You need the service to drive out evil spirits. They're ruining your life."

"How much does it cost?"

Rosita looked straight into her eyes, and again Adrianne felt as if she were being x-rayed. "You got money. Don't tell me you don't got money," she said. "You got a beautiful fur coat that cost a lotta money. I can see you got money, but that don't make you happy."

"How much?"

"One hundred and fifty. You got that with you, we can have the service tonight. Otherwise we wait until you get the money. My assistants are going out of town for a few days. I don't know when they're coming back."

"A hundred and fifty dollars?"

"Uh-huh. You make a lotta money on your job." Rosita pronounced the last word with a curling of her lower lip. "I can see what you do for a living," the gypsy's expression clearly said.

Did Rosita know that in the inner pocket of her purse she always carried six or seven large bills? What did it matter? Paper bills. Dirty gray-green paper bills. In return for copu-

lating, sucking off, pleasuring strange men, they gave her
bills which gave her certain powers. Why not? What did it
matter to whom she gave these dirty pieces of paper when she
was going crazy, sinking? "Can you use bills for toilet paper
on a mental ward? " Alfredo would say.

She unzipped the inner pocket and felt the bills with her
fingers. Con artist. Con. Run with her money.

"You don't got the money, we can do the service another
time."

"I've got the money," Adrianne blurted out.

"Okay. You gonna thank me. I know a lotta things about
you ... things you don't even know yourself. I'm gonna help
you, Adrianne, so don't be afraid."

The gypsy's voice was hypnotic.

"We gonna have this service in a little while when my
husband and the others get here. They're all good people.
We're gonna help you. Maybe you wanna lie down and rest
while you wait. You give me seventy-five dollars now and the
rest later."

Adrianne took out several bills.

"Okay," said Rosita after counting them. She put the
money inside her brassiere and led Adrianne to a dark velvet
couch at one end of the room.

A little girl about ten years old with skinny legs in a plaid
dress ran into the room giggling and covering her mouth.
Rosita cried out to her in a harsh language that sounded
strange to Adrianne. Then she had Adrianne take off her
boots and settled her on the couch, covering her with the fur
coat. Her hands lingered on the fur.

"You will die," a voice inside Adrianne murmured. Tears
choked her.

"That's okay. You cry, honey," said Rosita. She stroked
Adrianne's hair.

"Mama, help me," Adrianne pleaded inside. But her
mother was a cold woman who had withdrawn into the cocoon
of her own dreams.

"These are beautiful earrings," Rosita said, fingering the
one on her left ear. "Your man give them to you?"

"Yes. How did you know?"

"I know a lotta things. You love this man, but he hurt
you, he's no good for you. You even been thinkin' about killin'
yourself, right?"

Adrianne nodded silently while the gypsy continued to stroke her hair. The earrings were hurting her ears, and she wished she could take them off. But she didn't dare because they might get lost.

In the glow of the dim light the woman's face appeared kindly. Could she trust this gypsy?

All her separate thoughts converged like birds fighting each other with huge dark wings, and she felt sleepy. She dozed off and after a while awakened to the smell of frying chicken and footsteps in the kitchen.

Rosita brought her a plate with a small, greasy, cooked chicken breast and some rice, along with a cup of bitter tea. Afterwards, Adrianne fell into a sound asleep. When she woke up, the room was dark and she could tell that hours had elapsed.

"It's time," said Rosita softly as she turned on a light.

Adrianne could hear people talking in the kitchen, apparently arguing with each other in their harsh Romany language.

"Get up, honey," Rosita said. "Don't be afraid." She was wearing a long shabby velvet gown, and a silver amulet gleamed on her chest. The card table had been pushed into a corner, leaving some clear floor space.

Two men and a younger woman entered the room. The men wore short-sleeved sports shirts. The woman wore a long dark red dress and heavy gold jewelry. In her arms she held a baby.

Rosita wandered around the room lighting votive candles. She whispered something to the older man, whom Adrianne took to be Rosita's husband. Dark skinned, muscular, about fifty, he emanated sensuality when he smiled at Adrianne. The other man, who was perhaps in his early twenties, was slender, and his face was more reflective and sensitive.

A third woman about the same age as Rosita, stocky in a long gown with gleaming jewelry, came into the room.

The baby in the young woman's arms began to whimper, although she was trying to soothe it by rocking it against her breasts. "Ramón!" she cried. The younger man took the baby from her and turned it over on its stomach, holding it in the palm of one hand, while with the other he slapped its back. The baby gasped for breath, then quieted down, and he carried it off into another room.

When Ramón returned, Rosita led Adrianne to the space which had been cleared. The others grouped silently around her. "This girl, Adrianne here, needs all our help. Bad spirits have entered her. They got control, and they are making her sick. We are gonna drive them out. Don't be afraid honey, we gonna help you. We gonna heal you right here tonight, and you gonna thank us the rest of your life."

Adrianne watched a votive candle on the card table flicker.

Was all this a hoax?

Shadows flickered over their faces. Although she was scared and imagined herself running out the door now before it was too late, Adrianne felt hopelessly weighed down.

The young woman glanced at Ramón and seemed to be suppressing laughter. There was jeering laughter inside Adrianne's head. She glimpsed a multitude of shadowy figures all around them, as if she were in a dream. Although she had slept, she felt exhausted and feverish. Perhaps the tea she'd drunk earlier had been drugged.

"Don't be afraid," murmured Rosita.

Lower entities are not evil, Adrianne thought in a flash as the gypsies began to swirl around her, moving their bodies in a dance-like way. Lower entities are only ignorant. Compassion for these lower beings, spirits, or ghosts, whatever they might be, flooded her heart. She wanted to keep them inside her. Poor hungry lonely ghosts. She would feed and love them.

What was good and what was evil? It could only be good to feel compassion, and as for this physical life, it was soon over. Each person was like a husk that surrounded an island of emptiness, separating it from the vast universe.

Alfredo, I love you. I love even these poor crooked gypsies who were once vulnerable children. If they want to take my money, it's because they need it.

Take my money and kill me. Then I can float up to the sky.

"She is good," intoned Rosita. "She is a good person. Let her be," she gestured to Ramón, who looked as if he were about to slip off Adrianne's golden bracelet with its Tiffany imprint that a shabbily dressed trick had given her a few weeks ago. At the time she wondered if the trick had stolen it.

Rosita was stroking her forehead. Adrianne slumped and fell on the carpet.

Loud laughter blasted inside her head, and shades of gray and purple burst inside her. As she looked around at these people's faces, they seemed twisted, with dark eyes like wolves, evil mouths. Perhaps it was the evil inside her that was perceiving them like this, distorting their mouths and eyes. Perhaps they were going to kill her and throw her body into the Hudson.

The others began chanting. *"Pani pani lunjara . . . pani pani lunjara . . . mudares . . . mudares . . ."*

These words were repeated over and over again in a monotonous, threatening drone, like snakes hissing and snapping at her in the darkness. As she listened to the chanting, she could only make out fragments.

"Pani, pani lunjara . . . mudares . . . mudares . . ."

She grew dizzy and felt worn-out. She wanted to close her eyes and sleep.

"In the name of the Universal Spirit, I command you, dark spirits, leave Adrianne," Rosita said loudly in English

"Pani . . . pani mudaras . . . mudaras . . ."

An acrid odor seemed to fill the room as Rosita massaged Adrianne's neck and shoulders, infusing her with warmth. The gypsy pressed sharply on certain painful points. Then electric spasms seized Adrianne's body, and her arms and legs moved convulsively.

Claws were digging into her throat, and she could not breathe. She gasped for breath and began to scream while they, still chanting, held her down. They were angry with her. Light and dark waves swelled over her and filled her mouth with a sour-tasting substance. The claws kept digging into her throat, trying to destroy her. She screamed to rid herself of the claws, screamed to cleanse herself of the blood they were shedding inside her. Screamed louder and louder, while the people held her on the floor and continued to chant.

She struggled to rise, but they wouldn't let her. Breaths of all the men who had lain with her concentrated inside her into a huge dark cloud that came out of her mouth as she screamed again, so loudly that something shattered in the air around her. Then to her horror, she realized that her menstrual blood was soaking through her clothing onto the carpet. But no one seemed to notice or care.

She screamed louder. Hands were still holding her down, anchoring her.

"Universal spirit, protect Adrianne," chanted Rosita.

"Universal spirit, protect ... protect," the others chanted.

"Pani, pani ...mudares ..."

Golden light spears thrusting through blackness.

"Lower beings, come out of this girl," chanted Rosita. "Come out ...come out ...*pani mudares ...pani pani mudares ..."*

Someone clapped a hand over her mouth.

Ramón, the sensitive one, was holding a gleaming silver knife over her.

Then, with all her strength, she again tried to rise and get away, but they were holding her down with far too much force. "This is the end. Now I will die," she thought. She found herself trying to reach up with her mouth to bite the edge of the blade, but suddenly Ramón withdrew it and a few seconds later it thudded into the carpet.

She blacked out.

When she regained consciousness, she was covered with a blanket and hands were soothing her arms and hands and forehead. Warm hands held her icy, stockinged feet. She turned to her left side and vomited.

"At last," sighed Rosita. "Get up and wash yourself." She led Adrianne into a small, brightly lit bathroom. There Adrianne rinsed out her mouth with cold water. She washed her face then dried it with a lime-green towel on the rack. After she finished using it, Rosita grabbed the towel from her and threw it into the wastebasket.

Adrianne looked at herself in the bathroom mirror. Her face looked old. There were lines in her face that had never been there before. A film of sick perspiration coated her skin. Rosita must have drugged her tea earlier. How else could these hallucinations be explained? Yes, they drugged the tea. They did this at least once a week to unwary victims, and then the gypsies would laugh afterwards while they counted out their bills, just as she herself sometimes did when she counted out the bills from her tricks at three or four a.m.

When she returned to the living room, the vomit and blood had been cleaned up and only a damp spot remained on the carpet. But the stench still filled the air

She shivered. "I'm cold."

Rosita covered her with her coat and settled her down again on the couch.

"Universal Spirit, protect Adrianne. Surround her in golden light," chanted Rosita. The others chorused this. Then they began chanting again, "Universal Spirit, protect ...protect ... *Prajial te nan yo avel ...Prajial te nan yov avel ...yov avel ... avel ...avel.*"

Adrianne felt empty. As they continued to chant, a beautiful warmth enveloped her. Then sadness welled up and she began to cry. Rosita's arms wrapped around her. "That's good, honey. Cry. Cry. The evil spirits have left you, and you're healed now. You're *you.*"

The others chanted again, *"Prajail ...yov ...avel ...avel."*

She perceived something noble in their faces.

"You were possessed," said Rosita.

Possessed.

A strange word.

Its meaning slowly penetrated her. Had she truly been possessed? Or was this a game these people played?

"If you need help, come back, honey," said Rosita. "We're here."

Someone brought her purse, her boots, and her scarf. Hurriedly she put them on along with her coat. She felt ashamed and indebted to them and wanted to leave as fast as she could.

Out. Get out. Fast.

"It's not safe to be on the streets so late," said the older man. "I'll go with you to get a taxi." His voice tugged at her.

"No, I'll be all right!" she cried. She was so anxious to get away from them all that she pushed her way past them and rushed out the door.

Chapter 30

As she wandered down the dark street, Adrianne felt empty. No cabs were driving by, and it was very late and bitterly cold. Shivering, she wrapped her coat more tightly around her. Had it been a gigantic ripoff? What inside her had screamed so much that her throat was now raw?

She should have let Rosita's husband come with her to hail a cab. Although she walked alone night after night, she had never done so on such a deserted street. Something ominous hung suspended in the air; something sinister gleamed in the traffic lights. Or was it only her fear?

However, she felt purified of something evil that formerly had power over her. It was clear the life she and Alfredo led was degrading to them both. How could he respect himself while he lived as a pimp? It had been weeks now since he'd touched a canvas, and he went out during the day on mysterious appointments.

Surely if she confronted him as she was now, stripped of her deceptions, he would at last comprehend who she was and would understand how much she loved him. Her love would save them both.

"Alfredo, my darling, can you feel how much I love you?" she said silently, wondering if the waves of her emotion could reach him at this instant.

She had absorbed the poisons of all those who used her body. In fact, even now when she simply walked along the street, she was absorbing the poisons of frustrated and warped lives.

She must get away from all these people. Get a job as a cook in a sleepy bar again, or as a clerk in the back room of some office where there was the least possible human contact. Alfredo could work part-time again as a bartender.

He would understand that Michelle had to leave because the presence of a third person was destroying their life together.

She could feel pure golden warmth around her now as she walked down the cold, dark, deserted street, and she felt that at this instant she was understanding things with crystal clarity.

Alfredo was a god.

She was a goddess.

There were footsteps behind her. Muffled voices. Trying not to reveal any fear, she walked faster.

"Hey, Mama, wait for me."

"Gimme some of that nice soft pussy."

"Hey, Mama; hey, Mama!"

She broke into a run as she left the sidewalk and lurched into the middle of the street where it would be safer.

God help her.

"Hey, Mama!"

"Taxi!" she screamed. "Taxi!"

There it was, yellow light blinking, just around the corner. Look at me. Stop! Stop, she prayed.

The taxi screeched to a halt.

Chapter 31

"She says she had an exorcism."

"She's crazy."

They were whispering about her. Through the walls she could hear their voices as she lay on the old green couch.

When she had told Alfredo about the gypsies, he leaned back in his chair in the kitchen and roared with laughter. He pulled her down on his lap and held her while he rubbed his fingers up and down her spine. His breath smelled of liquor, and as usual he was intoxicated.

"You don't understand. Yet you keep talking about Gurdjieff and awareness. Something very powerful happened."

"*Loca!* You believe anything people tell you. You're suggestible!"

Falteringly, she tried to explain what had happened.

He grew angry, "You owe me three-nights' work," he said, pushing her off his lap. "When are you going to make this up to me?" After he had drunk a good deal, his mood changes were violent. Involuntarily, she took a step backward but resolutely continued with what she had planned to say.

"I'll be working. But look, I want Michelle to leave. We need to change our lives."

"Not now. First we need to get out of debt."

"We're in debt?"

"I borrowed some bread on what I thought was a sure winner."

"We're in debt?" She burst into tears. "There's no end to it!"

"You didn't tell those gypsies anything about me, did you?" He looked straight into her pupils, his own eyes narrow black slits.

"No."

He took a swig from the bottle of rum on the table. His hands were shaking. Why had he changed so much? It was her fault. She could not nurture but only poison the lives she touched. The exorcism was probably fake, and he was right to laugh at her. She was still filled with something evil.

"I thought you loved me," she said. "I thought I was working for *us*. If I'm not, then I should leave."

The words came out before she could stop them. They sounded so final that she immediately wanted to take them back, as if they were fish she could scoop up into a net. But it was too late. What if he were to throw her out? Arctic wasteland. Cold. No love. No life. Help me, God, she prayed.

Later, she bathed with a capful of bath oil called "*Baño del Amor y Delirio*" that she had bought over a week ago at a tiny Puerto Rican shop where magic candles, scents, and powders to produce spells were sold. The label on the dark bottle had grown greasy from being in her purse all this time, and tonight she thought the smell was too sweet. It was a cheap scent with a hint of musk.

She heard the door slam, then Michelle's footsteps. Alfredo was shouting, "Hey, baby, how'd you make out?" He said something else that she couldn't hear clearly, and they both burst out laughing.

The warm water lapped over her. She vowed to sleep on the couch until Michelle moved out.

Later she heard them tossing about in the bedroom. Michelle was moaning with pleasure, and Alfredo cried out as he climaxed. Adrianne felt as if she were being blown apart like a tree by wind. Its leaves were her flesh; its branches her bones. Its roots were her heart being torn out of the earth.

I will sleep, she told herself. But she couldn't. All night she lay awake. She went to the kitchen and poured herself a glass of Alfredo's rum. One drink. Another. Half the bottle.

On the all-night jazz station, Billie Holiday sang blues. The husky voice ate into her. She switched the station, then turned the radio off.

Sleep. Sleep, she told herself.

Still, she couldn't sleep, and at five a.m., weeping, she put on her comforting fox fur and went downstairs into the street where she walked and walked until finally she collapsed on a deserted piling by the East River. Pale sun rose in the sky. The streets began to stir again with traffic. When she returned to the loft, her throat was sore.

Despite fever and sore throat, she worked the next three nights, but on the fourth night she fainted just as she was about to walk out the door.

Alfredo was unexpectedly tender and insisted that she stay home to recover. The next few days she slept most of the time on the couch with the help of Courvoisier and codeine cough medicine.

One afternoon she watched Alfredo furiously sketch with ochre crayon on butcher paper. He was sketching a woman embracing a machine. She was pleased because this was the first time he'd sketched in weeks.

"What's that supposed to be?" she asked.

"Shit, Adrianne, don't bug me with stupid questions. And don't cringe like that. I hate it when you cringe like a beaten dog. Goddamn, stop crying!"

She huddled beneath the blankets and relaxed only when she could tell from the silence that he was working again.

Later, he sat down next to her on the couch. "These are my dreams I'm sketching, baby, my nightmares," he said, his long, slender fingers soothing her damp forehead. "You're burning up with fever. Now go back to sleep."

"I'm glad you're working again," she whispered.

He kissed her with more affection than he had shown in months. For a moment she felt the old bond between them, with all the invisible threads that had once bound them together.

But then Michelle leaned over her, too, and said, "Can I get you anything?" Her long hair swept over Adrianne's face. How perfect Michelle's breasts were underneath the gauzy white nightgown. An image passed through her mind of giant shears snipping off those breasts.

"Can I get you anything to eat, Adrianne?"

"No, thanks."

A few minutes later she heard Michelle and Alfredo in the kitchen. "Gimme those cigarettes ... gimme, you bitch!" She heard them laugh and scuffle.

Ground glass or roach poison or household bleach in their coffee could kill them. She could stab them in their sleep. God help her from having these thoughts.

Finally, the front door slammed as Michelle left for acting classes or auditions or a little hustling. How much *did* Michelle bring in, she wondered, before she drowsed off.

She awakened to feel Alfredo gently shaking her. A vague, disturbing dream fragment rose up then dissipated as he lightly kissed her her lips. "I brought you a cup of tea, sweetheart."

She turned over his wrist to look at his watch. It was one-fifteen in the afternoon. He wasn't high on anything yet; he was himself; he was the Alfredo she had first fallen in love with.

Just then the phone rang. She heard him talk to someone on the other end. His voice became tense. When he hung up he said, "I've got to go meet someone."

Agitated, he dressed to go out and put on his cashmere overcoat. Before he left, he fortified himself with more rum. Then he sniffed up a few specks of white powder on the back of his hand through one nostril at a time.

~~~

On the fifth day Adrianne was better, although she still felt shaky when she walked around the loft. Both Alfredo and Michelle were out. She noted with distaste how crammed the loft was with Michelle's belongings. Michelle's white panties and Alfredo's pale blue jockey shorts were entwined with the bed sheets. It all seemed unbearable! With regret, she thought of Max who had once been so kind to her.

For the past few days Max had been appearing in her dreams, and now she made up her mind to visit him. Did he still live in the rooming house? What day was it anyway? Sunday? Would he be in? With great hesitation she picked up the phone to dial the number. Suppose he had died?

Her stomach churned.

When the phone rang at the other end she had an urge to hang up, but she held on. "May I speak with Max?"

"Who's calling?" asked the landlady.

"Adrianne."

"Oh, hello. How are you?" the woman asked in her matter of fact voice.

"Fine. Is Max in?" Adrianne held her breath.

"I'll see."

At last she heard his familiar voice with its thick accent. "Adrianne," he said. "This is a surprise."

"I've been thinking about you, Max. Could I visit you?"

"Of course. When would you like?"

"Would today about five be all right?"

"Of course," he said. "Ah, but this is a surprise," he repeated. "Are you all right?"

"Yes, I'm fine."

All afternoon as she lay on the couch under blankets, she wondered and worried about what she was going to say to him.

After she showered and put on her makeup, she decided on a wool dress of virginal ivory with gold earrings and bracelet. Carefully, she combed and brushed her hair and applied dabs of Chanel Number Five. Little was left in her large bottle. Michelle must have been using it. She debated what coat to wear. The fox seemed too rich. The black rabbit fur was worn through in spots. When she leaned out the kitchen window, the air felt warm, and so she decided on her new beige trench coat.

Excited and nervous, she hailed a taxi. The sun was low in the sky. Spring buds were breaking out on the small street trees.

When at last she rang the doorbell outside her old rooming house, Max opened the door and stood there, thinner and more haggard than she remembered. He was not in his usual scruffy bedroom slippers but was dressed to go out in a brown suit. His shoes were well-shined, and he wore a blue and gold print tie.

"Max."

"Adrianne. *Meine liebchen.*"

As they embraced, she caught a whiff of his old man's smell. They stepped back from each other, and he said admiringly, "Adrianne, you look so beautiful. What do you want with me?"

"I ...I don't know."

"You are in trouble? You need money? You look so, well ... so beautiful ...such beautiful clothes ...but inside ...the girl inside ...you are all right, *meine liebchen?*"

"No," she blurted out.

"We go out for coffee, yes? Or better still, a bite to eat. Is it warm outside, or do I need an overcoat?"

"It's getting chilly."

He put on a worn grey overcoat and a hat. Then tucking her arm under his, he walked with her down the street. "You

will do me the honor of allowing me to buy you dinner, yes?"
His voice was warm and caring.

"I'm not very hungry."

"A little something ...a bowl of soup or a lamb chop, yes?"

"That would be nice."

They went into the same Horn and Hardart's where
they'd been last summer, nearly a year ago, and they both
had vegetable soup with crackers. While they were eating,
she suddenly felt nauseous and excused herself. She threw up
in the rest room.

Max, Max. What am I going to do with you? she wondered. She threaded her way back through the crowded cafeteria and spied him at their table, self-possessed, dignified,
and so lonely.

"What brings you to me? You are in trouble? That man ...
you are with him still?"

"Yes, but I'm not happy. I want to leave him."

"Tell me, what have you been doing? What kind of work?"

"Oh, just a job."

"A cooking job?"

"No ...a long story. I don't want to talk about it right
now." Her throat constricted.

"All right, *meine liebchen*." Timidly, he patted her hand.
"Why do you come to me?"

"I ...I want to get to know you better."

"Is much you are not telling me," he said. "But is all
right. You tell me what you want. I am so glad to see you. I
have missed you. You were like a bird with a broken wing.
Did I ever tell you that? I hope that now the wing it is fixed,"
he said tenderly. "I will not ask you more questions if you do
not want to talk. Ah, but you are so beautiful. You are a sweet
girl ...sweet like the springtime ...like my daughter Miriam.
If she had lived, maybe she would look like you. Excuse me."
He blew his nose. "I must forget the past. The doctor tell me
not to think always of the past. Is not good for me."

"Max, you're a kind man," she said. "You're a good man."

"Could you love me?" he asked, his eyes glittering as he
leaned slightly forward.

"I ...I don't know."

"Perhaps you will think I am too bold, an old man like
me. Perhaps I am crazy. You do not have to answer me now ...
only think about it. Would you marry me?"

She swallowed. "You're not crazy."

"Will you think about it, Adrianne? I have money to retire. I offer you all my love and a good life. I spend so little on myself, but I have money invested to last the rest of my life, and for both of us to be comfortable, to buy you beautiful clothes. We could live in the country, a simple life. You will think over my proposal?"

"I will."

Chapter 32

Adrianne gripped a black wrought-iron railing to keep from falling. Everything around her spun. She vomited onto the sidewalk and it felt as if her guts were spewing out. Nine o'clock in the evening on March 23rd. A clock chimed from a church tower near where she stood on Park Avenue and 49th Street. People's electric currents swirled around her as their bodies passed by. Someone took her arm to keep her from falling again, but she brushed him off and kept on walking.

"Time to leave Alfredo. Leave him. Leave, leave, leave," she chanted to herself as she walked past Grand Central Station downtown.

—

"What the *fuck* are you doing?" shouted Alfredo when he walked in the bedroom.

Adrianne stood there with her arms full of underwear. She was packing her suitcase, which lay on the unmade bed. Time slowed down. She took a deep breath. The light burned into her eyes as she blinked and lowered them, staring at a spot on the floor. "I'm through with this life."

He knocked the underwear out of her arms. Panties, brassieres, stockings, lacy slips flew all over.

Stunned, she watched while he lit a cigarette. He blew the smoke right into her face. "If you leave, watch your step. You might get into an accident. A car might run you down."

"I thought you loved me." She could not believe he was saying this.

"You *belong* to me."

"That's not love."

"You can't change any more than a leopard can change its spots. You're a *puta,* a cunt. You'll always crave different men."

He pulled the suitcase off the mattress and threw its contents on the floor along with her underwear. "Now put that shit away."

In shock, she picked up her scattered belongings while he went out for liquor. She stuffed her things back in the suitcase and quickly filled two other suitcases, stacking them in the closet just before she heard his tread on the stairs.

Later she lay in his arms, scarcely daring to move. "Adrianne, don't leave me," he whispered. "Stay with me. I love you. Stay, *mi amor*," he breathed into her ear.

Towards dawn, Michelle came in.

At seven-thirty in the morning while Alfredo and Michelle were sleeping, Adrianne dragged her suitcases down the five flights of stairs and hailed a taxi.

Part 3

April, 1960

Chapter 33

The following Thursday as soon as they had received the results of their blood tests, Adrianne and Max were secretly married by a justice of the peace.

Afterwards, he took her to a furnished studio apartment on West 86th Street which he had rented the day before. "Is only for a short time, *meine liebchen*. I want to live in the country far away from all this dirt and noise and from city life, if that would please you. You would like that?"

"Where, Max?"

"Vermont."

"Oh, yes," she said.

Awkwardly, he kissed her, and then slowly he removed her clothing. How beautiful she was with her soft white skin, full thighs and hips, and breasts like cantaloupes. With her tiny rosebud nipples, she was as beautiful as he had imagined—even more so—and she was giving herself to him. Could she truly desire an old man? Was that a pitying smile he saw on her face? Her golden hair brushed his cheek, her soft body pressed against his, and, incredibly, her mouth sought out his lips and then her tongue parted them while she grasped him tightly to her by the buttocks. Ah, such softness. She smelled sweet like the springtime, like apple blossoms. He was getting hard, and they moved to the bed. She lay beneath, pinning him tightly to her, and helped guide him into her moist, soft crevice. Once more he kissed her. Adrianne wanted to scream, bite his fingers, whisper, "I do this all the time, baby. Ten, twenty times a day."

What if he were to find out about her past?

She had screwed much older, much uglier men.

His fleshiness had something gentle, even feminine, about it, to which she began to respond. There was something soft and caring in his touch. She bit down on his lower lip. He began to thrust faster, climaxed, and in a little while it was all over. Afterwards he lay with his arms around her. To her surprise, when she felt the wetness on his cheeks she realized it was tears.

That night she dreamed of white clouds, sparkling streams and forests, and of searching for a house she used to live in. Finally, someone told her that she was standing in front of it, but it did not look familiar to her.

The next morning, Friday, Max went to work at the shop where he had repaired watches for so many years. Adrianne looked through the Want Ads in *The New York Times*. Perhaps she should get a job again. The cooking job hadn't been so bad. Besides, she would go mad inside these four walls.

Max had left her fifty dollars to buy a few groceries and to take care of anything else she needed. "Buy yourself something nice," he said, and she realized that this was coming from a man who renounced pleasure and luxuries for himself.

Saturday they took a bus to Vermont, to an inn where he had reserved a room for three days and nights.

As she sat on the bus next to Max, she thought, "This is my husband." It felt strange and unreal. The bus jolted on while she dozed.

Later, as the bus rolled along, she looked out the window at the countryside. She missed Alfredo intensely, but she was determined to be kind to Max.

"I am so much older than you," he said suddenly, breaking the silence as though he could read her mind. "If you do not fall in love with me right away, it is all right. In Europe where marriages are arranged, often the couple do not love each other until they get to know each other after they are married. Only in America and only in this century are the marriages romantic." Then his voice trembled. "Do you think you may grow to love me?"

"Yes, Max." She kissed his thin old man's lips, pitying him because he had known so many years of self-denial.

He dozed now, snoring slightly. In his lap lay a copy of *Der Zeitung* from West Berlin and beneath it a copy of *The Jerusalem Post*.

The bus droned on. Towns of old brick houses gave way to tall budding trees and green pasture land. It was April and the sky was blue. Lulled by the steady jolting rhythm of the bus, Adrianne again dozed off.

When they came to a stop, she awakened. They had reached Burlington. A fair-haired man in an old green Packard met them at the station and drove them to an inn far out in the country.

Adrianne and Max spent three calm and restful days.

"*Meine liebchen,* do you think you would be happy here?" They were walking through a meadow of fresh, green grass surrounded by forest. Max plucked a violet and handed it to her. Patches of snow still lay on the slopes of distant mountains.

"Maybe," she said. "I'd like to try living in the country."

Far away from Alfredo, she thought. Far, far away.

Chapter 34

In the synagogue on West Ninety-Third Street, Max glanced about anxiously. Adrianne was upstairs in the Women's Section, so he couldn't see her.

"God forgives," the rabbi had said. "God forgives, or else the souls he created would be totally destroyed." Perhaps Adrianne was a sign that he was at last forgiven, thought Max. Perhaps she was a sign like the twig brought back to Noah between the dove's beak after the flood.

Max put his hands on his thighs, feeling the shiny brown gabardine with distaste. Now that he was a married man, to please Adrianne he must buy himself nicer clothes. His left knee itched and he scratched it. His stomach felt heavy. The men around him were rising to their feet. He stood, too, and chanted the familiar Hebrew words. *"Adonai Israel ...Adonai Eluhenu ...Adonai ya Israel."* Usually he looked forward to the the weekly service, which had helped to sustain him all these years. But tonight, with the tumultuous emotions caused by his marriage, he could scarcely breathe. His longing to be in bed again with Adrianne was intense, and he could feel his heart pounding too fast.

The congregation sat down, and Rabbi Zimmerman, a frail, bearded man, began to speak. The pounding in Max's heart slowed, but his chest felt tight.

Dr. Goldfarb had advised him that he could retire early because of his heart condition. The doctor would sign documents enabling Max to begin drawing Social Security benefits, as well as his employer's pension now, so that he would not have to wait until he was sixty-five. Despite the manner in which he had been living, Max was not a poor man. Over the years, he had invested wisely and had built up a portfolio of stocks and bonds.

He wished right now that he could lean over and touch Adrianne. He would like to feel her soft cheek against his and luxuriate in her warmth. For so many years he had not held another human being.

What had her life been like with Alfredo, he wondered, and what had she done for a living. He did not want to pry, nor did he really care what she had done. He would simply love and cherish her, as he had promised in the marriage vows. Like a rose she would blossom, and in time she might grow to love him. How strange this service must seem to her.

Rabbi Zimmerman had begun to read from the Torah. The men near Max swayed slightly as they chanted under their breaths.

Giving into the moment, he was flooded with hope. God forgives. After all these years of atonement for his wife, no, his *former* wife, and children, God had brought Adrianne into his life as a precious gift. The lovemaking had gone even better than he dared hope, but he had a foreboding that things would not continue like this for long.

Upstairs in the balcony, surrounded by other women, Adrianne opened her prayer book to the page that her neighbor pointed out. The rabbi's speech sounded harsh, as if he were accusing her of something. She knew that her father's ancestors had been Jewish. Perhaps the memory of this service was in her genes.

She read the first two verses of the chapter on the side of the page that was printed in English.

"And Nadab and Abihu, the sons of Aaron . . . offered strange fire before the Lord, which he commanded them not.

"And there went out fire from the Lord and devoured them."

She glanced at the mysterious marks in Hebrew on the other side of the page. This was the language of her ancestors.

What kind of god would kill men for offering strange fire? Such a god must be cruel. Perhaps God and the Devil merged into a huge shadowy force. Had the gypsies really exorcised what was inside her? All these questions went through her head, making her conclude that perhaps Alfredo was right in his beliefs.

The new golden wedding ring on her finger gleamed. She twisted the other ring, the silver ring that Alfredo had bought her on Bleecker Street long ago. Against all reason, she still hungered for him. But she vowed to make Max happy, if she could.

Around her, the women whispered among themselves as they turned pages. Sometimes they chanted.

The cantor's deep voice rang through the hall. He was half-chanting and half-singing, unaccompanied by any instruments. The music resonated with a strange familiarity, although she had never heard it before.

An ache rose in her throat. She wanted to cry out, "I am one of you. My father's family was of your tribe." But she had lost the key. She would never belong to these people. Besides, her mother's family was Catholic.

She felt outside of everything.

"Papá, can you hear me?" she prayed. She sensed Julio's spirit hovering over her. She could almost see his face. His thin brows and the set of his eyes were like hers. "Adriana, you are my daughter, and no other man can have you," Julio seemed to whisper. Even though he had paid her little attention during his life, he had been silently possessive.

What would her mother say if she knew that Adrianne was here at the synagogue? Elena did not like Jews and always had held that part of her father's ancestry against him.

"God, love me," Adrianne prayed. But she could not sense God's love. She felt the sadness and longing of the people here.

Beneath her sat the men, their heads covered with *yarmulkahs*. When she looked for Max, he was not visible. She had a sudden urge to run out of the synagogue and back to Alfredo. Despite how he had treated her, she ached to be with him again. He connected with her in a way that no one else ever had. He knew her desires, her fears, her vulnerabilities. She couldn't con him, as she could poor Max.

Then the dream-mother of her childhood wafted through to her, the dream-mother of otter-soft walls. Her rich dark fur enveloped Adrianne. The dream-mother whispered, "I love you." Then she added, "Accept Max's love."

The women around her were standing up, and Adrianne stood, too, smoothing out her white wool dress. She noticed that most of them were middle-aged and old, dressed in clothing that looked many years out of style. They began to sing a plaintive melody.

The English words in the prayer book swam and danced in front of her. Lifting her eyes, she looked about the room. It was fairly large, with light green walls and a high ceiling. Its dark linoleum floors gave off a stale, gingery odor. There were folding metal chairs. How dingy the place was, Adrianne realized. How poorly the room was heated. She wrapped her black rabbit coat more tightly around her shoulders. Through small side windows she could see it had grown dark outside. Again she had an urge to run, to escape the collective sorrow of these women all around her.

Her neighbor nudged her and once again pointed to a page number. The woman was scrutinizing Adrianne, her eyes flashing as if to say, "I can see through you. You are an imposter."

Now the rabbi was speaking in English, but Adrianne could not concentrate on his words. Then she seemed to hear the faint sound of laughter. Apparently, no one else heard. Tremors ran through her nerves.

At last the service ended. Women buttoned their coats, readjusted their hats, and put on their gloves as they prepared to leave. Adrianne wanted to reach Max right away, but she had to follow the women who walked sedately, with muffled voices. Max was waiting for her by the foot of the stairs. He was engaged in conversation with another elderly man, but his eyes kept darting upwards.

"Adrianne!" he cried when he saw her. "Benjamin, I want that you meet my new wife!"

A strained look came over the man's face as he stiffly shook her hand.

She sensed people pointing her out and speaking about her. Some spoke in undertones while others did not bother to lower their voices.

"...a *shikse* young enough to be his daughter ..."

"...a man his age ...crazy in the head. His mother would turn over in her grave."

"She is Jewish?" Benjamin asked dubiously.

"No, I'm not."

"She has met the rabbi?" Benjamin, too, had a marked European accent.

"Here he is now," said Max. "Adrianne, this is Rabbi Zimmerman. Rabbi, my wife, Adrianne."

"Hello," said the rabbi. When Adrianne reached out to shake the rabbi's hand, his arms remained at his sides. "A woman does not shake the rabbi's hand," Max whispered.

"Are you Jewish?" asked the rabbi.

"No," said Adrianne.

The rabbi's look was severe. "If she is not Jewish, you cannot be married in this synagogue."

"We were married in City Hall," said Max. "Good evening, rabbi. *Shalom shabbat.*"

"*Shalom shabbat.*"

Max elbowed Adrianne out of the building into the streets. "They do not understand. For them it is a scandal you are not Jewish."

"Do you want me to become Jewish?"

"No," he said angrily. She had never seen him angry before. "Narrow minds they have. It is better we move to the country far away from these people. All these years it is this synagogue that keeps me in the city."

"My father's family was Jewish long ago, before they converted."

"Oh?" Max exclaimed eagerly. "Your mother's people, too?"

"She's Catholic."

"Then you are *goyim.*"

They continued walking. He was breathing jerkily, and she could tell he was still angry.

"I have been with this synagogue for many years, for almost as many years as you are alive, Adrianne. But now is time to cut the old ties and move away."

"I thought you wanted to move anyway."

"This synagogue, this rabbi I thought was my friend, all were keeping me here."

"Max, wait! Have you forgotten me?" They turned to see who was calling him. A plump elderly man in an overcoat and *yarmulkah* ran up to them. He heaved, catching his breath, and he and Max embraced. The man's spectacles had slid to the end of his nose, and he pushed them up. Under the street light, Adrianne could see that the man had a kind, ruddy face.

"Aren't you going to introduce me to the young lady they say is your new wife?" While this man, too, spoke with an accent, it was less marked than Benjamin's.

"Ah, she is indeed my wife. Adrianne, this is my good friend of many years—perhaps now my only friend—Morris Kaplan."

"Also his attorney," said Morris. "I have to stay on good terms with my client." He chuckled and gave Max a friendly pat on the shoulder.

Both men took off their black satin *yarmulkahs* and folded them into their vest pockets.

"We'll go out for a drink to celebrate this marriage. We'll have some schnapps, a cognac, perhaps a pastry for the young lady," said Morris. "I'm inviting you to Steinberg's Delicatessen."

"I accept," said Max. "Is all right with you, Adrianne, *meine liebe?*"

"Of course." She walked between the two men. It had grown much colder, and their breaths were frosty in the night air. When she slipped on a patch of ice, Max grabbed her arm.

Chapter 35

A month later Max and Adrianne rented a furnished house in Vermont, and at the end of May they moved in. Built late in the last century on the slope of a hill, the dwelling consisted of a living room, a small dining room and two bedrooms, one of which Max used as his study. The kitchen and bathroom had old fashioned fixtures. Faded wallpaper with tiny roses covered the walls of their bedroom.

They were about a quarter-mile from the center of a tiny village with a general store and a post office. In front of their house stretched a narrow tar road. No other houses were visible, and all around them grew thickly planted trees.

"Like the Black Forest," said Max with a sigh of contentment.

Adrianne, on the contrary, felt a menacing quality to the trees, and for a long time she felt ill at ease amidst the isolation, which was unlike anything she had ever known.

The menace of the trees manifested at night when she and Max went to bed. She tried to please him, to ignore her body's needs. It was hard. At times she sobbed quietly while he slept.

One night the jagged edge of his nail scratched her vagina so that she cried out with pain.

"I'm sorry," he whispered. *"Meine liebchen,* did I hurt you?"

"No, I'm okay."

His mouth pressed down on hers. She held back a wave of nausea as she inhaled his sour old man's breath. "Be a good whore, baby," Alfredo whispered in her mind.

Max had lowered his flaccid body and was licking her vulva. He had no sense of where her nerve endings were. She guided him with her hands, holding his scalp with the fine, wispy hair. After a few minutes he raised his body. "Is the

first time I do so to a woman," he whispered, and she cringed
from his voice in her ear.

"Fuck me," she murmured.

She stroked him until he hardened enough to enter her,
but she wanted to cry out with frustration when he came too
quickly, with a thin spurt of semen.

~~~

During the day, their life followed a calm routine. Breakfast was between eight and nine in the morning. They had
Sanka and frozen orange juice, usually with scrambled eggs
and coffeecake which Adrianne baked to satisfy Max's sweet
tooth. He had stopped following his diet so strictly. While she
prepared their meal, he would read his newspapers and
smoke a cigar. Sometimes he would turn on the radio to a
Middlebury station that played classical music. In rhythm
with the music, he would sway back and forth, a satisfied
expression on his face, as he looked out onto the trees.

Lunch was at eleven-thirty, which Adrianne found a trifle
early. His insistence on schedules annoyed her a bit, since
this habit of his had not been apparent before they married.
For the midday meal they usually had cold cuts, cottage
cheese, or soup with vegetables.

Supper around five-thirty in the evening consisted of a
roast or stew with potatoes, cooked vegetables or a salad, and
fruit. After a little reading or listening to classical music on
the radio, they would retire.

It was an uneventful life, but after a while Adrianne
began to find a curious comfort in its regularity. In the afternoon she would go for walks in the woods. When Max accompanied her, they had to stop frequently so that he could catch
his breath.

"We must buy a car," he said shortly after they moved
into the house. "Often I must see Doctor Goldfarb in New
York, and it is a long trip by bus."

He arranged for driving lessons. Three times a week a
young man drove out from Burlington, and they practiced driving. After several lessons, Adrianne, who had driven several
years earlier in Houston, was ready for her license. Max took
longer. "Many years ago, before the war, I drove a friend's car
in Hamburg. But it was so long ago. Most people then did not
own cars."

Twice he failed the vision test, so he had to get new glasses. After he finally obtained his license, he bought a used Chrysler with only seven thousand miles on it.

There were times Adrianne longed to call Alfredo. She would stare at the phone until it was all she could do to keep from picking it up to call him. The golden wedding ring on her finger gleamed in the light. On her other hand she still wore Alfredo's silver ring. Whenever she thought about taking it off and putting it away in a drawer, something prevented her.

"Tell me, *meine liebe,* what is the matter? Something is troubling you, what is it? Tell me," Max said.

"Nothing," she murmured. "You're a good man. I love you." Her lips brushed his cheek. Then she ran into the bedroom for her outdoor clothing, as she wanted to walk in the woods.

She contrasted Max's thoughtfulness—despite his clumsy manners, despite the occasional food spills on his shirt or trousers, despite his broodings over the past—with Alfredo's treatment of her. Max cared about her in a way no one, including her mother and father, ever had before.

Max used to sit in his rocking chair by the window in his study and half-close his eyes while he listened to music on the radio. Sometimes Adrianne would come in to talk to him while he was listening. One morning when she approached him, he slowly opened his eyes and said, "You startled me. I was dozing. I was thinking about you, Adrianne. Come here and hold my hand."

She had grown fuller, and she was now as heavy as when they had first met. Ah, how her fleshiness delighted him. She was wearing a navy sweater, a full grey skirt, and tiny hoop earrings. Her golden hair surrounded her face like an aura. She sat down in his lap. He reached out for one of her hands and turned it over in both of his. Her deep blue eyes seemed luminous. She was not stupid, nor was she as passive as she appeared to be.

"I feel peaceful here, Max," she said.

They sat in silence for a while.

"But for you I think something is missing," he said.

Despite all her pretense, he sensed her true feelings about their sexual life. Last night was one of the few times he was certain that she had experienced orgasm. He knew it from the relaxation that spread over her body and from how she had slept afterwards with the quiet, rhythmic breathing of a child. For a while he had watched her in the moonlight.

"No, Max. Nothing is missing."

He shook his head. "I do not think that is the truth," he said. "Adrianne, such happiness you give to me. I want that you too feel happiness. Is it college or books or a job ... or friends your own age? I am content with this life, but what are you doing to fill up the day? It is not enough to cook and clean and please an old man. *Meine liebchen,* you are young."

His tenderness moved her. After reflecting, she said, " I'd like to take piano lessons. When I was a child, I played the piano and had lessons from the time I was nine until I was twelve. Then my father died, and my mother sold the piano. I've always missed it."

"Meine liebchen, I shall buy you a piano."

"Oh, Max. Really!"

"My retirement money is not that much, but if a piano will bring you joy, we get one tomorrow." He stroked her breasts, enjoying their softness.

The next afternoon they drove to a music store in Burlington where Max rented a Baldwin baby grand, with an option to buy it. The piano nearly filled up their small living room. To make space, they pushed the coffee table and two overstuffed armchairs against the wall.

As she wanted to review everything from the beginning, Adrianne bought stacks of elementary music books. She began to practice Hanon finger exercises.

"You're so good to me, Max."

He beamed with happiness.

To her surprise, the daily routine of their life propelled her into practicing with an intensity she had never before experienced. She found herself gaining an ever deepening pleasure from her music. Each morning after the breakfast dishes were done, she would play. The first two weeks she reviewed several Clementi studies and a Bach prelude she had learned years ago. The third week she went on to practice a Schubert sonata.

Max would listen, nodding drowsily as he smoked his pipe, sometimes falling asleep, sometimes beating his fingers in rhythm. He enjoyed hearing her practice, he said, and no, it didn't bother him to hear her repeat over and over again the same chords, the same melodic fragments, and the same scale exercises.

Her wrist and finger muscles grew tired from practicing. She learned to be patient, as with daily effort the music began to sound beautiful.

Max suggested that she study with a teacher. They found a sparrow-like elderly woman in Middlebury who had once been a concert pianist. During Adrianne's first lesson, Max listened proudly.

Adrianne played the piano all day and into the evening, stopping only to make their meals and take occasional walks. It was getting colder; the days were getting shorter. Snow fell, covering the branches and coming up as high as the windows. She and Max bought snowshoes. Sometimes they would be snowed in for a day or two after a storm.

"You must memorize all that you learn," her teacher said at the beginning of the second lesson. "That way the music will always be with you."

"It takes so much time."

"You will develop the capacity to memorize. Your memory is like an unused muscle. If you are serious, you will think and dream music. You must go to concerts and hear musicians perform. It's quite different from just listening to a record. Will your father take you?"

"My husband," said Adrianne, reddening.

The teacher pursed her thin lips together and flicked a piece of lint from her skirt. Wisps of white hair escaped from her chignon. Embarrassed that the teacher had mistaken Max for her father, Adrianne faltered over the Bach prelude she was beginning to play. "I'm not interested in your personal relationships," said her teacher in a dry voice. "I want to see what you can do with the music."

Occasionally after this, Max and Adrianne would drive to Boston for a concert and spend the night in a hotel. Adrianne would listen to the performers with rapt concentration, as she tried to absorb all that she could.

Music began to fill her brain and the pores of her body. During that long winter and after the snow melted as summer approached, there was little else to do but play the piano, cook and clean up meals, take walks in the woods, tidy the house, and keep Max company. Her weekly lessons became the high point of her life.

Max did not like jazz, so she played mostly classical music. But she loved jazz, and at times she would play a Billie Holiday song or some classical blues, or something by Ellington or Miles Davis.

"This jazz is discordant, strange to me," Max would say.

"More than Schoenberg?"

"Ah, I do not like the Schoenberg either! When you finish with the jazz music, please play some beautiful Brahms."

She wrote to her mother that she was working as a waitress and gave only a post office box address.

About once a month her mother responded with notes on monogrammed paper, in which she described her activities at work as well as various social activities, such as dinner parties or theater.

Adrianne continued to improvise fictional accounts of her life for Elena, just as she had done when she was with Alfredo.

Ever since the time with Gerald, Adrianne had tried to shield herself from her mother. Odd as it was that a physician in his late twenties should seek out an eighteen-year old girl simply for companionship, her mother had appeared to believe this was the case. Finally, one evening after she and Gerald had broken up, in despair Adrianne had confessed the truth. However, she had omitted the part about her pregnancy and abortion.

"You will suffer the consequences," said her mother in a cold tone, pushing down hysteria. "May God forgive you. If Gerald does not want to marry you, perhaps you ought to go away."

During the next two weeks, Adrianne made preparations for her departure for New York. Elena never again referred to what had happened, but everything unspoken seemed to roll into an intangible mass of shame and guilt inside Adrianne. Adrianne felt her mother's condemnation, mingled with a strange, secret kind of satisfaction at her daughter's suffering.

It was then that Adrianne had gone to confession (again omitting the part about her pregnancy.) But the priest's coldness echoed her mother's.

~~~~

During their second winter, Adrianne and Max were invited to a Christmas party by a couple who lived nearby and who were potters. Among the guests was an actor from Boston. As he and Adrianne talked, a sexual current began to flow between them. Perceiving this, Max grumbled, taking her by the arm, and insisting that they leave the party.

That night, as she watched Max undress, she was struck anew by the whiteness of his body, his large chest, his spindly legs. He stood a little swaybacked. She was Max's prisoner, she thought angrily. She was still a prostitute really, giving her body to Max in exchange for all that he could offer, but not giving herself out of desire.

Yet Max could caress her in such a way that he almost mesmerized her at times. "Ah, my angel," he would murmur. "How happy you make me. I do not deserve such happiness. Never did I think would have such joy."

That night when they got into bed, his warm hands crept along her spine, kneaded her buttocks, and moved on to her vagina. On other occasions, when she felt more kindly towards him, she would let herself sink under the spell of his hands. Now she stiffened in resistance as she thought of the actor.

However, out of a sense of obligation she reached down between Max's legs. His penis was limp. Expertly, she massaged it until it came to life, and then she guided him inside her. While he thrust deeper into her, she watched them both from a point high above her body, as she used to long ago when she fucked strangers.

Finally he climaxed. "Ah, is so good," he sighed. She hurried to the bathroom to wipe off the semen, just as she had done in the past with tricks. Unable to sleep, she gazed at the moonlight shining through the curtains while he snored.

A few days later she came down with the flu, and painful memories of her life in Manhattan began to obsess her. One night she dreamed that the gypsy, Ramón, was plunging a knife into her heart.

Thoughts of all the men she'd been with tormented her. She loosened herself from Max's sleeping grip, got up, went into the kitchen, flicked on the light, took out a carving knife from the rack on the wall, and stared at it.

In his bare feet and robe, Max tottered in. "My angel, what you are doing?"

He wrenched the knife away from her. It fell to the floor. She, too, fell down on the icy linoleum and sobbed. Tenderly, he held her and caressed the nape of her neck. "Tell me, what is it, my angel?"

In bed again beneath the warm goose down, she whispered it all to him—or almost all. So that was how she had been living when she came to visit him in the beautiful white wool dress. That was how she had acquired her sexual skill!

"Is all right, *meine liebe.*"

"I'm not worthy of you, Max," she sobbed. He held her in his arms, filled with the sense that they were both impure. He, too, had used her young body and spirit. For her, perhaps he was no more than another trick. Did she love him at all, or had she only been pretending all along?

"I can leave if you want," she sobbed. "I can go back to New York, or Texas, or anywhere."

"No," he said emphatically. "I do not want that you leave."

For the next few days and nights they barely touched each other.

One morning as she was practicing a Brahms piece that he particularly liked, she faltered, then broke down and lay her head on the piano keys and sobbed. At that moment something in him melted. All along he had suspected something like this. Yet he had hidden this suspicion from himself. Poor child! A bird with a broken wing.

"It's all right," he said. He came over to her and held her, gazing full into her face.

With a shock, she realized the truth of his compassion. He loved her. He accepted her with all her faults. He forgave her the past. And perhaps she could forgive herself.

Music was a ray of light, a sunbeam on which she could float out of the darkness of her former world. Some classical music had almost unbearably sad passages. By not evading the sadness, she developed strength. She discovered parts of herself which had lain dormant.

Through the long winter, while the sky and hills were white with snow, she played the piano for hours on end. The harmony she found in music began to weave its way subtly between their bodies when she and Max were in bed. She would drift off to sleep listening to music in her mind, and sometimes felt as if she had been practicing in her sleep.

~~~

A spasm of coughing came over Max as he rocked in his oak chair. He should be smoking fewer cigars. Far away from the people he had known for so many years in his congregation, he was lonely. He missed the synagogue. Out here in the country there were none.

Adrianne does not love me as she would a younger man, he thought. She is kind to me, as she would be to a grandfather. She is nearly younger than my *kinder*. He stubbed out his cigar. Ah, but he liked what she was playing now, a Schubert piece. She faltered on a melodic phrase, played it again and again until she got it right, and the repetition soothed him.

Now she was going into an *arpeggio allegre,* and he followed it. He believed that she had the touch of a true musician.

His bank account was dwindling. However, he had enough set aside in stocks and bonds so that they could live comfortably on the interest. He must teach her something about finance, show her what securities he had and how to manage them, so that after he died she could live comfortably.

He sensed that he was going to die soon. In dreams a voice told him he was already dead and in a kind of gray no-man's land waiting for something. He was silent about his premonition because he did not want to frighten her.

One February evening when Adrianne came back from a long walk in the woods, she was so cold that she decided to take a bath immediately. The house was quiet. She thought that Max was probably dozing. After she finished her bath, it was still unusually quiet. Disturbed, she went into his study and there she found him slumped over in his chair. He was not breathing, and his skin felt icy.

"Max!" she cried.

Silence.

When she lifted his head, it felt heavy, and he was rigid. Terrified, she pushed her hands hard against his chest again and again with a rhythmical movement to start him breathing, but nothing happened. Then she thought of opening his mouth to blow into it, but she could not pry open his lips.

Although she knew it was too late, she called an ambulance.

The coroner determined that Max had died of a heart attack. Adrianne moved around the house barely conscious, at times heaving with sobs and crumpling to the floor, at other times curiously calm as though someone else were living out this scenario.

She gazed at Max's empty chair. His presence hovered over her and she could sense him with her, angry and questioning. *"Meine liebchen,* I did not want to die, not yet."

Chapter 36

She telephoned Rabbi Zimmerman at the synagogue Max had attended in Manhattan, and two days later Max was buried in a Jewish cemetery in Queens.

Adrianne viewed Max for the last time after he had been prepared for burial at a funeral home on West 93rd Street. Wrapped in a white shroud with a tallis over him, a faint look of disappointment seemed to spread over his face. The plain pine coffin was quickly closed by the people who had prepared the body, and it was draped with a black cloth. Adrianne placed red roses on the coffin and asked for more flowers.

"It's not the custom with a Jewish burial," said the funeral director.

The rabbi, who had come with Adrianne to oversee the last stages of the burial preparation, pinned a piece of black ribbon on her fox coat. His melancholy eyes sat deep in his pinched face.

It was raining when the hearse and two shiny black limousines carrying mourners drove from the funeral home on West 93rd Street to the cemetery. Inside the limousine with Adrianne were the rabbi and his wife, who was a small, nervous woman with a dark beehive hairdo, Max's friend Morris, and a white-haired couple.

"Will you sit *shiva?*" asked the rabbi's wife.

"Who, her, a *shikse?*" said the old woman, looking at Adrianne with sharp eyes that contrasted with her deeply lined face.

"What is sitting *shiva?*" Adrianne asked.

The rabbi leaned forward and gently explained that when a Jew died, it was the custom for people in the immediate family to mourn for seven days, seated on a low bench, while neighbors and friends brought food. However, since Adrianne was not Jewish and lived far away in the country up in Vermont, this would not be expected of her.

"But I want to sit *shiva*," she said.

"Mourning takes place inside the heart. You can burn a candle for seven days and nights. That is part of the ceremony. It will be enough."

They were driving through snarled traffic on the Long Island Expressway, past factories and then past miles of ugly row apartment buildings.

Finally, they reached the cemetery and drove through its grilled gates and onto a narrow concrete roadway, past miles of tombstones. Long ago Max had paid for this burial plot. "Max, why did you have to die? I don't want you here! I wish I had never even told the rabbi. I wish I had buried you in the Vermont hills," Adrianne thought.

The ground was muddy, with patches of dirty snow. Bare tree branches swayed in the wind. It was raining hard, with occasional wet flakes. Adrianne shivered. The hole where Max would lie had already been dug out and covered with a tarpaulin.

Standing a few feet from the burial plot, the rabbi put up his umbrella to protect himself from the driving rain. He opened a prayer book and cleared his throat, then began to chant the *kaddish*."

"...*Baruch dayan emei*.... Blessed is the righteous judge," he chanted. "Man is like a breath ...his days are like a passing shadow.... Thou dost sweep men away; they are like a dream, like grass, like grass which is renewed in the morning, in the morning it flourishes ...in the evening it fades and withers.... Teach us to number our days that we may get a heart of wisdom ...dust returns to the earth as it was, but the spirit returns to God who gave it ..."

Adrianne wept.

The rabbi closed the prayer book, placed it under his arm, and said, "Max Gottlieb had a hard life."

Several women sighed, and the mourners all seemed to look at Adrianne as if she were the cause of his hardship. Wind tore at their clothing, and sleet was pelting down.

"Max was persecuted by the Nazis. He lost his wife—his first wife—and his children in the Holocaust. He worked hard all his life, and he had little joy."

"But Max was happy with me, you bastards," Adrianne thought. Her heart pounded and tears surfaced as her grief found expression in rage. The rabbi went on talking, but she no longer heard his words, submerged as she was in her emotions.

Then she saw that they were preparing to lower the casket and that the edge of the tarpaulin was flapping in the wind. She became aware once again of the cold wind and rain blasting her face.

The cantor's wife, bundled in her heavy cloth coat, galoshes, and plastic rainhood, said, "Poor man," with a glance at Adrianne, as if it were she who had killed him. Adrianne could imagine them gossiping afterwards. "He died making love. Her fault. She provoked him . . . after his money . . . young enough to be his granddaughter."

Standing there in the cold, their faces wet with sleet, they all seemed to look at her with hostility, as if to question whether she had brought Max happiness or sorrow. They looked at her silver fox coat as if she had stolen it. "Yes, I hustled for it," she told them with silent fury. "Maybe I even screwed some of you. I'm certainly more desirable than your frumpy wives."

She was horrified by her thoughts. But they kept rising up.

The rabbi kept on chanting, sometimes in English and sometimes in Hebrew. The others wailed a mournful melody in Hebrew. Adrianne rocked back and forth, as some of the others were doing. She sobbed uncontrollably as the gravediggers lowered the casket and flung earth over it with their shovels.

Until now, she had not realized she cared for Max so deeply.

A gust of wind blew her silk scarf away. She watched it roll along the ground and land in a puddle. No one went after it.

The rain pelted down harder, and she shivered with cold.

Who will hold me at night, she wondered. Max, I love you, my darling. I love you, I love you, but it is too late. Can you hear me? Can you hear me after death?

An almost imperceptible current of wind, a touch like Max's hand touched her throat. She sensed his presence. *Meine liebchen, you will not lose me.*

Was this also an illusion? Like the old illusion that Alfredo loved her? She was scarcely aware any longer of the people around her, although she heard their chanting. Then the rabbi looked at her and said, "It's over. Time to go now."

She wanted to fling herself over the grave, but again she seemed to hear Max say gently, "Don't make a fool of yourself. You'll only get wet and cold and come down with pneumonia. I know you love me, as I love you, eternally. Ah, if only I had been a young man when we met." There was sadness in him even after death.

Afterwards, the others bombarded her with questions and superficial expressions of sympathy.

~~~

The next day she returned to their empty house in Vermont. Almost as soon as she had taken off her coat, she sat down at the piano and began to play the Brahms *ballade* Max had loved. The piano keys pressed down against her sorrow, and the beauty of the music soothed her. "This is for you, Max," she murmured.

"Meine liebchen," whispered his ghost, who caressed her hair as softly as a cool draft.

Without Max, who had sustained her, the prospect of staying here in the house was lonely and terrifying.

She decided to go back to New York.

Accordingly, she gave their landlord notice. She could no longer bear to be in this house without Max. Some of the furniture she sold to neighbors, and the rest she gave away to the Salvation Army. She returned the piano to the store from which they had leased it.

When she could finally bring herself to go through Max's papers, the securities he owned, the stocks and bonds were all confusing to her. Morris Kaplan said that Max had left everything to her, except for a small sum for his synagogue and another small sum for the State of Israel.

"If you manage these funds carefully, you will have enough money to go to college while you live on the interest. He loved you and wanted to be sure you would not have financial worries.

"I don't know what to do with all this money."

"For the time being, leave the funds invested as they are. He invested wisely. There's enough interest for you to live on. When you know more about finances, then you can think about shifting investments around."

"He was so kind. I can't believe it. It's hard for me to accept that he's gone, and that he's left me all this."

Morris blew his nose and patted her hand. "He was a kind man. Accept it, and thank God for your good luck."

Chapter 37

On a sunny afternoon in April, Adrianne loaded her suitcases into the the Chrysler. The house was bare of furniture
and she had cleaned it for the last time. She took her clothes
and a few personal effects, along with her music books and
Max's papers, after disposing of everything else.

The snow had melted. Everywhere around her things
were green and budding. Fragrance filled the air and birds
chirped. A little over two years ago, on a fine day like this, she
and Max had gotten married.

At four o'clock she began her drive to New York. Compul-
sion guided her hands on the steering wheel, her feet on the
pedals, her hand on the stick shift. She drove for hours
through the country. The sun sank. Lights were turned on. As
she approached the city, traffic grew much thicker. At ten
o'clock she drove onto East River Drive and into the midst of
heavy late traffic.

She had to see Alfredo. Had to see him, at least one last
time. What if he were out? What if he had moved?

Lights were on in his loft. She drove slowly around the
block to find a parking space, and she found one near his
Cadillac. The car looked dusty under the streetlight. There
was a large dent in the trunk.

She wondered if Michelle were still with him or if he had
found someone else. *"Last chance ... mustn't ... shouldn't ...
Max, forgive me. I have to do this."* Conflicting emotions
whirled through her.

When she tried her old key to the street door, it no longer
worked. "Alfredo," she yelled. "Alfredo!" No response. She
finally took her compact out of her purse and threw it up
against a window. It smashed in pieces on the sidewalk.
"Alfredo, let me in. Alfredo, it's me, Adrianne," she shouted at
the top of her lungs.

Still no response. A dog barked inside. She gathered her coat more tightly around her and waited. Then disheartened, she yelled once more and was about to walk off when a voice she recognized as Alfredo's called out, "Who's there?"

"It's me. Adrianne."

"Are you alone?"

"Yes."

"Just a minute."

The dog barked again. After a couple of minutes she heard the bolt slide back. The door opened a crack and Alfredo peered out. She drew back, frightened, as a large black mongrel barked and snapped at her ankles. This was like the dog of her nightmare long ago.

"Easy there, mutt," said Alfredo, pulling at the dog's leash. "Come inside, baby. The dog won't hurt you."

As soon as she entered the dark corridor, he bolted the door and took her into his arms. "*¡Preciosa!* You finally came back to me. Where have you been, Adrianne?"

"It's a long story."

"No one saw you come in?" he asked with anxiety.

"No."

This fear in him was something new.

His arms around her tightened; he kissed her wetly on the mouth. She breathed in his old familiar scent of sweat, alcohol, and tobacco while the huge mongrel growled at their heels.

He pressed against her as they climbed the creaking wooden stairs. His door had a lock on it, with a bar that hooked into the floor. Under the electric light she could see that his eyes were bloodshot and his face haggard. He wore a black leather jacket, a black T-shirt, and jeans. Around his neck hung a shark's tooth on a silver chain.

Alfredo unsnapped the dog's leash. It growled again and she shuddered. "Easy there, big boy," he said to the dog. "Adrianne isn't going to hurt you." Tentatively, she stroked the dog behind its ears. It sniffed her again and then slunk off, still watching her.

The studio walls were almost bare, discolored in areas where canvases had been hanging. Paintings were stacked against walls, and the place was full of big wooden packing crates.

They sat down on the old green couch. Alfredo's hands shook visibly as he lit a cigarette for her, then one for himself. When she had first met him there was a light in his eyes. That was now gone. His smile seemed forced. Yet he still had charm. She wanted to reach out and caress his face. After hesitating a moment, she did.

"So you came back to me, Adrianne."

"I wanted to see you again"

"You've grown even more beautiful." He stroked her, feeling the silky fabric of her dress. "Relax and take your shoes off, baby. Can I get you something to drink?"

"Yes."

While he was in the kitchen, she looked around and noticed with a shock a slashed canvas propped against the wall. She walked over to examine it. A man who looked like Alfredo, surrounded by a jeering crowd in the midst of barren land, had been slashed into several pieces. Beneath this she found an old portrait of herself which she always loved. It was ripped from her left temple through the bridge of her nose and down through her cheek and jaw. Other canvases had also been slashed.

"Who destroyed the paintings?" she asked when he returned with two glasses and a bottle of rum.

"I did." A strange look flitted through his eyes.

"Why?"

"I was high on drugs."

"Why did you do it?"

"I was angry," he said. "I wondered what the fuck I'd been struggling for all my life. The paintings didn't seem good enough."

"Oh, Alfredo, I'm sorry. "

"You don't give a shit."

"I care about you."

"You're full of shit!" he snorted. Then, more softly, "Tell me about yourself. Where have you been hiding for the last two years?"

"I married Max. Do you remember him?"

"That old creep!"

"He was wonderful!" she said, flushing, tears flooding her eyes. "I'll always love him. He bought me a piano. We lived out in the country and I played the piano for hours every day. I've become a musician." Her voice trembled with emotion.

"Why did you leave him?"

"He died of a heart attack."

"Hmm." He finished off his glass then took her face between his hands. "I treated you badly," he said. "I never realized how much I loved you until after you were gone."

Her heart pounded. She swallowed. *"Beware, meine liebchen,"* Max whispered.

Alfredo gazed into her eyes with his old magnetism then let her go. He stood up and began pacing back and forth, just as he used to. He had lost weight, and his jeans bunched around his waist, held up by a thin belt.

"This fucking city. Why did I treat you so badly? Why did I destroy my work? I don't know. I borrowed cash from Dominic, and he's been breathing down my ass.

"Harris just strung me along at the gallery. Do you know how many of my paintings he sold? Two! He told me at the beginning how much he believed in my work, but then he stuck my paintings in the basement. Six months ago I took them back. Shit!"

He ground out a cigarette on the floor.

"Can you fix the canvases?" she asked. The rum, poured straight, was going to her head. She hadn't eaten since this morning.

"Maybe a few," he said. "But I'm splitting. Everything goes in storage. If you'd come three days later, you wouldn't have found me here. You must have sensed this because you're intuitive. In your bones you wanted to be with me, baby."

He stood still and gazed at her. "Adrianne, this time we'll do things differently."

"Where's Michelle?"

"She split a long time ago. When she left, she stole a lot of shit. Money I'd hidden. Grass. Some of your jewelry. You left a lot of stuff here."

He sat down beside her and stroked her thigh. "You're like a Botticelli."

"I've gained weight."

"It doesn't matter. You're beautiful."

Just then the phone rang and the dog barked.

Alfredo answered it in the kitchen. She could hear him talking in a low voice, but she couldn't make out the words.

When he came back, he looked shaken. He lit another cigarette.

"Alfredo, what happened?"

"Nothing. Now tell me about you. Tell me about this marriage of yours."

"Alfredo, who phoned you?"

"Shit, Adrianne, lay off! Tell me about your marriage."

She talked about her life in Vermont with Max, although she could see he was preoccupied. Finally, she stammered, "Alfredo, for me, music has become what painting is for you."

"Great, baby," he said without conviction.

The phone rang again. "Fuck that phone."

It rang and rang and finally stopped.

"You haven't changed underneath," he said. His voice had turned hostile. "You still belong with me, and that's why you came back, because you're still my woman. That old man bored you silly when he was alive, right?"

"I loved him."

"Did he ever fuck you like I did?"

He pressed himself against her, and she could feel the bulge underneath his jeans. Despite herself, she experienced a stirring of sexual excitement.

"Two years ago when I left, you threatened to hunt me down and kill me."

"*Preciosa*, you know I didn't mean it. I was upset because I loved you."

She felt like a traitor to Max because she could not prevent herself from responding to Alfredo. He had crouched so that his swollen cock was throbbing between her thighs. "I'm not a slave anymore," she said while he pressed her even more tightly against him.

"You're my woman," he murmured, caressing her until desire overwhelmed her. She let him take her into the bedroom. He tore off her clothes and removed his own. He had grown so thin that his ribs protruded.

"Max, forgive me," Adrianne said inwardly.

"*Meine liebchen, this man is no good for you.*"

Alfredo was bony against her heavy breasts and belly. His penis felt huge as he thrust, filling her, and his angry, electric force swept through her. Long ago she had wanted him to submerge her with his force like this, but now she resisted. He labored over her for a long time before he finally came, but she held back. Afterwards, she stared at a light from the next building which shone in through the air shaft. She thought of how Max, even when his penis was soft, placed his hand between her thighs and held her there until she had an orgasm. Most of all, she remembered the gentleness of his touch.

Alfredo lit a cigarette, passed it to her, and got out of bed.

"Can you get me some water," she asked.

"Sure, sweetheart."

She heard him piss in the bathroom then go into the kitchen.

When he returned with a glass of water, he smelled more strongly of alcohol. He offered her the nearly empty bottle of rum. She shook her head, but he took a swig before he lay down again, putting an arm around her shoulders. God, why had she come here, she wondered.

"This time we'll do things right," he murmured into her ear. "As soon as I can get my affairs straightened out, I'm leaving New York, and I want you with me because you and I belong together."

Once she had longed for this more than anything else in the world.

"You've got to help me," he continued. "Dominic's friends are after me for the money I owe him. If I don't get out of here soon, they'll hurt me real bad, or they'll kill me.

"I've been out of work now for a long time. I need you to hustle just for a few days for *us*. I need money for storage space, and we need money to live on for a while. We'll drive to Mexico City. Then we'll go on to Vera Cruz and take a freighter to Rio. I'd like to to go Cuba, but Castro's been doing some weird stuff down there."

She lay rigid, her breath choked up in her throat.

"I can't do it."

He got to his feet and stood over her, looking down with eyes that were glacial.

"I can't do it. I'm not a slave anymore."

"You're my woman. You'll always be my slave.

"I thought you'd changed," she said, sitting up and wrapping his worn silk robe around her.

"No more than you have," he said. "You're still a hooker."

"Alfredo, that's not true!"

"I know you to the marrow of your bones."

"You're talking about someone else, not about me." she said. "You can never make up to me for what I've suffered with you. There's no way you could make it up to me. Even if you were *my* slave for ten lifetimes, you could never pay me for the pain I've gone through."

"Bullshit! You were bored out of your skull with that impotent old asshole."

"He wasn't impotent, and I loved him!"

"You used to fuck twenty men a day. You miss being out there on the streets. That's why you came back." He loomed closer.

"Get away from me! I love Max! He was so good to me." She broke down into tears.

"So, you came back to tell me you're in love with a corpse? He's dead, baby. You and I belong together."

"No," she said.

He grabbed her wrists. "You're my slave!" he said. "I need you. Adrianne, I NEED you to help me out! Can you get that through your fucking dumb skull?"

"NO!" she shrieked, breaking away from him. "NO MORE!" Shaking all over, she began to dress. "Alfredo, I'm leaving," she said. "You won't see me again."

"Just give me a chance."

"You still act like I'm something to be used, like I'm a piece of furniture."

"Cut the crap." He yanked her head back and looked down directly into her eyes. "In a few days you and I are going to drive south across the border. You'll just be working for a few days, bitch. You've got to help me out!"

"Let me go!"

His hands closed around her throat until she couldn't breathe. "I could choke you to death," he said, staring at her with cold angry eyes. His grip tightened. She tried to pull his hands away, but she couldn't. He kept staring at her, as if in the grip of some outside force, and she prayed for him to let go. Finally, he blinked and took his hands away. "I'm going crazy here," he muttered. "Got to get out."

She sank onto the pillows, struggling for breath. Meanwhile, he had turned on the overhead light and was rifling the contents of her purse. "Money ... money ... ten ... twenty ... thirty ... forty ... two twenties ... the old man's or did you turn a few tricks on your way down here? Aha, a Vermont license!"

Then he unfolded a sheet of paper on which she had jotted down notes of a melody.

"That's my music! I wrote it!"

"Fuck your music."

"Alfredo, you're an artist!"

"And you're a whore, baby. I'm the only artist around here."

He dangled her car keys. "What kind of car you got?"

"A Chrysler."

"Let's take a ride."

"It's over in a lot on Tenth Avenue," she lied.

"He left you everything, right?"

"The will is in probate, and it probably won't be settled for a long time," she said, lying again. (Privately Morris had told her that Max arranged things so that the will would skip probate. "How he loved and worried about you," Morris had said, taking off his spectacles to wipe his forehead. "What a *mensch.*")

Alfredo flung the contents of the purse on the floor.

"Pick up your shit."

In shock, she bent over to gather her cosmetic case, the empty wallet, crumpled kleenex, a stick of cologne, and the folded sheet of music.

When she had put everything back into her purse, he pulled her by the haunches back onto the bed. He drew her up against him, moistened her with a little saliva, and forced his thick cock inside her anus. She cried out with the sensation of burning pain. He had never fucked her like this before. After he climaxed, he held her in his arms. His touch sent volts of fear through her. Finally, in the early morning he fell asleep. Gray light shone into the room. He was snoring when she got up. Quietly, she dressed then picked up her purse and her shoes and carried them into the studio. The dog growled in its sleep.

She noticed the dust on the floor. The windows were covered with grime. A bunch of purple chrysanthemums had withered in a vase. Petals had fallen and lay on the floor mingled with dust. On a small table, a watercolor had been spread out to dry. It was a somber self-portrait, which caught the essence of Alfredo. The expression in the eyes was haunting. She thought it was one of the best pictures he had ever done.

On top of a crate lay sheets of butcher paper filled with charcoal drawings of a nude—a long, slender girl with black hair and an Oriental slant to her eyes. She wondered who the girl was.

Then she tiptoed into the kitchen, nearly tripping over the dog's bowl. On the kitchen table lay a mass of papers. An overdue notice from Con Edison stating that unless the $32.40 past due was paid by the twentieth of the month, the electricity and gas would be turned off. A New York Telephone bill for $56.23. An overdue car payment notice from Chemical Bank for $79.00.

Want ads with jobs for bartenders were circled in red ink.

She glanced at an old photograph of a beautiful dark-haired woman, dressed in the style of the thirties, who held a small boy in her lap. An older boy of six or seven stood behind them. The woman gazed down with affection at the child in her arms. There was a lonely look in the older child's eyes. This must be Alfredo's mother and younger brother, she decided, and the lonely one looked like Alfredo. There was a photograph of a brick apartment building in Queens with a family standing in front, probably his relatives.

Finally, she studied a larger photograph of a pale man with dark hair and features that resembled Alfredo's. Written on the back in faded ink was "Havana, 1929."

The dog growled again and stirred in its sleep. Adrianne held her breath. As she tiptoed past the bedroom, she took a last look at Alfredo. He was sleeping on his side with one arm flung over the pillow. Neither Alfredo nor the dog made a sound when she unbarred the front door.

She drove through the Holland Tunnel to get to the New Jersey Turnpike and didn't stop for gas until she reached Newark.

Part 4

April, 1962

Chapter 38

Adrianne filled the gas tank at a Shell station on the outskirts of Newark and ate breakfast at a coffee shop. In the restroom she surveyed her tired face in the mirror. Then she telephoned her mother. It was nine o'clock on a Saturday morning, and probably Elena would be home from work.

"Mama, it's me, Adriana. I'm coming home to visit you."

"*Verdad?* Adriana! You haven't written to me in such a long time." Elena's voice sent tremors down Adrianne's spine.

"I need to see you." Adrianne had an almost incontrollable impulse to blurt out that she had gotten married and that Max had died, but she bit her lips, trembling with the fullness of all that she had concealed.

The next four days Adrianne drove, spending the nights in motels along the route. On the fourth afternoon she arrived in Houston during rush hour. The highways were clogged, but she finally reached the outskirts where her mother lived. She felt frightened and a bit numb. After she had parked the car in the double driveway next to Elena's station wagon, for a moment she sat still and gazed at the carefully tended rose bushes, the lush grass, and the willow tree. Using the rear view mirror, she combed her hair and freshened her makeup. At last she left the safety of her car. The air was cool. Dark clouds had massed in the sky. She rang the bell, and her mother opened the door.

"Hello, Adriana," said Elena, and she embraced her daughter rather formally.

Her mother's cheek was as soft as Adrianne remembered, and she smelled of the same lavender cologne. However, she had forgotten how fragile her mother's body was. Once again, Adrianne was aware of her own heaviness. Evidently, Elena had just returned from work and was wearing a blue linen dress with a string of pearls. Her hair, pulled back in a chignon, had grown almost completely gray. The lines in her face were more marked and she looked older.

"How are you, Adriana?"

"I'm all right, Mama."

"You wrote so seldom," Elena said.

The house was as immaculate as always, with its gray-green carpeting and ivory drapes. Silver candle holders, passed down from her mother's parents, gleamed in the dusky light. Her father's photograph stood on the mantel-piece. Like Adrianne, he was large-boned, but darker. Several framed photographs stood on top of a small corner table. There was a wedding snapshot of her parents, along with one of herself as a little girl of six. An old-fashioned oval picture of Elena's parents in a silver frame completed the collection. Elena had been their only child.

When Adrianne carried her suitcase into her old bedroom, she was shocked for a moment because it looked so bare. Her furniture was still there, along with the white ruffled bedspread and matching ruffled skirt of the dressing table. But none of Adrianne's personal effects remained. Her clothes, her books, her pictures, and her small radio had all disappeared and her closet was empty.

Disturbed, she unpacked a few items, showered, and changed.

Her mother was preparing dinner. "I'm making *paella*," she said when Adrianne came into the kitchen. "But I've only got frozen shrimp, and it should be fresh."

"I'm sure it will be good," said Adrianne, sniffing the spicy cooking odors. Elena poured them each a glass of Chilean wine.

"Where did you put all my things?" asked Adrianne, sipping her wine.

Elena was draining the shrimp and didn't seem to hear, so Adrianne repeated her question. Her mother looked straight ahead as she responded, "I gave them to the Salvation Army. I didn't know if you were ever coming back."

"Oh, no!" Adrianne cried. You could have shipped them to me!"

"I didn't know you wanted them."

"You never asked! You got rid of the piano, too—just like that. You never asked me how I felt."

"Those scales and those pieces you used to practice over and over again wore down my nerves," said Elena.

Adrianne burst into tears. "You never considered how much the piano meant to me."

Elena stepped back, bumping into the stove. "*Cállate!*" she cried. "You've just arrived, with practically no notice. I'm making you a special dinner. Is this the thanks I get?"

Adrianne retreated into the hallway and stood there for a moment, listening to the sound of her mother's heels against the kitchen linoleum. She had wanted so much for this to be a good visit. She would try to smooth things over, she thought, as she went into the dining room. Finding the silverware in its familiar place in the sideboard, she set the table.

Elena came out to the living room with her glass of wine and a bowl of olives. "Will you join me?" she asked.

Adrianne nodded. They sat down on the couch in front of the coffee table, which was piled with books on gardening in English, along with recent books in Spanish—short stories by Borges, novels by Marta Lynch and Silvina Ocampo.

"What have you been doing?" Adrianne asked, pushing down her anger.

"Exactly what I've done for years." said Elena. "I work at the library. I go to Church. I see a few friends. I read and tend my garden."

Adrianne could imagine her mother in her office at the Central Branch, where she worked as an administrator. On the job, her mother seemed to clothe herself in a distinct personality, much as she might put on a dress. Adrianne had caught glimpses of this personality whenever she visited her mother at work. There her mother was efficient and courteous. She never gazed off into space, as she was doing now.

Adrianne sipped her wine and gazed at her mother's profile, at the small, aquiline nose, at the soft skin marked with tiny lines,

While they ate, Elena and Adrianne made polite conversation. Their knives and forks sounded against the bone china plates.

"This *paella* is good," said Adrianne. In truth, the saffron rice, the chicken, sausage, and tiny shrimp, usually a favorite dish, stuck in her throat.

After dinner as they were drinking tea, Adrianne said, "I brought you a gift." She ran into her room and back again with the pearl brooch that she had bought Elena en route at a jeweler's in Atlanta.

Her mother opened the white box with its tissue wrappings and turned the brooch over, examining it. "This must have been expensive."

"I wanted to get you something nice."

Elena looked her full in the face, and then gazed past her, as though she were able to peer into Adrianne's mind but did not want to deal with what she saw.

"Are you still working as a waitress?"

"No, I'm not. I got married," Adrianne blurted out.

"Married? Adriana, why didn't you tell me?" Her mother sounded on the verge of tears.

"I don't know," Adrianne mumbled. Then she spoke haltingly about Max, their life in Vermont, her study of the piano, and finally his heart attack.

"How sad," said her mother. She stirred her tea with a tiny silver spoon.

"That's what you wanted, Mama. You wanted me to get married."

"*Niña,* why didn't you ever tell me any of this?"

"I don't know. I was afraid of somehow jinxing things if I did. I wanted to wait awhile, and then it was too late."

"Were you happy with him?" Elena asked.

"Yes, I was. He was much older than me, but we were happy together and I loved him."

"He was Jewish, you say?"

"Yes, he was."

"I see." Elena's disapproval was obvious.

"Papa's family was Jewish long ago."

"Your father was Catholic!" her mother emphasized angrily.

"It doesn't matter what Max was. He loved me."

"So much has happened to you. How sad that he died." Elena's voice trailed off.

"He was such a good man. I've never known anyone so good."

"You've gained weight," said her mother, scrutinizing her.

"He thought I was beautiful."

Just then the phone rang and Elena went into the other room to answer it.

"*Ah, Alicia,*" she heard her mother say. "*Me gustaría ir al cine pero mañana en la noche no es posible porque mi hija está de visita.*" She went on talking in Spanish, her voice warmer and more full of life than Adrianne was accustomed to hearing.

Then her mother returned to the table. "A friend from the Women's Church Guild," she said, furling her napkin. "Alicia from Peru is the only other woman there who speaks Spanish."

"Do you miss speaking your own language?" asked Adrianne.

"English has become my language."

"Do you ever want to go back to Chile?"

"No, I don't." Elena's lips trembled. "My parents are dead, and I never did get along with your father's family. There's no one there for me."

She gazed off for a minute as if she were in a trance. Then she said in a softer tone. "I am sorry about your husband. Now perhaps you know something of what I went through when Julio died."

Adrianne helped her mother wash the dishes. Immediately afterwards Elena excused herself, saying that she felt very tired.

That night Adrianne couldn't sleep for a long time. When she finally did get to sleep, she had disturbing dreams which she could only vaguely recall.

The next day while her mother was at work, Adrianne rested and read a few poems from an old volume with yellowed pages by Gabriela Mistral that she found among her mother's books. She could not understand some of the words, and she felt sorry for her loss of her Chilean past. Later on, she listened to some of her mother's Brahms' chamber music and to the recording of Satie's *Gymnopedes* that she had brought with her. The music calmed her. She found herself playing the Satie on an imaginary piano with her fingers as she lay on the couch.

In the afternoon she went out to buy groceries, and while her mother was still at work she prepared their dinner: Chili, rice, salad with avocados, and for dessert, chocolate ice cream and blackberry pie. The old craving to eat had returned in full force.

Later, she looked at herself naked in the bathroom mirror. Her face and body had grown fuller. She despaired over her stomach and heavy breasts. No, she was not the daughter her fragile-boned mother wanted.

Again she had difficulty in sleeping. She got up and consumed the rest of the blackberry pie. As she was going back to her bedroom, she saw from a crack beneath the door that her mother's light was still on.

She knocked.

"Mama, can I talk with you?"

"Come in, Adriana." Her mother sat in bed, propped against lacy pillows. A black prayer book was in her hands. She wore a pale-blue nylon nightgown, and her long hair hung loose. "What do you want to talk about?"

"May I brush your hair?"

Elena looked startled. "If you'd like."

On the dresser lay a worn bristle hairbrush made of silver with an engraved crest, from her mother's family. Adrianne picked up the brush, sat on the edge of the bed, and began brushing her mother's silvery hair. How soft it felt. She plaited her mother's fine hair into a braid.

"Why are you doing this?"

"I want to," Adrianne said. She put down the brush.

Her mother reached over to a jar on the nightstand and applied cream to her face, rubbing it in with slow, circular motions. Then she turned so that she was facing Adrianne, but she was gazing beyond her in that way she had. Something in her mother's vague air cast a powerful spell around Adrianne.

It was hard for her to speak, and when she began, she felt as if she were choking on the words. "Mama, I want to be closer to you. We never have been close. This is the first time I've ever brushed your hair." She paused, then forced herself to ask, "Do you really love me?"

"*Claro*, of course I love you."

"Tell me the truth. How *do* you feel about me?" Adrianne stared directly into her mother's eyes, daring her to tell the truth.

Elena looked away and after a moment began to speak, deliberating over her words. "You were so different from what I thought you would be. I longed for a child who would be my friend. But from the very beginning you were a burden. You were a disappointment, just as your father was."

"Were you angry with him?" asked Adrianne. The room seemed unusually bright, and things seemed to be in slow motion.

"At times, I was furious."

Her mother gazed off into space again. "I nearly died giving birth to you. Afterwards, I was very depressed. Julio wanted more children. But after you, I couldn't have any more. The doctors said I might die if I went through another pregnancy. You weighed more than five kilos, and you were far too big for a woman of my slender build."

"I couldn't help how big I was," said Adrianne, flooded with sadness.

"No, you couldn't. But somehow it colored my feelings towards you. It shouldn't have, but it did. And now you think you can just come home when you please and take up where you left off. Don't you realize I have a life, too?"

Every word of her mother's was like a blow, but tonight Elena was speaking truths that she never had before and might never have again. Adrianne needed to press on.

"Mama, when we still lived in Chile, and Papa left— before we joined him—did you have a breakdown? I remember my nurse telling me you were sick."

Her mother gripped the black prayer book. "It was nervous exhaustion."

"I see," said Adrianne. "Sometimes I've felt close to breaking down, too."

"You always were high-strung."

"Like you."

"No, not like me!" said her mother angrily. "You're different. When you were two-years old, your presence kept me from joining Julio in the the United States. That wasn't anything you could help, but the situation was too difficult for me." Elena paused, looking down at her fingernails.

Through Adrianne's mind flashed an image of her mother long ago, blonde and elegant. When Adrianne was a child, Elena had seemed as beautiful as a movie star.

Raising her voice, Elena continued, "All those years I raised you—whether I did it well or badly, I took care of you. I wasn't happy when Julio went off on business trips. I was lonely, but I couldn't join him because of you."

"I'm sorry, Mama," cried Adrianne, impulsively hugging her so close that she could feel the shape of her mother's bony body and small breasts. With a cry, Elena pushed her away.

"I'm sorry," Adrianne said, bursting into tears.

Elena gave her a stony gaze.

Moving back a safe distance, Adrianne straightened her body. "I want you to know what happened to me while I was gone," Adrianne said defiantly through her tears. "I hustled men for a living." Ignoring the horrified look on her mother's face, Adrianne continued. "I was a prostitute. Before I married Max, I was in love with a pimp."

Her mother gazed at her in stricken silence.

"As for Lucille, she was more than a friend," Adrianne added.

For just an instant Adrianne thought she saw a strange flicker of joy in her mother's eyes, the trace of a smile. Or was she imagining it? Was she herself going crazy?

Then her mother shrieked hysterically, "You shouldn't be telling me these things! I don't want to hear them! Why are you telling me?"

"I want you to know the truth." Summoning all her courage, Adrianne took a deep breath and forced herself to go on. "Three years ago I got pregnant. Gerald arranged an abortion. It would have been a girl."

Her mother gave a cry of anguish and clutched her prayer book. Her face was white. "You are a murderer. I don't want you under my roof. *¡Solamente Dios puede salvarte!*"

"Mama!"

"I don't want to hear anymore. Just leave. Leave me. Right now." Her mother closed her eyes and whispered, *"La niñita está muerte. Pobrecita."*

Adrianne fled.

In her bedroom, Adrianne contemplated slashing her wrists or hanging herself with an electric cord. She could leave right now and find a motel room, but it was after two a.m. Rolling her body into a ball, she clutched her knees and sobbed convulsively. Finally, she began to doze off. Softly, the dream-mother comforted her. *"Meine leibchen,"* murmured Max's voice, floating near her. Then he vanished. After a brief, restless sleep, she awakened with the thought of seeing Lucille. How could she have cast Lucille off so heartlessly

when Lucille had shown her more compassion than her own
mother?

At eight in the morning she phoned Lucille's house.
Lucille's husband, Barney, answered.

"Hello. This is Adrianne," she said. "Is Lucille still in the
hospital?"

"Lucille died six weeks ago."

Completely overwhelmed, Adrianne left the house without eating or drinking anything and drove around for hours.
Several times she barely escaped colliding with other cars on
the highway.

Late that afternoon she drove back to her mother's house.
Elena's station wagon was in the driveway, but the house was
empty. When Adrianne peered through the blinds of her bedroom window, she saw her mother bent over in a faded gardening dress. She was digging up earth around a white rose
bush.

In a daze, Adrianne packed and put her suitcase in the
car. Then she walked back into the garden. "Mama, I'm leaving," she said.

Elena stood up and turned around to face Adrianne. In
her gloved hands she gripped a pair of rose clippers. "Where
are you going?"

"I want to go to California and study music."

"What will you live on? Your earnings as a prostitute?"

"Max left me enough money to live on for a few years. I'm
sorry. I'm sorry I caused you pain." Adrianne took a step
towards her, but Elena backed off with an anguished look.

"*Qué Dios te salve,*" Elena murmured. Then she went
quickly into the house, shutting the door behind her.

Chapter 39

Adrianne drove west. Cities became prairie which gave way to desert. There were few cars now, and heat rose in shimmering waves from the road. Drops of sweat rolled off her face; the steering wheel was slippery. As the sun rose higher and the light became more brilliant, the heat intensified. Days later on a deserted stretch of highway in southern Arizona, she turned off at an exit where a faded sign advertised a diner. The diner was boarded up, but she kept on driving, hoping to find a restaurant further along. Instead, she found herself in isolated country, rimmed by distant mountains. The car began to make noises, and she grew uneasy. A rabbit scurried across the road just in front of the car. Far off she could see what looked like buildings or trees, but she knew they were mirages.

Suddenly she smelled burning and pulled over. Smoke was pouring out from underneath the hood. When the smoke finally stopped, she opened up the hood, but she couldn't tell exactly what was wrong. Hoping the engine hadn't been damaged, she was dismayed at seeing a puddle of water underneath the car.

Around her was a vast expanse of flat earth with a few clumps of brush that merged into a cloudless sky. For almost an hour she waited. The car was so uncomfortable that she got out and paced back and forth along the road, then sat down on the ground in the full glare of the heat. Although the dust made her cough, she didn't dare drink the last of the water in her thermos.

Finally, she saw a pickup truck in the distance coming towards her. She waved her arms and shouted. The truck stopped just behind her car. A stocky man of medium height who appeared to be Mexican or Indian got out. He had graying black hair and a copper-colored, lined face.

"Car break down?" His voice was husky, almost hoarse.

"Yes."

After looking inside the hood, he said, "The radiator hose is okay. I think the radiator sprang a leak."

"Is the engine damaged?"

"Can't tell."

When she coughed, he got out a canteen and handed it to her. She gulped down big, cold mouthfuls of water. "Thank you," she said. "I'd just about run out."

He tucked his fingers inside his broad, leather-tooled belt and looked at her, squinting his eyes against the sun's glare. "You from these parts?"

"No, I'm not. I'm on my way to California."

"You're fifty miles from the nearest town, and then it's only a truck stop. No hotels. It gets mighty cold out here at night. You can spend the night at my place if you like. I've got room. Tomorrow I'll haul your car to town. The one thing they've got in that town is a garage. My son works there."

"That's kind of you. But I think I'll stay here and wait for the police."

"No telling when they'd get here. If you're almost out of water, I wouldn't stay here overnight."

"I'll go with you," she said, not quite sure that she was making the right choice. From the trunk of the car she took out the small suitcase which held her overnight things, and he hoisted it into the back of his truck. He opened the passenger door, and she got in. The ledge beneath his windshield was littered with small white stones and rough turquoises. There was a pungent odor. "What's that smell?" she asked

"That's sage and other herbs. I gather plants from the desert to sell in Tucson.

She pushed back the straw hat she was wearing. Sweat was on the inside of her open-necked blouse. Her skirt, too, was damp with sweat, and her hair clung in strands to her face.

"My name's Manuel. What's yours?"

"Adrianne."

"Don't be afraid," he said, as the truck picked up speed. "I won't harm you. I told you I've got room, and I'll leave you alone." His deep, rough voice was somehow reassuring.

She looked over at him. His hands were square, with straight nails. He seemed genuine. He was wearing a gray, short-sleeved shirt and a white sombrero.

"I've lived in these parts all my life. One of my daughters lives just beyond that rise over there. My youngest son works at the gas station where I'll be hauling your car tomorrow."

"Are you married?" she asked.

"My wife died a few years ago."

"I'm sorry."

"I am too."

They were silent, and she looked out the window. Shadows were lengthening. Although her watch had stopped, she guessed it was about five in the afternoon when they pulled up at an adobe house with a small trailer in back. In the front yard was a cactus tree, several enormous aloe vera plants, and a few spindly plants held up with stakes.

He got out her suitcase and lifted armfuls of gray-green branches out of the back of the truck.

"You can help me carry these inside," he said.

The fragrant dry leaves brushed against her skin as she carried them into a bright, sunlit room and lay them on top of bundles of drying herbs. The odor, which made her think of wind, filled her nostrils.

He gave her a tour of the house. "I built it myself, with the help of my sons," he said proudly.

The house had white walls and dark tile floors. One of the bedrooms was used for drying and storing the herbs he collected, while he slept in the other bedroom. His bed was unmade and a few articles of clothing were tossed over a chair. "Excuse the mess," he said. "I wasn't expecting company."

"It's not messy at all," said Adrianne, and in truth she was impressed with the cleanliness of the house and with its spare furnishings.

Then he showed her the trailer, where she would sleep. It was tiny, with a berth-bed and yellow curtains. From a built-in cabinet he took out sheets and woven Mexican blankets for her .

A wave of dizziness swept over her. "I'm so tired. I'd like to lie down," she said.

"Go ahead. I'll cook up some dinner."

Hours later, she awakened in darkness and wandered inside the house.

They ate rice, beans, and tortillas, along with a salad of green peppers and tomatoes from his garden. Manuel offered her beer, but she declined. Then he offered her a cool drink made with rice water.

Halfway through the meal, she got up and vomited in the bathroom.

"You are unwell," said Manuel, when she returned to the table. "Are you pregnant?"

"No, I don't think so."

He felt her feverish forehead, and his touch was gentle. "You got too much sun."

"I was waiting for a long time," she said. "It was so hot inside that car that I got out and waited outside."

"Go and lie down."

She went back to the trailer, put on her nightgown, and lay beneath the blankets, but still she shivered. Throughout her journey she had been in turmoil over her mother, and this emotional pain permeated everything.

Manuel knocked at the trailer door and came in with a damp compress which he applied to her forehead. It felt cool and smelled refreshing. He sat down on a stool beside her and placed one of his hands gently on the top of her skull. She felt the power from his touch surging through her. It swept warmth through her entire body so that her chills vanished. When she looked up into his dark eyes, they beamed compassion. He won't hurt me. I can trust him, she thought, as she closed her eyes and let the relaxation fill her.

"Sleep," he said. "You'll be all right in the morning." Then he left the trailer. However, she still felt his force sweeping through her body, filling it with fresh currents, as though he were still touching her. Her dreams were vivid, but when she awakened, the memory of them vanished.

The next morning the house was empty. His truck was gone. On the table she found a slip of paper with looped, large, almost childish handwriting.

Adrianne, I am taking your car to fix the radiator.

Manuel

When she walked outside, she saw that the sun had already risen high in the sky. A breeze blew her hair, and she was hungry.

On the kitchen counter she found a stack of tortillas wrapped in a cloth napkin. A pot of beans and coffee were on the stove. She warmed up the food and consumed everything hungrily. Afterwards, she decided to go for a walk.

As she made her way across the land, she felt impeded by her heavy thighs and large, pendulous breasts and by the weight of her entire body, which ached when she tried to run. So she stopped and sat down to rest. A tumbleweed rolled across her field of vision. The previous night she had dreamed something disturbing about huge black birds.

Absorbed in her thoughts, she continued walking. When she turned to look behind her, the house was no longer visible and she felt a pang of fear. However, she decided to rest again before she retraced her steps. Red-faced and sweating, she sat down on a rock.

The vastness of the land now made her perceive her own emotions as trivial. Those emotions seemed like the gophers and jackrabbits and other small desert animals that darted past her. It was so hot that tensions in her brain melted. She felt as though hands were pushing down on her. Far off she heard the bleating of sheep. Objects around her started to pulsate. Sagebrush, rocks, pebbles, and bushes expanded and contracted. Their forms shifted. Shimmering waves of air rose from the earth. There seemed to be an ocean in the distance. A mirage, she knew.

Then there was a gust of wind, and inside the wind she seemed to hear her mother's voice. From a tumbleweed hurtling across the ground, a shape emerged. Adrianne gripped the edge of the rock. *"You're damned, doomed. You deserve to die,"* her mother murmured. The vision faded, but Adrianne felt something pulling on her.

Heat continued to penetrate her.

"Adriana," sounded her father's thin voice, although perhaps it was the wind which blew his meaning through her bones. Tall, heavy, and stoop-shouldered as he had been in life, he whispered that he wanted her to remain his alone.

She seemed to hear Lucille's voice. *"Honey, come with me."*

Her clothing was sticking to her with perspiration; her head throbbed. In spite of herself, she dozed off. When her eyes opened again, she had half-slipped off the rock. Max's soft hands were on her neck. *"Come, Adrianne, come. You are my soul. You are my missing part."*

"If you love me, let me live!" she cried out.

"Meine liebchen, I love you." His voice was thick and guttural, as it had been in life. On one of his fingers flashed a ring with red and blue stones.

When she rubbed her eyes, he disappeared. All she saw were waves of air rising around her, but still she heard his voice mingling with other voices, enticing her. Then again she seemed to see the shadowy form of her mother beneath some rocks. Elena smiled in that strange way, with the glimmer of satisfaction that Adrianne had seen for the blink of an eye during that last night. *"I knew about Gerald,"* her mother whispered inside the wind. *"I knew a lot about you. When I gaze off, I see things beneath the surface. You have lived out my secret dreams, and now this heat will get you and you'll die."*

Her mother was rocking a tiny carcass against her breasts.

Adrianne stood up. Through her fear, she knew she had to stay awake. The voices fused, pulling her in different directions. *"Come with me ...with me,"* they all echoed around her. Were they coming from inside her brain? The wind intensified, blowing branches of the sparse desert brush. She felt them flow through her with the wind, fill her, and then pass beyond.

Finally, she was empty, and in spite of the heat she shivered as she had the night before underneath the blankets.

"Not yet to die, meine liebchen. Not to die. Not to die."

The ring with the red and blue stones flashed.

Just then she heard a bird's cawing. She blinked and saw a vulture circling overhead. Exerting all her will, she forced herself to run. Her legs felt like tree trunks. Her full breasts ached as they bounced against her. Gasping for breath, she made herself keep running. The murmur of voices continued around her. With a sudden gust the wind blew off her hat, rolling it against a bush. Adrianne retrieved it. Prickly plants hurt her skin. The sky was radiant blue. The wind had died down, and she felt strangely light. A fly landed on her arm. When she looked up, she saw that the vulture was circling lower. She knew she had to keep on walking, walking. Her ankles were covered with scratches and her exposed skin had turned bright red.

Keep on moving, moving.

Finally, she saw the house. As soon as she walked inside, she collapsed on the cool tile floor.

Hours later she awakened in semi-darkness. Then again she fell into a feverish sleep.

She dreamed that she was making love. A sea wind billowed in through white curtains as she and the young man, her lover, fused in love. His eyes were the same deep blue as hers. His face and body were beautiful to her. With magical hands, he caressed her all over, her breasts, her belly, her cunt, until she felt as if flames were licking her. His cock filled her, as if it were a soft bright flame unfolding its petals through her torso and limbs. She and her lover pressed tight against each other, smooth and slippery with sweat. Flashing light energy flowed between them, opening up her body and mind, as they floated through space. On her right middle finger gleamed a ring with red and blue stones, like the one she had seen Max wearing in her desert vision. Then she fell through darkness, awakening with a jolt, as one of her legs jerked in a spasm.

For a moment she did not know where she was or even who she was. Slowly the room spun into focus, and she realized she was lying on Manuel's bed. At that moment he walked in the bedroom door and looked at her with concern.

"At last you're awake," he said. "I was worried. You were burning with fever."

He put a glass of water to her lips, and she sipped a little of it. Although she was sweating, chills swept through her. He ran a lukewarm bath for her in which she soaked for a long time. Then she rested a while longer.

"You need to be more careful," Manuel said at dinner. "The desert and the heat can kill you."

She told him about her visions that morning.

Manuel said, "I should have warned you. You shouldn't wander alone here. This land has a special kind of power. I want you to show me where this happened."

After they had eaten, they walked outside, accompanied by his sheep dog which bounded back and forth. When Adrianne showed him the place where she'd had her visions, she was filled with a sense of unease. She told him a little about her life and about the recent visit with her mother. Although he didn't probe, she had a sense he grasped far more than she told him. She talked about how she was now going to study music in California.

While they walked, the murmur of voices sounded again. This time she let the voices pass through her, not clinging to them. That way they had no power. She felt the ground beneath her feet and the cool air around her.

Swiftly, the sun sank beneath the horizon, suffusing the sky with a vivid rose light. It grew dark, and the first stars appeared. A coyote howled. She shivered inside Manuel's leather jacket and walked faster to keep up with him. She felt herself changing as she stepped across the land, which now gleamed ghostly white in the light of the rising moon. She felt herself changing, changing. The stars looked especially large and clear. The old self was slipping away like a skin being shed, and this frightened her. She wanted to hold on to her old self, but the immensity of the surrounding land and sky somehow forced her to let it go.

"Sometimes I think God is dreaming us, and we are dreaming our lives," he said in his deep voice. "What we take in through our five senses is like a dream. God is this desert. We're like grains of sand or like the stars."

His words sank into her mind.

"When we die," he continued, "We fade the way shadows fade when the sun goes down." He was silent for a moment. Then his voice took on a different tone as he asked, "Do you wonder how I found you?"

"Yes," she said.

"After your car broke down, you got scared with that killing heat and your lack of water. You weren't ready to die. The feeling you sent was so strong, I picked it up like radar. So I got in my truck and drove until I found you."

"I see," she said, pondering his words. On and on they walked. "It's so quiet," she murmured.

"Words can get in the way. They often lie." His presence strengthened her. Reaching for her hand, he held it for a moment in his warm grip.

Rays of golden purple light from the evening sky enveloped them, and inside the light she felt safe. She felt, too, as if an enormous burden were being lifted from her. They continued walking in silence until they reached his house again, brilliant underneath the light of the moon and stars.

The next morning they drove to the gas station. Manuel introduced her to his son Pablo, a slender young man whose eyes were almost pure black.

"I sealed up the radiator," said Pablo. "I also put a new hose on because the old one looked worn-out. You're lucky the engine's okay."

She thanked him and paid the bill. Manuel took her suitcase out of the pickup and put it into her car.

"Hey, Dad, take a look at your carburetor," cautioned Pablo, peering inside the hood of Manuel's truck. "Come and take a look."

"Goodbye, Manuel. Thank you for everything," she said.

He reached into his shirt pocket and handed something to her. It was an antique silver ring set with two small stones, one a deep rich red and the other dark blue. The stones glimmered, just as they had in her dream.

"This ring came down to my wife through her family," Manuel said. "Somehow I think you're meant to have it."

"Oh, Manuel," she said. "It's so beautiful."

"The silver needs polishing. The stones are sapphire and ruby."

When she slipped the ring on her middle finger, it fit perfectly.

"I'll think of you when I wear it."

"Think of the desert," he said. "Don't let anything drive you *loca,* you hear?"

She smiled and shook his hand. Then he went over to his truck to look at the carburetor. When she started up the engine he tipped his sombrero, and she waved goodbye.

She drove on and on. Towards afternoon the wind died down completely. Nothing stirred. The sun was brilliant. Far off in the distance a vulture soared. When she glanced at her ring, the stones flashed in the light. As she drove, she felt as if she were one with her body, with the moving car, with the earth, the sky, and the flying bird.